WHISPERING HEARTS

V.C. Andrews® Books

The Dollanganger Family
Flowers in the Attic
Petals on the Wind
If There Be Thorns
Seeds of Yesterday
Garden of Shadows
Christopher's Diary: Secrets of Foxworth
Christopher's Diary: Echoes of Dollanganger
Secret Brother
Beneath the Attic
Out of the Attic
Shadows of Foxworth

The Audrina Series
My Sweet Audrina
Whitefern

The Casteel Family
Heaven
Dark Angel
Fallen Hearts
Gates of Paradise
Web of Dreams

The Cutler Family
Dawn
Secrets of the Morning
Twilight's Child
Midnight Whispers
Darkest Hour

The Landry Family
Ruby
Pearl in the Mist
All That Glitters
Hidden Jewel
Tarnished Gold

The Logan Family
Melody
Heart Song
Unfinished Symphony
Music in the Night
Olivia

The Orphans Series
Butterfly
Crystal
Brooke
Raven
Runaways

The Wildflowers Series
Misty
Star
Jade
Cat
Into the Garden

The Hudson Family
Rain
Lightning Strikes
Eye of the Storm
The End of the Rainbow

The Shooting Stars
Cinnamon
Ice
Rose
Honey
Falling Stars

The De Beers Family
"Dark Seed"
Willow
Wicked Forest
Twisted Roots
Into the Woods
Hidden Leaves

The Broken Wings Series
Broken Wings
Midnight Flight

The Gemini Series
Celeste
Black Cat
Child of Darkness

The Shadows Series
April Shadows
Girl in the Shadows

The Early Spring Series
Broken Flower
Scattered Leaves

The Secrets Series
Secrets in the Attic
Secrets in the Shadows

The Delia Series
Delia's Crossing
Delia's Heart
Delia's Gift

The Heavenstone Series
The Heavenstone Secrets
Secret Whispers

The March Family
Family Storms
Cloudburst

The Kindred Series
Daughter of Darkness
Daughter of Light

The Forbidden Series
The Forbidden Sister
"The Forbidden Heart"
Roxy's Story

The Mirror Sisters
The Mirror Sisters
Broken Glass
Shattered Memories

The House of Secrets Series
House of Secrets
Echoes in the Walls

The Umbrella Series
The Umbrella Lady

The Girls of Spindrift
Bittersweet Dreams
"Corliss"
"Donna"
"Mayfair"
"Spindrift"

Stand-alone Novels
Gods of Green Mountain
Into the Darkness
Capturing Angels
The Unwelcomed Child
Sage's Eyes
The Silhouette Girl

V.C. ANDREWS®

WHISPERING HEARTS

POCKET BOOKS
New York London Toronto Sydney New Delhi

Pocket Books
An Imprint of Simon & Schuster, Inc.
1230 Avenue of the Americas
New York, NY 10020

Following the death of Virginia Andrews, the Andrews family worked with a carefully selected writer to organize and complete Virginia Andrews's stories and to create additional novels, of which this is one, inspired by her storytelling genius.

This book is a work of fiction. Any references to historical events, real people, or real places are used fictitiously. Other names, characters, places, and events are products of the author's imagination, and any resemblance to actual events or places or persons, living or dead, is entirely coincidental.

First Pocket Books paperback edition August 2021

For information about special discounts for bulk purchases, please contact Simon & Schuster Special Sales at 1-866-506-1949 or business@simonandschuster.com.

Interior design by Erika R. Genova

Manufactured in the United States of America

10 9 8 7 6 5 4 3 2 1

ISBN 978-1-9821-7875-8
ISBN 978-1-5011-6261-9 (ebook)

WHISPERING HEARTS

PROLOGUE

"You walk out that door now, you walk out of this house and this family forever," my father shouted, standing in our entryway like the statue of Lord Nelson in Trafalgar Square, punching his fist toward our front door. He wasn't close enough to touch it, but in my mind I could hear the pounding.

My father always seemed predisposed to keep parental controls tighter on me than on my sister. One would think he had seen defiance in me the day I was born.

A forefinger poking the air was his way of showing anger or disappointment; a fist was absolute rage and was often accompanied by rose-tinted cheeks, flaming wide eyes, and a tight jaw. Sometimes, he would speak through his clenched teeth and have a way of hoisting his shoulders that made him look even more frightening. I knew all of it was meant to intimidate me. When I was much younger, his reactions always succeeded in sending me into retreat, but eventually I did what he himself often advised: I grew a little more backbone.

From what my sister told me months later, that morning, "as if he had been sitting on a large spring," he had popped up and out of the living room when our short stairway creaked beneath my feet, revealing that I had begun to descend.

I continued down, carrying my small suitcase, my brown leather Coach drawstring bag hung off my shoulder, clutched under my arm as tightly as I would cling to a life preserver. It had been my maternal grandmum's; I had often been told that I had inherited her cheekiness. Julia had been given her ivory brush, and we shared her sterling silver hand mirror. I would never tell her, but sometimes I saw my grandmum smiling at me over my shoulder when I gazed into her mirror. She would be whispering, *Your perfect features should be captured in a cameo*. If I did tell Julia about that, she would only accuse me of being conceited.

I had lowered my head after taking my first step on the stairway this morning and had held my breath from the moment I left my room, anticipating the confrontation with my father. I knew this would be the worst altercation ever between us, and there had been some fierce ones recently. I had put my hair in a braided bun earlier, looking at myself in the mirror and taking periodic deep breaths while I chanted, "You can do this. You must do this, Emma Corey. Do not retreat when he growls."

I had dressed in my new light-blue pleated skirt suit that I had bought with an employee's discount at Bradford's Department Store and had saved to wear on this day. It was practically the only thing I had purchased for myself during the two years I had worked there, anticipating how much money I would need for the journey across the Pond to New York City.

When I reached the bottom of the stairs, I ignored him and instead looked into the living room and saw my mother and sister sitting beside each other on the sofa, their hands clutched in their laps, knuckles white. Absolutely terrified, neither dared glance toward the door. It was as if the whole house had frozen. Clocks were holding their breaths, hands trembling.

It was one thing to talk about my leaving for America and hear his objections, his protests and threats, but far another to actually do it. I was as determined as Mercedes Gleitze, the first British lady to swim across the English Channel, in 1927. My father wasn't going to block me and stymie my ambitions, either.

For months I had been talking to my mother and my sister about my going to New York to work and to audition for opportunities to develop my career as a singer. I was trying to prepare them and boost my own courage simultaneously. My excitement sprouted and blossomed as the time for leaving grew closer, and my resolve strengthened.

My sister didn't help. She was never supportive of my pursuing a career as an entertainer. In fact, for as long as I could recall, she did her best to discourage me.

My mother's silence whenever I discussed it telegraphed her utter dread of anticipating my father's reaction. Whatever she did say was almost always discouraging.

"You really don't know anything about that world, especially in America," she told me. "You'll be a poor little lamb who's lost her way."

She was always on the verge of tears when we conversed about the subject. Her lips trembled, and she wove her fingers around each other so nervously and tightly that I thought she might break one. Everyone always said she had bones as thin as a bird's. It would merely take a brisk wind to crack one.

"From what I've read, no one really knows that world, Mummy, here in England or there in America. Most everything depends on a lucky break, but you've got to be at it to get that to happen, and if you're too frightened to try, you'll always wonder if you could have succeeded. Regret is worse than failure, because failing at least means you had attempted to do something. Not seeking to develop your talent is a sin. I can't imagine years and years from now staring into the memory of this time and wondering forever about what might have been."

I explained how I hoped to get into a Broadway show, to be seen by a music producer, and to be contracted to do an album, just as Barbra Streisand had done. My voice was often compared to hers, so I envisioned myself on television shows performing as well.

I loved singing, loved to bask in the expressions on the faces of my audiences and thrill to the way I could touch them. I was able to get people to pause in their busy or troubled lives and travel comfortably with me along the paths of the melodies—some joyful, some wistful, but always taking them to another place, even if only for a few minutes. For as long as I could remember, I was told I had a special gift. Why didn't my family believe as I did that it was as important to develop and share it? If you were given a gift, surely it was immoral to ignore it.

"Totally ridiculous," Julia said when she heard my plans. "You're still just a child full of imagination. You've never gone fifty miles from your home without me or our parents or some school chaperone. Be realistic. Grow up, for goodness' sake."

Julia was wrong. What I wanted wasn't some pipe dream a teenage girl grows in a garden of fantasies. My plans were stable and mature. I was especially disappointed that she, who already was working as a teacher, didn't see this. It was supposed to be in a teacher's DNA to encourage young people, to push them to try, to experiment, and to be courageous so they could become all they were capable of becoming.

But then again, maybe she did envision all I could do; maybe she was simply jealous that I had the courage to step out of this house alone to try something so big, something she couldn't do. She knew I was lead singer in the church chorus for years and lead singer in the school chorus as well. She was aware of all the praise I had received from the moment I had sung my first note as a child. She accompanied my parents to every school performance and was always in church whenever they attended and heard me sing. A cloudburst of compliments soaked us all before we walked down the steps to go home.

Most important, she was aware that it hadn't stopped there. I had earned praise in other ways. On weekends since my sixteenth birthday, I sang in pubs in Guildford and at some social events, even a wedding, but I really felt professional when I sang in taverns and was paid for it. In the U.K., you are considered an adult by the age of sixteen. Not only can you drive, but you are allowed to have beer, wine, or cider with a meal in a pub if you are with an adult, and so singing in one wasn't unusual for someone my age.

Many people told me that the pubs had better attendance when the word was out that I would be singing in them. I would do all the traditional favorites like "The White Cliffs of Dover," "Pack up Your Troubles," and many songs written by Cole Porter, as well as songs sung by Streisand. In particular, the Three Bears tavern did so well that the owner advertised me in the local paper occasionally and on flyers left at store counters.

I avoided joining anyone's garage band, even though I was constantly invited to do so, and by some of the best-looking boys in our school, too. My interest wasn't in their kind of music. I was heavily into pop songs, big-band tunes, and show tunes. Besides using Barbra Streisand as my touchstone, I wanted to be on my own like Jewel, Mariah Carey, or Sarah McLachlan, who were popular at the time. I was convinced that was my future.

But I suppose the person who influenced me the most and did the most to encourage me to pursue a singing career was my secondary-school music teacher, Mr. Wollard. He had been teaching for over twenty years and told me that I was the best singer he had ever had during all that time. Unlike most teachers his age, he kept up with what was happening in the current music scene and convinced me I had the voice for it, not that I needed a great deal of convincing.

"You could definitely be the next Streisand," he said when I told him she was my idol.

From when I was fourteen years old until now, I brought home his compliments gift wrapped in confidence and joy and often revealed them at dinner. Most of the time my father ignored them or muttered something like "The man should be careful blowing up a young girl's image of herself." In the early days, never anticipating that I would take the big leap defiantly, my mother would remind him how beautifully I sang and how so many people had complimented them both about it.

"Don't say you aren't proud of her, Arthur. I see the joy in your face when you hear the praise."

He'd grunt reluctant agreement about that but made sure to point out that I didn't have real competition, thus, deliberately or otherwise, belittling my achievements.

"You can give her a head full of air. It's not like she's singing in London on the West End," he would say, and then turn to me and wave that thick right forefinger. "And one in ten thousand, if that many, makes a living doing it. You mind your grades and think about finding a decent way of earning a living like your sister wants to do."

Julia had already determined she would be an elementary-school teacher, which our father approved of so enthusiastically in my presence that there could have been bugles and a marching band accompanying him. At dinner he would raise his arms and look toward the ceiling as if the answer to the question he was about to bellow was scrolled across it.

"Why should I have one daughter with her feet solidly on the ground and another who is flighty? It's beyond me. I didn't bring one up differently from the other."

"I'm not flighty, Daddy," I protested. "I'm very serious about the singing profession."

"Profession," he said disdainfully, and shook his head. He looked at me with a softer expression, catching me off guard. "You're a pretty girl, Emma, and you do well in school. Don't go chasing pipe dreams. The world is not a friendly place to those who don't have a solid footing. Remember that. You rarely get a decent second chance in this life."

I knew he wanted me wrapped like a fish in brown paper, his responsibility as a father done and off his list of worries. If I did anything that particularly annoyed him, he would rant, claiming that sometimes he believed children were rained down upon us "like stinging hail." However, the more he fought the idea of my pursuing a singing career, the more I clung to it, and not simply out of spite, either. I was that confident in myself.

I never told anyone in my family that Mr. Wollard had a friend in New York, Donald Manning, who managed a restaurant in Manhattan and who had offered to help find me a place to stay and a job at the restaurant so I could support my efforts. I knew if I had mentioned it, my father would have made some formal charge against Mr. Wollard and maybe even have caused him to be sacked.

The day after my eighteenth birthday, I called Donald Manning. I had saved up enough money to get to New York and set myself up for a while. It had always been my intention to do it immediately after secondary school; otherwise, I might lose my nerve. He put me in touch with Mr. Leo Abbot, the landlord of the apartments that were walking distance from the restaurant he managed. After I had spoken to him, I sent him a cashier's check for the first month's rent and deposit. All he had available was a two-bedroom, which was more expensive. The initial payments took up half my savings, but he said I should have no problem finding a roommate to share the expenses.

"New York is always burstin' with young ladies lookin' to hitch themselves to a star," he said.

I didn't like the way he had said that. I didn't want to be part of a generic pack of lemmings running headlong over some cliff of fantasies. I knew it was going to be hard, very hard, and I would swim in a lake of disappointments. Eventually, I might drown in rejection, but I decided to do it anyway. Was that courage or blind stupidity?

"The apartment is furnished and has a passable set of dishware, pots and pans, and silverware," Leo had told me. There was a pause, and he added, "Not real silver, you understand."

When I announced it all at dinner the night before I was to leave, my parents and my sister were astounded and upset that I had done all this planning and arranging so quickly without their knowledge. I had hoped that they would be proud and impressed that I had taken care of so many details on my own. I had tried to be businesslike, explaining the costs for travel, the rent, and what I could make in my temporary side job. I even had a liabilities-and-assets statement for my father to peruse. However, when my father saw it, he crunched it in his fist and slammed his other hand on the table so hard the dishware and silverware bounced. He stabbed his right forefinger at me, forbidding me to follow through.

"Get that deposit back, cash in those plane tickets, and quickly. I didn't raise a daughter, give her good room and board, clothe her, and get her educated to have her turn into a cock-up and embarrass this good family name."

He spun on Mummy, still pointing his finger like the barrel of a pistol.

"I told you, Agnes Lee Moorhead, that permitting her to sing in those pubs before a crowd of worthless and wasteful lumps who don't know a *do re mi* when they hear it would come to no good. They blew her full of herself. She's just another impressionable young girl someone is going to exploit."

"You can't say she hasn't got a beautiful voice. You've heard her in church and in school, Arthur," Mummy said softly, light tears starting to swim in her eyes. "And you've heard how much she was admired. Maybe, if she continued to sing here in the pubs and—"

"Because she sang in church and school? That's cause to waste young years, not to mention the real money she could be earning in a useful position? It will come to no good, and I won't be part of it or have it be part of my family here or anywhere. I forbid it," he said, then left the table, which was very unlike him, for he wouldn't stomach anyone wasting his food. He told us his father used to make him eat for breakfast whatever he had left over at dinner.

Mummy turned to me, her face as crimson as it

would be if she had stood too close to a fire. "You'll have to reconsider, Emma. Maybe wait until he's warmed to the idea."

"He'll never warm to it," I said, looking after him as if there was smoke in his wake. "He wants me stuck in some bank-teller job or something and then have a brood of children to mind. Just because he buried every dream he has ever had doesn't mean I bury mine. I'm eighteen and in charge of my future now. I've got to pack," I said defiantly, and, like him, rose and left the table.

"They're two peas in a pod," I heard Mummy tell my sister. "Both stubborn and butting heads."

Now he stood there in our entryway, the threats dripping from his eyes, his lips quivering with rage. I was trembling, too, but I wouldn't let him see that.

"I'll call you, Mummy, when I arrive in New York," I shouted past him. She looked up and at me, tears streaming down her face.

"No, you won't. You won't call this house if you step out of it with that suitcase," my father said. "I forbid your mother to speak with you, and your sister as well, if you leave. Send no letters, either. They'll be burned at the door."

Despite how hard I was shaking inside, I stood as firmly as he ever had stood whenever he had forbidden us from doing something. Maybe he saw himself in me, in the determination fixed in my eyes, and that told him he wouldn't win the argument today, no matter what.

"Burn what you want," I said. "I'm going to do what I'm meant to do, Daddy, with your blessing or without."

"It's without!" he screamed behind me when I opened the door.

I gazed back at him. He looked made of stone. I would never deny that I was afraid. I had never defied him as much as this, and I was about to set out alone for a world in which I didn't know a soul. Julia was right about that. For a girl from a small city in England who had never even been to London except only on a school trip to see a West End show, this was the same as being rocketed into outer space.

In my purse I had pictures of my mother, my sister, and my father. I had the gold locket they had given me on my sixteenth birthday. I had my birth certificate, my passport that my father never knew I had, and a little more than three and a half thousand pounds that I would exchange for United States dollars at the airport currency kiosk. I had packed a fraction of my wardrobe in my one suitcase, thinking most of my clothes were not really suited for an entertainer in New York City.

I had called for a taxi to the airport, and the car was there at the curb waiting for me. Even at this moment, I couldn't believe I was really doing it. But I was.

I looked back into the house.

"I love you, Daddy," I said, and closed the door behind me before he could reply.

It was the last thing I would ever say to him.

And he had said his last words to me, words that would reverberate over thousands of miles and haunt me all the days of my life.

ONE

When I was a little girl, in the late afternoon or early evening right after the sun set—or what my father referred to as "the gold coin slipping down a slippery sky to float in darkness until morning"—I would edge open the window in the bedroom that I shared with Julia. No matter what the temperature outside, I would crouch to put my ear close to the opening so that I could hear the tinkle of the piano in the Three Bears, a pub down our street in Guildford. During the colder months, when Julia came in, she would scream at me for putting a chill in the room, but she would never tell our father because she knew he likely would take a strap to me for wasting heat and costing us money. Like his father and his father before him, he believed "Spare the rod and spoil the child."

In our house money was the real monarch. Everything in one way or another was measured and judged in terms of it. We could easily substitute "Long live our savings account" in our royal anthem for "Long live our noble queen." I suppose that was only natural and expected: my father was a banker in charge of personal and business loans. He often told us he had to look at people in a cold, hard way and usually tell them that they didn't qualify because they didn't have the collateral. He didn't sugarcoat it, either. He made sure they left feeling like they had cost the bank money just by coming there to seek a loan, for he also believed that "Time is money." He called those whom he rejected—who had convinced themselves they could be granted credit despite the realities of their situation—"dreamers." And he wasn't fond of dreamers.

"They don't have their feet squarely on the ground," he would say. "They bounce and float like loose balloons tossed here and there at the mercy of a mischievous wind."

Sometimes, when I looked at people passing by our house, I imagined them being bounced about like that, and in my mind I would tell them not to go to see my father for financial assistance, to go to another bank. My father was so stern-looking at times that I was afraid to confess I had experienced a dream when sleeping. He might point his thick right forefinger at me and say, "You're doomed to be a balloon."

He wasn't a particularly big man, but he gave off a towering appearance. When he walked, he always kept his five-foot-ten-inch body firm, his posture nearly as perfect as that of the guard at Buckingham Palace with his meticulous stride, even though my father never had military training. He was truly our personal Richard Cory, "a gentleman from sole to crown," just like the man in Edwin Arlington Robinson's poem. And that wasn't simply because of the similarity of his surname. Even on Saturdays and Sundays, he would put on a white shirt and a solid blue, gray, or black tie, no matter how warm the weather. When I asked my mother about it once, she said he simply felt underdressed without his tie. Then she leaned in to add in a whisper, "It's like his shield. He's a knight in shining ties."

He didn't care that so many men his age dressed quite casually most of the time, even at work. But I'd have to admit that when he stood among them, he looked like someone in charge, someone very successful and very self-confident. He did everything with what my mother called "a banker's precision." He shaved every morning with a straight razor, making the exact same strokes the exact same way, and never missed a spot. Sometimes I would watch him make his smooth, careful motions as if he was another Michelangelo, carving his face out of marble. He had his black hair cut or trimmed more often than other men, and he wouldn't step out of the house wearing shoes unless they were shined almost to the point where you could see your face in them. He always carried an umbrella, the same one he had since our mother and he married.

"He brought it on our honeymoon," she said.

But I gathered that he didn't keep it and care for it for romantic reasons. It would have been a waste to do otherwise. He felt justified carrying it no matter what the weather.

"The biggest unintended liar in the U.K. is the weatherman or woman," he would say. He used the umbrella like a walking stick on sunny and partly sunny days, but he was always poised, like an American western cowboy gunman, ready to snap it open on the first drop that touched his face and defeat the rain that dared soil his clothes.

Other people saw him this way, too, as Mr. Correct or Mr. Perfect. Those who couldn't get any bank money from him called him Mr. Scrooge, but everyone would agree that he lived strictly according to his rules.

"Your husband moves like a Swiss timepiece," Mrs. Taylor, our closest neighbor, told my mother once. She was fifteen years older than my mother and had thinning gray hair. In the sunlight she looked bald. Her face had become a dried prune, but her eyes still had a youthful glint, especially when she was being a little playful. "I'd bet my last penny that he takes the same number of steps to work every morning, maybe even the same number of breaths."

"Oh, most probably," my mother replied, not in the least offended. No one could tell when she was, anyway. She was that good at keeping her feelings under lock and key when it came to anyone who wasn't part of our immediate family. Like my father, she believed that your emotions and true feelings were not anyone else's business. "Arthur believes 'Waste not, want not. A penny saved is a penny earned.' He knows just how many dips in the hot water one tea bag will go, and he won't tolerate waste. He always says any man who watches his pennies can be as rich as a king." She did sound a little proud.

Mrs. Taylor pursed her lips and shook her head slowly. "He's like a doctor of finances," she admitted. "When my accounts are a bit sick, he always has a remedy to suggest, and it always works." She laughed. "I've gotten so I try not to waste my energy when I'm walking, even from one room to another. I'm afraid Arthur will see and take me to task."

One day when I was accompanying my father to the greengrocer, I actually counted his steps, and the next day when I watched him go off to work, I realized that he did take the same number to the corner. For a while, everywhere I went with my mother and sister, I counted mine. I watched other people, too, but no one on our street paced their gait with the same accuracy each time as did my father.

Years later, when I was in secondary school, I'd sit by the same window in our bedroom and remember the things that had fascinated me when I was a child, seemingly unimportant memories, like the way my father walked. I'd hear the same music, see similar things, and smell the same flowers, but my reactions were different. I realized that everything had been more intense back then. Even the same colors had been richer, darker, or lighter. It was like thinking about the world in the way a complete stranger would see it. Maturity steals away the baubles, bangles, and beads and leaves you terribly factual and realistic. Nothing was more than it factually was anymore. I thought that was sad. A part of me, a part of everyone, should be a child forever. In a child's eyes, everything is also bigger and more important, especially his or her home. When I look back on it now, I realize how small ours really was.

We lived in a brick two-story, two-bedroom, end-terrace house that shared a common house wall with Mrs. Taylor's house. She was a widow who lived alone, even though her daughter and son wanted her to live with one of them. She said every time they visited her, they began with the same request, but Mrs. Taylor was stubborn and determined not to be dependent.

"I'll be passed around like a hot potato the moment I express an opinion," she said. "When you find your place in this world, dig in."

If I was present, she would nod at me after she spoke, as if she was alive to bestow her wisdom only to me. Maybe that was because I was more attentive in comparison to my mother or my sister. My father once told me never to ignore what people say no matter how insignificant it first seems. "It's the doorway to their secrets. Somewhere between the lines, you'll see what they really think if you listen with both ears."

My father had me believing that it was good to be suspicious of anyone and anything because everything was such a mystery. Shadows falling from passing clouds were there to hide Nature's secrets. People avoided your eyes when they didn't want you to see their deepest and truest thoughts. That was the real reason no one wanted to be surprised when he or she was alone. They wouldn't have time to put on their masks and disguise their real feelings.

"Look at a man's shoes first," he told me when I was older and more interested in boys. "If they're nicked and scuffed, that tells you he's disorganized and irresponsible. Even a poor man can look neat and clean. If a man doesn't respect himself, he won't respect you."

It did no good to tell him that most of the boys in school wore sneakers now, and everyone's were scuffed. To him what was true a hundred years ago was true today. The truth simply wore different clothes. "Scratch the surface of something, and you'll see it hasn't changed no matter what color the new paint. What was true for Adam and Eve is still true for us. Don't fall for shallow and unnecessary changes just because they are in fashion at the moment."

My father was truly more like an Old World prophet, suspicious of so-called modern innovations.

He was like that with all the things in our house, demanding order, defying what he thought were needless alterations. He could tell if my mother moved a candlestick on the mantel or a chair just a little more to the left in the living room. He hated when she changed where something could be found in a closet or a kitchen cabinet. He believed that in a well-kept house, a man could find what he wanted even if he had suddenly lost his sight.

My father wouldn't rage if something had been moved without his knowledge. He would simply stand there with his arms crossed against his chest and wait for my mummy's explanation. If it wasn't good enough, he wouldn't move or look away from her until she had put it back where it had been. No one could say more with silence than my father could.

She'd shake her head afterward and tell me, "Your father remembers where each snowflake fell on our walkway last winter."

Our house had been in my father's family since his grandfather had bought it. My parents had lived in an apartment with Julia until my grandfather's death. My grandmother had died five years earlier. The house had an open hallway in the entry, with a family heirloom, a five-prong dark-walnut rack for hanging coats and hats, on the wall. Our living room was on the left. We had a brick fireplace, but we didn't use it as much as other people used theirs. My father had read an article that revealed that fireplaces sucked up the room's heat and sent it up the chimney along with the pounds we spent on heating oil. He called it "quid smoke." There was another fireplace in our dining room, and that one was used even less, usually begrudgingly after my mum's pleading when we had dinner guests. The dining room had a large window that faced the rear of our house, where we had a small plot of land that my father insisted be used to grow vegetables and not used as our little playground.

"There's no value in anything that doesn't produce or have the capacity to produce," he said. He would often stop in the middle of doing something and make one of his wise pronouncements, even if I was the only one in the room. It was as if he had to get his thoughts out, or they might cause him to explode. He always lifted his heavy dark-brown eyebrows and straightened up before making his statements. How could I not be impressed, even if I didn't agree with him? He was Zeus speaking from Mount Olympus.

At the rear of the house was a patio big enough for us to set a table and dine alfresco in the summer. There was a rear gate that opened to the street behind us as well. Julia and I took that one on weekdays because it put us closer to school, and by this time, she was mimicking our father's own ten commandments, one being, "If you can get somewhere in a shorter time with less wear on the soles of your feet, take it. Make your shoes last longer."

My father permitted my mother to plant flowers along the edges of the yard. She had magic hands when it came to nurturing Blue Dendrobium or Minuets. She planted Mums Surprise in front, where we had evergreen fern as well as Leylandii hedging.

My parents' bedroom was on the first floor, and ours was upstairs. Their bedroom was nearly twice the size of ours and had two views, a side view and a rear view. My mother was proud of her kitchen, which had a Bosch gas stove and oven, an integrated Bosch dishwasher, and a Worcester Bosch combi boiler. We had a basement that my father converted into his home office and another bathroom. Both the upstairs and downstairs had the original wood flooring, which my mother cleaned and polished twice a week.

My father believed that if you took care of old things, they would never be old. People would think you had recently bought them. "Treat everything as if it's destined to become a valuable antique, and you'll never go wrong," he said. "Nothing, no matter how small, should be neglected."

We were a short walk from High Street, which was the English way of saying Main Street. Julia, who eventually became the elementary-school teacher she had intended to become, was always showing off her knowledge, even when she was only fourteen. She loved correcting my grammar and leaped to explain things before our mother could take a breath.

"High Street, you know," she told me once, "is a metonym."

"A what?" I said. I was all of ten.

"It's when something isn't called by its own name but by the name of something closely associated with it," she recited.

"Oh," I said, still not understanding, or, more important, not caring.

"It's like calling Mummy's best dishes china. It comes from its association with Chinese porcelain. We often say 'the crown' when we're referring to the queen. Understand?"

"Yes, yes," I said, before she could go on.

"I'll ask you the meaning in two days," she threatened, because I dismissed her so quickly.

We were quite unalike in so many ways, most of all in how we looked. Julia took after my father more. She was bigger-boned, which gave her "forever wide hips." Her hair was lighter than mine, more a dull hazel brown, and no matter what she washed it with, it was always coarser. She had light-brown eyes and a bigger nose and wider chin but thin lips. I felt sorry for her when people would remark about my good looks and completely ignore her. Sometimes, it felt like we were from two different families.

Ever since I could remember, people would flatter me about my raven-black hair and violet eyes. They called me a young Elizabeth Taylor. My hair was naturally curly, and along with my high cheekbones and full lips, it made me "movie-star material," according to Alfie Cook, who was two years older than me.

When I was in the seventh grade, he vowed he would someday be my boyfriend. He stood there and predicted it with the authority of the prime minister. However, he never was my boyfriend, because I never wanted him to be. He was too serious about it for me, and that diminished any romantic possibilities. He was that way about everything and had his whole life planned out when he was just a little more than fifteen. He did accurately predict that he would go to school to become an accountant, just like his father, and when he graduated, he would become part of his father's company.

"I'll probably be married by twenty-three and eventually have three children, more if one of them isn't a boy. Got to carry on the family name, right?"

I thought that having such a definite plan for yourself meant you had no ambition. Ambition required more risk, more exploring. Of course, my father believed Alfie was the most sensible boy in my school, but I don't think I was ever interested in sensible. To me, being sensible meant denying yourself what you really wanted or wanted to do. There were always good, logical reasons not to buy something or not to do something. I learned that truth from my father after listening to his review of people who came in for loans. He always considered what would be practical, and more often than not, he didn't take any risks.

It's always easier and safer to say no, I thought when I was older, but people who live on noes never explore and never discover. Maybe they need fewer Band-Aids in life, but without any risks, they had less of a life to me. These were my secret thoughts growing up. I don't think there was a day when I didn't fear my father looking at me more closely and then leaping to his feet, his accusing finger pointed at me like a revolver, crying, "You're a balloon. My daughter is a balloon!"

I stopped worrying about it when I was older. I was too intent on becoming a professional singer. Even in grade school, I stood out whenever it was time to sing. Everything seemed to move gracefully for me, carrying me toward that one goal, so I believed it was meant to be. I didn't demand it or even compete for it, but I was quickly singled out in chorus.

Julia blamed herself for my pursuit of a singing career in defiance of my father. She had taken me and my girlfriend Helen Dearwood to the Three Bears to eat. We both could order a pint with our food. Before we were finished, they started the karaoke competition. Helen urged me to go up, and Julia didn't stop me. And after I sang, the pub's owner invited me back to sing. I did a few times, and then he offered me ten pounds for Friday and ten for Saturday. My total singing time wasn't more than a half hour or so in the beginning, but gradually, I sang for longer periods.

How many times would I hear Julia say, "If I had only stopped you that night"?

"It wouldn't have mattered. When you're destined to do something, you do it," I told her, but

I think she liked blaming herself. Maybe it made her feel more important in the family and definitely more aligned with our father's view. When she continually said that, I began thanking her for taking me to the Three Bears, and that put a stop to her mentioning it. I didn't think it was something anyone should be blamed for anyway. When my father wasn't around, my mother took some credit for my singing, revealing she sang when she was younger, but quickly added she would never have considered singing as a career.

"Such a thing never entered my thinking," she told me. "And if it had, I'm sure it would have popped like a soap bubble."

When she said that, I thought I heard a note of regret, not that she would ever admit to it. There was something terribly sad about her whenever she reminisced about her childhood. I could almost smell her thinking about missed chances. I often wondered, if she could have a second go at it, would she still have married my father? She was surely pretty enough to attract most any man. Whatever good features I had, I had inherited from her. But that was all I really wanted to take from her.

Most girls would want to be something like their mothers, but deep in my heart of hearts, I knew I didn't. My mother was full of compromise. She lived solely to be sure my father was happy and content. I loved her, but she was too eager to think less of herself. It's often a good thing to think about someone else before yourself, but there are parts of yourself that you must cherish and nurture if you want to be proud or simply be satisfied with life as you know it. I would never tell anyone that my mother was really unhappy. She was; she just didn't realize it, or want to realize it.

I knew I would never be happy if I didn't set out to see where my future was. Hopefully, it was waiting for me on a stage, behind a microphone, or in front of a television camera. When I left my house that day years later, it was as if someone who had been living inside me for all my life had finally fully emerged. It was her body now; she was taking the footsteps to the taxi, she was boarding the airplane, and she was looking out the window when the New York skyline appeared and, although no one else could see it, fireworks were exploding in the sky.

Emma Corey was coming.

Get ready, world.

This rebirth didn't happen overnight, of course. It took me years to work myself up to the point where I could be so independent and determined. As soon as I was sixteen, there was a second big event in my life that helped me become so. My father knew who owed the bank money, and because of that knowledge, he had influence with many of the smaller businesses in Guildford. As soon as my birthday celebration was over, he informed me that he had found a nice weekend position for me at Bradford's Department Store on High Street.

"Mr. Bradford himself has seen you walking to and from school and thinks you're a perfect fit for his perfume counter. You can take that as a compliment," he added. "He knows you're still in school, of course, so you'll work nine to five Saturday and Sunday. He'll pay you twenty-five pounds a day at the start. In six months, if you work out, which I'm sure you will, he'll raise it to thirty quid. That's a tidy sum for doing nothing more than squeezing scents at women who think an aroma will overcome their ugly faces."

"Oh, what a terrible thing to say, Arthur. Beautiful women wear perfume, too," my mother said.

Daddy grunted, which was really all he would do when Mummy corrected him.

"What about church on Sunday?" my mother asked.

"She can go to the early service if she wants."

My father was not really a churchgoing man, but he did attend services on Sunday occasionally, more, I thought, to chin-wag with some of the successful businessmen who did business at his bank than to pray to be forgiven for his sins. He looked at everything in life from the point of view of profit and loss, even prayer.

"When will she do her homework?" my mother asked him. "They get homework to do on weekends."

"In the evenings. She has both free."

"I'm singing on Fridays, Saturdays, and probably Sundays soon at the Three Bears," I told him.

He stared as if he was trying to decide if I really was his child.

"They give me ten pounds, Daddy," I said proudly, but mainly to measure it in the terms he would appreciate.

"Now, let's see how good you are in math, then. Here," he said, holding out his right hand, "is Mr. Bradford offering you twenty-five to start, and here," he said, holding out his left hand, "is your ten pounds at the pub. How much more will you have if you work at Bradford's and do your homework at night, forgetting about the pub?"

I looked away, and then I smiled. I held out my right hand. "Here's my twenty-five quid at Bradford's, and at night," I said, holding out my left hand, "is my pub ten. That gives me ten on Friday, Saturday, and maybe Sunday, thirty-five on Saturday and thirty-five on Sunday at Bradford's added to it eventually. And when I get my raise, that becomes forty a day. So I'll do my homework early in the morning on Saturday and Sunday or at night when I return from the pub. I could be up to ninety quid over the weekend, including Sunday and my pay raise."

"We have Sunday tea. Forget about the pub on Sunday," he snapped, annoyed that I was using his kind of logic successfully. "It disrespects your mother and me to miss Sunday tea."

"Subtract ten, then," I said with a shrug. "I'm still ahead quite a bit."

"If you're tired when you are at work at Bradford's and drag yourself around yawning in the faces of customers, he'll let me know bloody fast," my father warned. "You don't embarrass me out there, hear?"

"Yes, Daddy. Don't frown so much. You'll get wrinkles and look like an old sod."

I glanced at Julia. She was always astonished at my cheeky way of responding to our father. She would never have dared utter the smallest defiance. Secretly, I thought she wished she was more like me.

Ironically, in the long run I really had my father

to thank for enabling me to go to New York. He'd never have given me a penny for the trip, but by working in Bradford's and with the additional pounds I made singing in the pub and other places, as well as gifts of money on my birthdays, I was able to save a tidy sum, enough to give me the confidence to go forward. My father thought my miserly way when it came to spending my own money was simply due to his good influence.

Probably some of it was his influence, but I wouldn't dare thank him, although at the moment I was leaving and he was raging at me, I was tempted to do it. I wanted to throw something back at him that would put him on his heels and stop him from stringing along his threats. He'd stutter and stammer like an old car engine.

I always tried to swallow away the images and words of that day. It wasn't how I wanted to remember my father. Although he was a stern, unforgiving man, he was generous when it came to dispensing his wisdom, and I would never deny that he was doing so to ensure our welfare. Probably, that was the most I missed from him or about him the day after I had left my family: hearing his advice, his prophetic declarations and firm conclusions. No matter where I went, I would hear his voice often. And in New York, I would meet many men who reminded me of him.

I suppose the greatest bit of wisdom he didn't have to preach to me to get me to believe was that no matter where you go or who you become, you cannot really escape your family, not that I ever really wanted that. They are forever part of you, and whether you realize it or not, they determine who you really are.

But I would meet people, including the man I eventually would marry, who lived to do just that, escape their own families and, in a true sense, escape who they really were.

TWO

Despite my determination, I almost turned back a few times before boarding the plane for New York. Besides the fact that it was my first airplane ride, the sight of all these people coming and going was almost overwhelming enough to send me home. I never really grasped what writers meant when they wrote "a sea of humanity" until I saw the crowds at the airport. People from so many different countries were coming at me and passing by me in waves full of conversations, laughter, hugs, and kisses, many dropping loved ones off and many, out of breath from excitement, rushing to greet arrivals.

There was no one there to bid me a fond farewell, and there would be no one waiting in New York to welcome me. There would be no kisses and hugs. The tears I left behind were so full of sorrow that they would look like droplets on a hot stove, sizzling with sadness. I had kept my travel details secret from friends, but now, at this moment in the airport, I never felt like more of a stranger in a strange land, someone truly alone, and technically, I hadn't yet left England. I wondered if I had made a mistake being so secretive after all.

I tried desperately to hide how much of a novice I was when it came to traveling. If I didn't build up my self-confidence before I left, what would I be like when I arrived in a city with a far larger population mainly quite different not only from me, but many from each other? More often than not, I had been told, New York was a city of strangers rushing by and around one another. I would see someone lying on the sidewalk, maybe on a piece of cardboard with a sign advertising how desperate he or she was, and I would witness how easily people walked by as if no one was there.

"In New York, people are quite invisible," Mr. Wollard had warned me. "It's the way of big cities. They make people afraid and therefore indifferent simply to avoid trouble. Don't expect to make new friends quickly."

Mr. Wollard was the only one in whom I had confided about my final decision to go. He did continually inquire about whether my parents were aware. I didn't want to lie to him. Instead, I admitted, "No, but they're suspicious. I will give my mother and sister all my details before I leave and then tell my father as well."

Mr. Wollard still looked concerned. "I don't know if that's wise, Emma."

"I'm eighteen, Mr. Wollard. I don't need to get

permission, and I'm using only my own money. I have to try, and they'll only try to stop me."

"True, you're an adult, Emma. I'm hoping something good will come of it. I've told many of my students who were in my musicals the same thing when they asked if they should continue pursuing a career in show business. If you have to ask, the answer is no. You were one of the few who didn't ask that. Instead, you asked what do you do next. You knew what you wanted, and that reveals persistence, determination, and courage. Besides, you're a talented young lady. If the Americans aren't total nincompoops, they'll realize it fast."

He shrugged. "You can always come back and try here or go to a school with a performing arts program like our own University of Surrey. I just think you're head and shoulders above their best graduates already. You not only have the beautiful voice, great range, but you have the personality that brings smiles when you sing, and you have the poise." Then he confessed, "I wish I would have had the courage when I was your age."

He had told me about the theater actors' publication *Playbill*, in which open auditions were advertised. He explained that it was difficult getting an agent right from the start, but if I was fortunate enough to land a part, an agent would most likely follow. He said he had never taken the first step and looked melancholy for a moment.

Everyone has a secret ambition. Some are planted in a garden to grow, and some are smothered, I thought. But as I walked toward the boarding gate,

I heard his words again and wondered if my father wasn't right when he said Mr. Wollard should be careful "blowing up a young girl's image of herself."

Was Mr. Wollard living his dream vicariously through me? It made me shudder to think so.

My father was right about so much, I thought, but I wouldn't let him be right about this.

My second moment of hesitation came when they announced the boarding of my flight. I stood there for a few moments staring at the attendant, a young woman who looked not much older than I was. She smiled and lifted her shoulders, asking with her expression, *Are you going or not?*

My upper body surged forward in my impulsive lunge, forcing my legs to catch up.

She laughed and checked my ticket. "Have a great flight," she said. As I started toward the gangway, she asked, "First time?"

"Yes," I said. "How did you know?"

"I looked the same way on my first," she said. "Good luck in New York."

"Thank you."

I felt my whole body relax. Maybe, just maybe, the world out there wasn't as cold and as indifferent as I had been told. I had the same feeling reinforced after spending the journey next to a woman who wasn't much more than in her mid-thirties. She was posh, with her designer clothes, beautiful watch, pearl earrings, and matching pearl necklace, but from the warmth in her blue-gray eyes, I would hesitate to call her arrogant or snobby. Her name was Lila Lester, and she told me she worked in public relations for an up-and-coming women's cologne and perfume company. She showed me a gold bracelet the owner had given her on her recent birthday. It had an inscription, a quote of Coco Chanel's: "A woman who doesn't wear perfume has no future."

"Oh," I said. "I worked at a perfume counter in a department store in Guildford but never bought any of the expensive perfumes, even at an employee's discount. I was saving all my money for this trip."

I had sprayed on my inexpensive cologne, which probably had evaporated by now.

"Don't look so worried," she said, and reached into her purse to produce a small perfume sample from her company. "Here. This will get you through the day."

"Thank you," I said, and smelled it. "Very nice. A little like Norell."

"Very good," she said. "It is."

After that, she told me about herself, about what it was like growing up in Milwaukee, Wisconsin, and what her high school and college life was like. She described how she had met her husband, who now worked at an insurance company in New York, and told me so much about their twelve-year-old daughter, who was showing talent on the piano, that I didn't feel reluctant at all about describing what I was doing. She thought it was exciting. She told me I was quite brave because I didn't really know anyone across the Pond.

"You must really want it," she said.

"I do. Oh, I so do."

She nodded and smiled. "If there weren't dreamers, nothing new would happen."

I didn't say it, but my father would strongly disagree.

When we landed and left the plane, she said good-bye, expecting I would fall quite behind going through customs, but somehow I was moved through quickly. Lila Lester was still waiting for her luggage and waved to me from the carousel.

"Slow today," she said when I reached it to pick up my suitcase. Just then, the bags started to come. "Guess they were waiting for you."

Hers came first, but mine was right behind it.

"How are you getting into the city?" she asked.

"I guess a taxi."

"I have a car waiting. We'll drop you off," she said. "No worries. I live off Central Park West. It's not terribly out of my way."

I wasn't sure where I was going to live exactly, of course, but I had given her my new address. In the limousine, she described what it was like for her, someone from Milwaukee, Wisconsin, to come to New York to live.

"I wasn't much older than you are now and just as frightened."

"Oh, I'm not really frightened," I said.

She smiled. "Sure you are, but it's nothing to be ashamed of. In fact, if you weren't, I'd say you were in for a worse time because you won't be careful."

She told me that not long after she had gotten married in Wisconsin, her husband was promoted to an executive position at the insurance company, so they moved to New York.

"I think I trembled for weeks whenever I would go out alone with my daughter."

After her daughter had reached the age of eight, Mrs. Lester decided to pursue her own career and quickly went from a small public relations firm to her present position.

"So don't let anyone discourage you," she said. "If you're determined, you'll find your place."

I tried to listen to her, but my eyes were being drawn to everything we were passing, especially when we arrived in the city. Of course, I had seen pictures and movies set in New York, but actually being here, my new home now only a step out of the car away, was more than just exciting and intimidating. It was almost unreal. I felt like someone who had stepped into a storybook.

I should have been very tired from the journey and the time difference, but I couldn't stop my heart from pounding. When we passed some Broadway theater marquees, I was totally gaping. I'm sure I looked like what they called a "rube." Mrs. Lester laughed and squeezed my hand.

"Being with you," she said when we reached the address of the apartment building, "is like reliving my youth. Good luck, Emma. Just keep telling yourself, 'I can do this. I can do it.' And before you know it, you will."

"Thank you," I said.

The driver pulled to the curb and got out to open my door and get my suitcase out of the trunk. She slid over to wave. I took my suitcase, smiled and thanked her, and then turned to look at the doorway to my new home.

The building was nothing like I had envisioned. It was a narrow brownstone about four stories high, with a short stoop to a small gray concrete platform with black pipe railings. The street itself was quite busy with traffic and pedestrians. No one gave me much more than a passing glance as I carried my suitcase to the steps. It was obviously a busy rush hour. Everyone was hurrying to get somewhere, and the taxi drivers and other drivers on the street were impatiently pressuring one another. Someone double-parked and caused a cacophony of horns and shouts. When I looked at the faces of those upset, I thought I saw a dozen potential serial killers. The double-parked driver emerged indifferently and opened his car trunk to take out someone's luggage, moving at his own slow pace. The horns grew louder.

Patience is obviously not a virtue here, I thought. The driver glanced back at the traffic behind him with indifference and moved casually into his vehicle. When he pulled away, it was like watching a clogged pipe empty out. How different from the traffic in Guildford, I thought.

Get used to it, Emma Corey, I told myself. *This is going to be your new world.*

I started up the stoop. At the side of the door was the directory. I saw there were eight units, all having names beside the buttons. Which one was going to be mine with whoever I talked into sharing the cost with me? I wondered. The bottom slot listed Leo Abbot, manager, so I pressed that button and waited, expecting him to come to the door to greet me, but instead, I heard a buzzer, which I understood to mean the unlocking of the front door. I stepped into the short entryway, where there was a second door opening to the hallway. I quickly realized there was no elevator.

A door on my right opened, and a short, balding gray-haired man, with glasses that had lenses so thick that they looked like deep-sea goggles, stepped out. He was about my height, very slight in build but with large hands. He impressed me as someone who had shrunk with age, every part of him except his hands. He was wearing a well-worn dark-brown leather vest over a faded white shirt and black slacks, with a pair of what looked like black, furry leather slippers.

"Emma Corey?" he asked.

"Yes."

When he smiled, he looked more like someone's granddad than a landlord. There was warmth and delight in his eyes. I never knew how important it was to have someone look and see you when he or she spoke to you. Most of the people along the way were practically robotic. This was like a warm embrace, and with the way my heart was pounding, I needed that.

"You got here faster than I thought. Good for you. C'mon. I'll show you the apartment. I put some water, bread, eggs and butter, and some coffee and milk in the kitchen for you. Donald Manning sent it over earlier today from his restaurant. He also sent over some fresh bedding and some towels and hand towels. Soap, too. Someone's looking after you. Donald's a good guy, heart o' gold, but he ain't no pushover when it comes to working for him," he warned. "I eat dinner at his place on occasion and see how he cracks the whip."

He paused and looked at me more closely.

"You don't look much more than sixteen. You're

eighteen, right? You're gonna need proof of it at times."

"That doesn't bother me, sir," I said.

He smiled. "Oh, you can call me Leo." He leaned toward me to speak in a loud whisper. "'Course, there are a few tenants here that have other names for me, names that would dirty your ears. Let me carry that for you," he said, reaching for my suitcase.

"I'm fine, thank you." I did think I was stronger than he was.

"Always take advantage of people who want to do something for you," he advised. "This here is New York. It's as rare as a two-dollar bill."

"Oh, I don't wish to take advantage of anyone, Leo."

He laughed and shook his head. "Eager and trusting. Youth is wasted on the young," he declared, and smiled. "You're on the third floor. You ain't gonna gain weight here."

He started up. I followed behind. The walls, the stairs, everything looked well worn and in need of some good repainting and polishing. There were apartment buildings in Guildford that were twice this age, I was sure, that looked much newer, but one of the things Mr. Wollard warned me about was the overall grittiness of New York compared to what I was used to seeing.

"New and well-kept-up places are way out of your league right now, but you'll be comfortable enough. You'll be out working and pursuing your career anyway. Where you live, as long as it's safe, is incidental," he said. "It's one of the reasons the song about New York says, 'If you can make it here, you can make it anywhere.'"

However, the moment we entered the apartment, I could see my mother crying for me. It was much smaller than I had envisioned. The furnishings weren't inexpensive so much as they were worn and looking more like things from a secondhand shop. The kitchen had a small dark-wood table and four matching chairs, two in particular looking stained and chipped. There was a living room with a brown sofa and two chairs with cushions, an oval wood coffee table, and two lamps with shades that looked discolored by something I didn't want to imagine. A television set on a table that seemed too weak to hold it was in the far right corner. A splash of a dark-brown area rug was in front of the sofa.

The bathroom was between the two bedrooms. Each had a double bed. One was totally stripped. The mattress looked okay, but without bedding, the room looked very depressing. I hoped it wouldn't keep someone from moving in to share the rent. Both rooms had dressers and closets with mirrors over the dressers, but the furniture here, too, needed a good polish, and there were nicks and scratches on everything. The wood floors were worn down to the stone or tile beneath them in places. Area rugs would do well to cover the blemishes, I thought. I'd have to do a lot to make it look warm and cozy.

As I gazed at it all, I had a flush of sadness and regret, thinking about the beautiful bedroom Julia and I shared in Guildford. I visualized the flowery pattern of our wallpaper, the Wedgwood-blue floor siding and cornices, and our beautiful silk curtains. Everything in our house was always sparkling clean.

And it was certainly ten times quieter. Right now, even though the windows were closed, the traffic sounded as loud as it did on the street.

"In New York 'specially," Leo Abbot said, perhaps because of the expression on my face, "it ain't so much what the apartment looks like as it is about location. 'Location, location, location,' that's the song the real estate agents sing here.

"You can walk to the restaurant and to Broadway from here quickly. You don't even hafta ride the subway. There's a supermarket 'round the corner and a drugstore on the same street, as well as a bank. Everything's at your fingertips, which is why you should have no problem findin' a roommate. In fact, Donald Manning told me he posted the openin' in his restaurant for you today."

"That's wonderful and kind of him."

He looked around and nodded. "I know you're far from home, Emma. You don't hesitate to come knockin' on my door if you need to know somethin' or want somethin'. I'll leave two sets of keys on the kitchen table. Oh," he said, turning back. "If you want that phone in the kitchen turned on, let me know. You'll need it to get calls from producers, I'm sure," he said, smiling. "I'll put your name in the directory tonight, too. Okay? Any questions?"

"I'm not sure how to get to Mr. Manning's restaurant," I said.

"Oh, right. You're startin' tomorrow, right?"

"I am."

"Okay. I'm sure you know it's called the Last Diner. It looks like one with its booths and long counter. It's two blocks east and one block north.

Probably no more than a ten-minute walk for someone your age. It takes me double that."

"Thank you."

He studied me a moment. "You ain't much younger than my wife was when we first met."

"My mother wasn't much older than me when she married my father."

"Bet your parents weren't happy to see you leave and go so far, eh?"

"No, not happy."

He nodded. "Yeah, well, that's only natural. Don't lose the love of your family, Emma. No one champions you as much as they do."

He paused. I could see he wanted to say more, that he wanted to trust me with more personal information.

"Been a widower for close to four years now. Still not used to it."

"I'm sorry."

"I have two married daughters and five grandchildren, all of whom keep me busy from time to time," he said.

"That's very nice. Do they live in New York?"

"No. One, Toby, lives in Massachusetts, and the other lives in Nevada. My oldest grandchild, Jordan, is goin' to attend college at Columbia next year. He's the one lives in Nevada. His mother's not taking his leavin' home so well. I promised I'd see lots of him, and I'm sure I will." He leaned toward me like someone about to utter a deep secret. "Until he finds a girlfriend or somethin'," he added, smiling.

"Oh, I'm sure he'll never stop coming to see you."

"We'll see. Mothers have to be understandin'. Children need the freedom to grow and develop as individuals on their own. Fathers make like it's easier for them to let go, but it ain't so.

"Anyway, now you've got a future to build. Good luck," he said, and walked out, leaving the keys on the kitchen table.

I didn't move.

What he had said caused me to worry even more about how my mother had reacted to my leaving. Most of the time, she was so tight about her feelings. I knew that holding it all inside wore down your heart. I didn't care what my father had said and threatened. I would call her this week, maybe even tomorrow. She'd be worried that I hadn't arrived safely. I was sure of that.

I began to unpack. After I hung up my things, I fixed my bedding and then decided that I was too excited simply to go to sleep. I would take a walk around the neighborhood and maybe get a bite to eat. I also thought I might find that supermarket and get some cleaning materials. My mother would call this flat a pigsty for sure, but I didn't want to say anything that might insult Mr. Abbot.

I picked up one of the sets of keys and headed out and down the stairs. What I felt stepping out of the front door was like what I imagined a newly hatched chicken felt when it stepped out of a cracked egg. The city was still quite in-your-face with its traffic, pedestrians, and bright lights. Didn't the traffic ever slow down? Or was that description literally right, "the city that never sleeps"?

Although it was a warm June night, I felt a chill. I knew it was just a chill of fear. *It will pass, Emma,* I assured myself.

Now, the wide-eyed newcomer, I started down the street, my gaze going everywhere. In fact, I was so hypnotized by all the movement around me, the lights and tall buildings, I accidentally bumped into a man. Or maybe he bumped into me. I heard something splatter at my feet and looked down, astounded. He had dropped a paper bag that had a bottle of some whiskey in it, the liquor spilling out around the dampened bag and shards of glass. Some people slowed their walk, and some paused to look.

The man looked disheveled, homeless. His shirt was missing buttons, and his pants were held on with a piece of rope. His gray beard was longer in places and quite untrimmed, hair growing even from the crests of his cheeks. His eyes were red, and when his lips parted, I saw he was missing quite a few teeth. His hair was straggly, dirty, and even knotted.

He bellowed like a wounded dog, sending my heart from a flutter to a drumroll. "You made me drop my bottle!" he screamed. "That's twenty dollars."

I gasped and stepped back. "I'm sorry," I said.

"Twenty dollars!" he cried, and held out his grimy right hand.

"Like hell she will," a stout man with short rust-colored hair said, and brushed me aside to step beside me. The disheveled man staggered. "Don't give that guy a penny," the man beside me said, and to demonstrate I shouldn't, he pushed my purse back a bit, holding it so the homeless man couldn't seize it and run. He looked like he was just about to do that. My rescuer was dressed in dark-brown jeans and a T-shirt and had tattoos on both his forearms.

"Let's see what this is all about," he said, and leaned down to touch the liquid on the sidewalk. He brought it to his nose. "This is water, you bastard. Move on, or I'll break your scrawny neck."

The disheveled man cursed and started away.

"You okay, miss?"

"Yes, thank you."

"That's one of them new scams in town. Tourists are fallin' for it all day. Watch yourself."

The people who had paused walked on. He started away. I wanted to shout to him, *I don't know your name!* but he was already crossing the street and quickly disappearing in the pedestrian traffic. I looked back to be sure the homeless man was gone and then hurried along, walking now as fast as anyone else in New York. *Either become one of them, or tuck your tail between your legs and hurry back to Guildford*, I thought.

I was still shaking when I found the supermarket. I went in, located the cleaning things I had wanted and a blueberry muffin. That would be my dinner tonight. All I wanted to do was get back and off the streets.

When I reached the cashier, I took my things out of the cart and watched her ring them up. Then I reached for my purse. I was surprised the clasp was undone. *How careless*, I thought. I opened it and reached in for my wallet.

It wasn't there.

I could feel the panic flow down my face and seize my heart. I hadn't taken it out at the apartment, and of course, I had it with me on the airplane.

"Anything wrong?" the cashier asked. There were people waiting behind me.

"My wallet's gone," I said. "I think it was pinched."

She smiled. "Pinched?"

"That means stolen," a tall man in a jacket and tie two people back said.

"Oh. Well, you've got thirty-two fifty-eight here," the cashier said indifferently. She might as well have said, *Pay up, or get out of the way.*

Fortunately for me, I had listened to advice my father had given me when I had gone on my first school trip. "Never keep all your money in the same place, Emma. Split it up so if you lose some or some is stolen, you'll be all right."

I had put over three hundred dollars in my wallet, which also had so many other important papers and pictures. I quickly located some of the money I had wrapped in a handkerchief and took out a fifty-dollar bill. Still stunned, I gathered my bags and started out. I was really walking in a daze and couldn't stop trembling again when I started back to the apartment. My eyes were searching every alleyway and every person walking toward me to be sure I wouldn't run into the disheveled man again.

"Miss?" I heard coming from right behind me, and stopped. It was the tall gentleman who had explained the meaning of *pinched* to the supermarket cashier. Getting a closer look at him, I thought he wasn't much older than I was. Seeing someone this young in a jacket and tie was reassuring because it reminded me of the young men who worked in the bank with my father. For a moment, I imagined it was my father who had followed me to America just so he could protect me. Wishful thinking.

"Yes?"

"Are you all right?" he asked. Then, before I could respond, he asked, "Where do you think you were robbed?"

I looked around. "About here," I said, and told him what had occurred. "I hadn't taken out my wallet since I left England last night."

"Last night?"

"Yes."

He just stared at me a moment with a grin frozen on his face. He was slim, maybe six feet tall, with interesting eyes. They were charcoal but with a hint of green. I hadn't noticed in the supermarket, but he had a dark complexion, strong, firm lips, and an almost perfect Roman nose. His hair, swept neatly to the sides and just a trifle below his earlobes, was a café noir shade.

"That's terrible," he said. "I mean, terrible that you were taken advantage of just hours after arriving. I've heard stories about tourists being scammed. Is this your first visit?"

"Yes, but it's not a visit. I'm here to begin a career," I said.

He nodded. "Well, what happened from what you described was you were a victim of a double scam." He spoke slowly and didn't sound like he was born in America. I couldn't figure out his accent, however. "The homeless guy was probably partnered with the man who rode in on a white horse. You were distracted while he ventured into your purse. That's what teams like that do. One distracts, and the other picks pockets or whatever. It almost happened to me on a subway in Rome once. A couple across from me began to get hot and heavy with their kissing while an older lady beside me was moving her fingers into my pants pocket. Luckily, I looked down and saw it happening."

"I didn't," I said a bit mournfully. I hated sounding so pitiful.

"Yes, obviously not. You should report it to the police. How much did they get?"

"A little over three hundred U.S. dollars and my English driving license, passport, national health cards, and pictures of family."

"Except for the dollars, the rest is in some garbage bin for sure."

"Yes, well . . . what did you do when you saw the elderly lady's fingers in your pocket?"

"Looked at her. She withdrew them quickly, and I kept my mouth shut. I wasn't about to accuse an elderly Italian lady of pickpocketing me. Not in that subway." He smiled. "You still look pretty shaken up. Where do you live?"

I hesitated. It was like a blinking marquee on the entrance to Heathrow: *Don't Talk to Strangers, Especially in New York*. Was *naive, trusting little fool* written on my face? I had within hours of arriving suffered one disaster. Was I about to suffer another?

"Not far. Thank you for your concern," I said, and started away.

"Hey. Wherever you're going, you're in my neighborhood. I'll walk with you, if you like." He saw the hesitation in my face and smiled. "Okay, I'll give you references."

He shifted his bag of groceries to his left arm and reached into his inside pocket to produce his wallet. Than he flipped it open and showed me his driver's license. His name was Jon Morales. He moved a wallet insert to show me he was an assistant investment manager at the UVE Group. The card had his picture on it. He put his wallet back into his pocket and shifted his grocery bag back to his right arm.

"Is that a bank, UVE?"

"No, it's an investment managing company. I'm training to be a CFP, a certified financial planner. I've been living in New York for only two years. My family lives in San Juan, where my father is in banking."

"So is mine. He's a loan officer."

"So we're practically related," he said, widening his smile.

I had my first real laugh since I had arrived. Suddenly, however, I was feeling quite tired. The jet lag and emotional experience had taken its toll. My body felt like it was sinking in warm mud.

"I'm just around the corner," I said, even though I really wasn't in the mood for company the rest of the way. I just wanted to get to my apartment, have a cup of tea and my muffin, and go to sleep. I'd start cleaning tomorrow after I worked my first day at the restaurant.

"Works for me."

We started down the sidewalk.

"So what career are you beginning?" he asked.

"I'm a singer. But tomorrow, I start in a restaurant."

"Which one?"

"The Last Diner."

"I know it. Have lunch there from time to time. I have a potential client who invests in Broadway shows."

I looked at him suspiciously again.

"You'll never hear me make a promise that's not supported with substantial collateral."

I stopped at my stoop.

"Substantial collateral? Well, what do you know," I said. "I never left home after all."

He had a broad smile smeared across his face. I hadn't looked before, but now I did. His shoes were clean and shiny, one of my father's first tests of a young man's quality.

I started up the steps and turned at the doorway. "Thank you for escorting me, Mr. Morales," I said. "Good luck on your career."

"Good luck on yours," he called when I opened the door.

I nodded. Yes. If I didn't believe it before, I believed it now. I would need lots of that.

Tons, in fact.

And from the way I was introduced to New York, I knew that luck, like money, didn't grow on trees.

Thanks for that one, too, Daddy, I thought, and went into my new home, right now like someone condemned to it.

THREE

Even though I was exhausted, when I finally laid my head on the pillow, I remained with my eyes wide open for at least an hour. The sounds from the street did calm from what they were when I had first arrived, but for me they were still close to the noise of a holiday parade in Guildford. I couldn't shut them out. I had to leave the window open a little, or else the stale odor in the room would also keep me up. I thought I might get some fresh flowers after I had given the whole apartment a good cleaning.

I had left a light on in the bathroom, but neon lights from grand signs across the street flickered on the walls. They seemed strong enough to come right through them. That and the light from buildings outside poured through the sheer old cotton curtains and kept darkness at bay. Realizing I didn't need it because of that, I rose and turned off the bathroom light. The room still seemed to be on fire.

If Daddy were here, I thought as I returned to bed, he'd be ranting about the waste of electricity in those buildings. Why was it necessary to keep the lights on so brightly in empty offices stories high? Was everyone afraid of burglars, even at those heights? How long would it take me to get used to this?

I decided I just had to get thicker curtains for my bedroom. These were too dodgy anyway and might fall apart after one wash. There were sure to be other expenses I had not anticipated. If I took too long learning how to be a waitress, I could run low on funds quickly, especially after having been robbed. This wasn't going to be as easy peasy as I had convinced myself it would be. Another saying of my father's flashed across my mind: "A fool spends no time at all convincing himself of something he knows in his heart to be untrue."

Oh, put a sock in it, Emma Corey, I told myself. *Just imagine your father's look of self-satisfaction if you went running home after only a day in New York. You'd have to get rid of mirrors because of the disappointment that had sunk into your face. Every time he had a chance, your father would remind you of the money you had wasted, not to mention time, which was the same thing to him.*

I won't go home even for a short visit, I vowed, *not until I've had some success that would quell his criticism.*

Who knew? When I returned to New York after that, I might have his blessing. He could even begin to brag, although the few times I had seen my father admit to being wrong, he looked like he would choke. His face would redden, and my mother would have to say, "Breathe, Arthur, breathe."

Still, the thought of all that happening someday filled me with encouragement.

However, when I finally fell asleep, I didn't sleep well. There were so many unexpected sounds to wake me periodically. People in other apartments in the building apparently either worked at night or were serious insomniacs. Sometimes, the footsteps were so loud I sat up, thinking someone had broken into my apartment. I was really looking forward to a roommate, hopefully someone used to all this and therefore someone who could reassure me at night, as well as ease the burden of expenses.

Consequently, I almost overslept and leaped out of bed when I looked at the desk clock I had brought from England. It had been a gift from Mrs. Taylor on my fourteenth birthday. I could still hear her say, "Any daughter of Arthur Corey better know what time it is." She had bought me one that matched the blue in Julia's and my room. Right now its hands were clapping, and its face was screaming, *Get up; get going. You wanted a new life. Start it!*

Not knowing my way around New York, I knew I had to leave myself more time to get to the restaurant. I rushed about, gulping only a glass of milk for breakfast. I wasn't satisfied with the way I looked when I had left, but as Daddy would chant, "Priorities, priorities, when it comes to precious minutes." As I hurried down the stairs, I thought, *Now the apartment building is so quiet?* Maybe the other tenants were all vampires.

As soon as I saw a phone booth, I stopped to call home, because my phone wasn't hooked up yet. I had left earlier as well to make the call, remembering we were five hours behind the U.K. Before I stepped in, I groaned with disappointment. Someone had vandalized the phone and cut the wire connecting the receiver.

I started to panic when I couldn't find a public phone that worked. One after another either had its cord cut or smelled so much like a dirty bathroom that I couldn't imagine going in and closing the door behind me. And with all the noise from traffic and jackhammers, I thought I would surely have to shut myself in the booth and maybe put my finger in my other ear. There finally was a relatively clean working one on the same block as the restaurant. After I stepped in, I realized that I would need quite a few quarters, and I didn't have that many, so I tried a collect call first.

Because it was late June, Julia was off work and answered on the first ring, like someone sitting there beside it and waiting for it to chime. She accepted the charges. Of course, I had no intention of revealing what had happened to me my first night in New York if she asked how I was. I was determined to sound happy and excited.

"Hello," she said in a deep whisper.

"It's me, Julia, Emma."

"I know it's you, you silly goose. Are you calling from New York?"

"Yes, of course."

She sighed so deeply that I thought it might blow out the phone like some light bulb.

"Daddy's going to know you called when he looks

at the phone bill, and I'm going to get into trouble for accepting it," she whined.

It was hardly the response I was hoping to hear.

"I'm sorry, Julia, but I wanted you all to know I had arrived safely. I thought you'd be concerned. I've moved into my apartment, but I don't have a phone hooked up yet, and—"

"Come home, Emma. You made your point. We'll get Daddy to forgive you. Just come home. Please."

For a moment, I was taken aback by the way she was pleading. It was quite unlike her, especially when it came to telling me to do something. But I quickly recovered.

"I have no intention of coming home. I just arrived, Julia. I haven't even begun to try, nor have I begun my job yet. You're the silly goose. Where's Mummy?" I demanded.

"She's lying down. She refused to eat breakfast, even though I brought it to her. Daddy isn't talking to either of us. He still blames us for what you've done. He thinks we knew for weeks and didn't tell him. He called your announcement at dinner the night before another example of a family Pearl Harbor. Mummy couldn't eat and cried all through dinner. Thank you, Emma Corey."

"Is she all right now?"

"No," Julia said, punching the word over a few thousand miles. "How can she be all right now? Daddy's still not talking to her. Aren't you listening?"

Julia was never one to sugarcoat anything, and in that way, she was far more like our father than I was.

"He's not right blaming her or you. I'll send him a letter and tell him so."

"He won't read it, Emma. He really will burn it first as soon as he sees the postmark."

"Then I'll call him at the bank. He'll have to speak to me."

"I wouldn't make a wager on it, Emma. He's probably already told his secretary, that nosy parker Mrs. Weeks, not to transfer any calls from you to him. He's not hiding his anger from people, either. If anyone asks him what you are doing or planning to do, he says, 'I wouldn't know.' That's what he said to Mrs. Taylor already. If he could, he'd take an eraser to your memory right now, and I'd be an only child."

"I'll call and give a different name."

"Brilliant. He'll still hang up on you the moment he hears your voice unless you were calling from this house, and even then I couldn't be sure. Meanwhile, Mummy's upset, and it's making her sick. Just come back."

"I can't, Julia. At least, please tell her I'm safe. I have my apartment, and I'm starting work today, and soon I'll have a phone with a telephone number, probably today. I left a note for the landlord to have that done. He's very nice, by the way, sort of like Mr. McGregor. Remember? The shoe repairman?"

"Telephone? Thanks for reminding me. This call is costing a fortune, I'm sure. Daddy will be even angrier that I spoke longer than a minute to you. Come home. You're acting like a fool and a spoiled brat," she said, and hung up.

The shock of hearing the click and the dead sound threw a chill over me as cold as a pail of ice water. I had been looking forward to hearing my mother's voice and how I would comfort her and assure her I would be fine. For a moment, I simply stood in the phone booth holding the receiver. Then a man in an overcoat and a wide-brim hat knocked on the glass so hard I thought he'd shatter the glass all over me.

"Sorry," I said, opening the door. He grunted. I stepped out quickly and passed him to hurry away. I seemed to be rushing away from everyone right after the moment I had arrived here. I thought I probably already looked like a New Yorker to anyone else who had just arrived. It wouldn't have surprised me to have someone stop me to ask directions to somewhere in Manhattan.

When I reached the entrance to the restaurant, I paused and sucked in my breath the way I would just before I swam underwater. Then I walked in and stood there gazing at the booths, tables, and counter filled with patrons. There was some music vaguely audible over the clang of dishes and conversations. The walls were crowded with pictures of what I imagined were celebrities who had eaten here, spaced in between large photographs of New York City scenes, including the East and Hudson Rivers, as well as the Statue of Liberty.

By the authoritative manner in which Donald Manning came walking toward me the moment I entered the Last Diner, I knew it was he. He was a tall, lean, dark-brown-haired man with a thick dark-brown mustache. He was wearing a gray tie and a black sports jacket with charcoal-gray slacks. I didn't think he was smiling so much as merely pressing his lips in tightly at the corners. I didn't move or so much as grin, unsure of the greeting I was going to receive. I knew I wasn't late, given the time I was told to appear the day after I had arrived, but I so desperately needed a bright welcome.

"Emma Corey?"

"Yes."

He looked me over and nodded. I was afraid he was going to tell me there was no job for me after all. I knew I looked younger than eighteen, but he finally smiled. I released the air nervously trapped in my lungs.

"Billy gave me a good description. I can see why you won his heart," he said, and leaned closer to add, "but he was always a softy for a pretty face."

"I'm not just another pretty face," I said, sounding a bit too indignant. It was not a good way to meet your boss for the first time, but there it was again, that part of my father in me, self-pride not afraid to reveal itself.

Donald Manning surprised me with a laugh. "No, I don't imagine that's all you are." He stopped smiling. "Just know that New York is full of pretty faces. It's no ticket to Broadway on its own, but I suspect Billy made you aware of that. You ever wait tables?"

"Only at home," I said. "My sole job's been behind a perfume and cologne counter at a department store in Guildford. And singing at a pub, of course."

"Well, we'll save your singing for your auditions. How's your apartment?"

"It's fine, sir. Thank you for what you've done. I'll pay you back."

He folded his arms across his narrow chest. "It wasn't me. It was Billy Wollard who had all that set up for you. He sent me a money order, and I did what he asked. Not that I wouldn't have done what he wanted anyway. He did me a lot of favors when we were classmates and studying music at Surrey."

"You studied at Surrey?"

Just hearing the name of a school in Guildford brought me comfort.

"I spent a few years in the military, ended up living in the U.K., and enrolled in some courses because I thought I'd be the next Louis Armstrong."

"So you play the trumpet?"

I had learned a while back that singers and musicians are more comfortable in the company of other singers and musicians. It was as if we all shared a secret.

"Haven't for about ten years. It's buried in a closet. I think I broke Billy's heart more than my own when I gave it up. I got into the restaurant business over there first in London and then returned to sanity here."

He nudged me out of the way of some incoming customers and then took on a more somber look.

"Now, I respect Billy's opinion when it comes to you, but there are teachers like Billy all over this country who believe their protégés can make it on the Great White Way. I've had at least a dozen waiting tables here. None right now, however. They're not the best employees. Their heads are in the clouds, and they don't appreciate the work and what's required of them. Billy thinks you will, says you come from a very respectable family where you were taught to be efficient, responsible, and you have a good work ethic. Since you're the first he's ever sent over here, I will take his word for it."

"Thank you," I said, but I could see he was all business, just as Mr. Abbot had warned.

"I hope you won't let him and me down," he cautioned.

"I won't. I promise."

"Hmm. New York's full of promises, but the people making them don't always fulfill them. Okay. Here's the deal. I'll pay you a dollar over minimum, but you make most of your money with tips. For the first two weeks, you'll train with Marge Arnold over there," he said, nodding toward an attractive blond woman who flashed smiles at the customers at her table as if they were long-lost friends. She was taller than me, with a figure that was struggling to survive the addition of years.

"Marge has no other ambition aside from dating and marrying a millionaire, so she's the best to break you in. But I warn you, she's serious about what she does and how it's to be done. Just mimic her, and you'll be fine. She's doing me a favor by taking you under her wing."

"I understand," I said. Like my father, I hated accepting too many favors. He always thought of it as debt accumulating severe interest.

"It's as simple as that," he said, nodding and smiling at some customers coming into the restaurant before turning back to me. He looked serious again. "I know why you're really here. I'll let you go to any audition you want if you give me fair notice. You'll be going to what they call open auditions until you get an agent."

"I understand."

"Yeah, well, they can take all morning. You'll see the lines down the sidewalk sometimes. I've heard the complaints a thousand times from those employees trying to be the next hot item on Broadway, but you can make up the time by staying longer with your regular daily schedule. We're open twenty-four hours, so you'll always have time to compensate. You can even work on your day off. Got it?"

"Yes, sir."

"Call me Donald. I learned to hate the word 'sir' in the army. Go through the door to the kitchen, and take the door to your immediate left, where you'll find a uniform that should fit. There's a dozen or so hanging up there. There are lockers there, too. Just put your valuables in one with your clothes and take the key. Learn to lock everything up in New York. Thieves smell naivete."

"I'm afraid I learned that the hard way last night," I said, and described the incident and what was stolen.

He shook his head. "It happened to you that fast? Something of a record, I think. Sorry to hear it, but you can't dwell on it. Think of it as you would an audition that didn't pay off."

"I already have. You needn't worry," I said firmly.

He smiled. "Maybe you'll make it here. The Brits do have grit. They held Hitler back until we got into it."

He looked down at my feet. "Those shoes won't work," he said. "You're going to be on your feet ten, twelve hours a day and walking to and from here and all over the city to audition for this and that. Ask Marge where to get the right shoes, and get them this afternoon either during your lunch hour or after work. I'll have my bookkeeper, Mary Springfield, get your information today. She hasn't smiled since she was slapped on the ass at birth, so don't be put off by her manner of speaking. Her 'good morning' can bring you to tears. She doesn't make mistakes, so I overlook it.

"Oh," he said as he was turning to leave me. "I have a name, a number for you to call, someone who wants to share the apartment and expenses with you. She was in here yesterday for breakfast and saw the posting. I think she fancies herself a dancer. Maybe you'll drum up an act together. I'll get it to you later."

"Thank you."

He waved at Marge Arnold and then pointed at me. She studied me a moment, nodded, and smiled at Mr. Manning.

"Go to it," he said. "Get the uniform first. She'll do the rest, and she'll let me know when you're ready to wait tables, so be a fast learner. No real money until then."

"Thank you, si—Donald."

"Billy Wollard," he said, nodding at me. "He was a dreamer, too, but got a case of realism faster than I did. He's got the instincts, but New York is full of very talented people."

If I heard that one more time, I thought I'd scream. I think he saw it in my face.

"Anyway, good luck, Emma Corey."

He walked toward the counter, and I headed for the kitchen door, my legs trembling with every step. I found a uniform that looked like it would fit.

It was a bit shorter and tighter around my bosom than I had anticipated, but as my father often said, "Beggars can't be choosers." I wasn't a beggar, but I was close enough to it. I put my things in a locker and took the key. Then I sucked in my nervousness and stepped back into the restaurant. Marge Arnold was at the counter talking to one of the short-order cooks. She beckoned to me, and I hurried over.

"Emma, is it?"

"Yes."

"I'm Marge, and this is Ralph Buckner, one of the day cooks. We call him Buck."

"How ya doin'?" he said.

"Fine, thank you for asking."

He laughed. "See?" he said to Marge. "There are people who give you a nice answer and not 'What's it to you?'"

"She'll learn," Marge said.

"With you as a teacher, she will."

He went to put on a hamburger, and she turned to me.

"End of the day, after you start taking orders, it's wise to give him a five. He'll make sure to treat your orders quickly, even before some of the others here who don't tip him. Word to the wise, tip well, live well. That's New York, sister."

"Works well in England, too," I said.

She laughed. I was going to quote Samuel Johnson in Boswell's *Life* of Johnson, but I doubted she'd read it. Johnson said he got a better, bigger cut of meat by giving the waiter an extra penny.

"Okay. I got a new table. We're doing the first five booths from right to left and three of those tables across from them. You don't let anyone slip over one of your tables. Some of these birds will peck away your customer if they see a chance. Never neglect one. If you're busy, you tell him or her you'll be right with them. You don't let people think you're too overwhelmed to give them good service, get it?"

"Yes, I do. Thank you. I appreciate what you are doing for me."

"I like your accent. Work it right, and it will get you bigger tips. That, along with a good smile," she said. "Let's get you familiar with the menus, breakfast, lunch, and dinner. You'll taste everything over the next week, so if a customer asks about a choice, you can respond without sounding like a phony. You should know what's in everything, too. People come here with allergies, salt restrictions, whatever."

"The ingredients? Of everything?"

"Yes. What's the matter?" she asked, seeing the expression on my face. She smiled. "The job's more than you thought it would be?"

"A little," I admitted.

"I know. Anyone who doesn't do this kind of work thinks we just jot down a few words, tell the chef, and make sure the customer gets what he or she ordered, always with a fat smile. Then they write us a big tip. Not always big. By the way, you can get stiffed here, especially here. It's New York, the place that made 'Charity begins at home' famous."

"Stiffed?"

"They'll leave you nothing if they have some complaint about the food, the chair, where they're sitting, your attitude, how long it took to get the food . . . on and on. And remember: the customer is always right, even when he's a big idiot, or she is. Women are often the worst tippers. Another thing: we get lots of Europeans here, and they're used to the tip being included. I usually underline 'gratuity' before I give them the check."

She smiled. "All right, relax, Em. You're turning pale enough to ruin someone's appetite. Just follow me around for a while and listen," she said, and headed for a table.

Em, I thought. Only my girlfriends in school called me that. Julia never would, and Mummy certainly wouldn't, especially in front of my father.

Marge paused and tilted her head. I hurried to catch up to her.

Treat it all like a part in a play, I told myself. *Memorize and perform*. Every time I heard how difficult something was here, I could envision my father's face, full of *I told you so*.

By the time my day ended, Donald Manning's prediction had been hammered home to my feet and ankles. Marge, on the other hand, seemed energetic to the end, even getting stronger as the day wore on. The restaurant was always busy, and she barely took a break. She never lost her smile, even though a few of the customers were demanding and nasty. She raised her eyebrows and nodded at me.

However, many of the regulars who came into the Last Diner made sure to sit at her tables. No matter what work you do, I thought, you could become an expert at it. My father wouldn't consider her profession something to pursue, but he would be fair enough to recognize she was good at it.

When we had a chance to talk, I told her about my ambitions. Donald Manning had already told her about Mr. Wollard and their history together. She listened with a strange, thoughtful smile on her face as I told her about my singing history and accomplishments. It was a strange smile because she didn't look that pleased for me. She looked like someone who had heard a similar story so many times that it had become just another sack of nonsense, and by this time at the end of the day, her opinion had become important to me.

"I have to give it a try," I said. It was as if I was underlining it all and following that with a herd of firm exclamation points, but I wanted her to see I was different, more determined than anyone who had worked here to support his or her ambition.

She shrugged. "What do I know about show business? But I don't discourage anybody from doing anything," she said. "All I'll tell you is it's not the end of the world to have to do something else. In the end, most of us do something else."

She looked at my feet and then at her watch. "C'mon. The shoe store that has the best price for the ones I'm wearing is on my way to my subway station."

"You don't live nearby?" I asked, surprised. If I was lucky enough to get a place that was within walking distance, why couldn't she?

"I live in the Bronx," she said. "With my mother and my four-year-old daughter, Jodi. Saves on rent. Jodi's in a preschool. It ain't cheap. Before you ask, Jodi's father's a deadbeat. I don't even know where he is these days."

"Oh, I'm sorry, Marge."

"Yeah, well, some mistakes you pay for, and some you never stop paying for. Got a boyfriend?"

"No."

"Good. You know the joke about taking an aspirin on a date, if you should go on one?"

"No."

"Keep it between your legs until you get home."

"What?" I started to laugh.

"Let's go. Your innocence is bringing me to tears."

We went back to change our clothes, and then I followed along to the shoe store. I studied how she walked and how she avoided people, or, I should say, how she got people to avoid her. She didn't bump into anyone who was oblivious and in her way, either. She could part the Red Sea, I thought, and told her so.

"Always look like you know where you're going, even though you don't. The babe-in-the-woods look attracts the mosquitoes."

I revealed my dreadful experience after I had arrived in New York. It brought her to a complete stop.

"Baptized hours after you arrived?" She shook her head and then smiled and said, "Good."

"Good? Why good?"

"It won't happen to you again. You have been forced to wise up quickly. Trust no one, even if they sign a promise in blood."

I was beginning to miss Guildford in more ways than I thought possible within forty-eight hours of arriving here.

"Let me do the talking in here," she said when we reached the shoe store.

Perhaps because she pitied me because of what had happened to me, she went into the store with me and bickered with the sales manager, moaning about how we were hardworking girls surviving on a few dollars just like him. She went back and forth with him until he dropped the price another four dollars.

"Think of every dollar you save as a tip, and you'll be a better consumer," she said as we left. It was something my father would certainly say. "Know your way back?"

"I . . . yes," I said quickly. I wasn't positive, but I felt relatively sure, and by now, I didn't want to show any more hesitation or indecision, especially to her. I was afraid she'd pounce and declare I wasn't ready for New York and tell Donald Manning to send me back like a fish too small. Even though she admittedly knew nothing of show business, I sensed that the opinion of someone like her, someone battling to survive here, was more important than anyone else's when it came to predicting my future. I was determined to prove to her that I had what it took to turn all this into what we called a doddle, a cinch.

"That's it, honey. You're set as far as your feet go, at least."

"Thank you, Marge."

"Welcome to America. See you tomorrow," she said, and gave me a quick hug. I didn't even have time to raise my arms to hug her back. Now I would call it an American hug.

She hurried off more like someone making an escape. I smiled, watching her a moment, and then I walked back to the apartment building in my new walking shoes. My feet were feeling better already. When I entered, Leo came out of his apartment as if he had been listening for me at his door.

"There's a woman coming here in ten minutes," he said, looking at his watch. He looked at a slip of paper. "A Miss Piper Hurley. She was here earlier, but I didn't want to let her in to look over the place until you were back."

"Oh, right. She saw the advert at the restaurant this morning. I was supposed to call her, but I forgot to stop at a pay phone. Thank you, Leo."

"You have a phone of your own now. It was hooked up. The bill will come this week or so. Your number," he said, handing me a slip of paper, "is written there."

"Thank you very much."

"You don't need to call this Piper Hurley. She'll be here. Looked anxious to find a place. How'd the first day go? Better than yesterday?"

I smiled and nodded. "Harder, but yes, much better. I think anything would be."

"That's the spirit," he said. "Come get me if you need any information for her," he said, and returned to his apartment.

I went up quickly and did what I could to make the apartment more presentable. I imagined it was a good sign that this Piper Hurley was so anxious to see it. And it was good that she was trying to be in show business, too. We would have a lot in common. Perhaps she had just arrived in New York as well.

A little over ten minutes later, I heard the buzzer at the outside door and pressed the button to open it. Then I waited, listening for her footsteps. I didn't even wait for her to knock. I hoped I'd like her, but right now that wasn't a priority. She was, as my father would say, "as good as money in the bank."

"Hey," she said when I opened the door. She was a tall strawberry redhead, very pretty, with a body that looked sixty percent legs in her tight black pants and green jacket with a hood. She wore black leather shoe boots and, from what I could see, no makeup to cover the patches of freckles on the crests of her cheeks, nor did she add any lipstick to enhance her naturally orange-red lips. Her hair was pinned back. With her small features and kelly-green eyes, she had the face for it.

"Hi." For a moment, I wasn't certain she was the person seeking to share the apartment. Perhaps she was a neighbor stopping to say hello. My look of confusion widened her eyes.

"I'm Piper Hurley. Your grandfather wouldn't let me see the place without you."

I laughed. "He's not my grandfather."

"Yeah, well, if he's not, he should try out next audition for grandfathers." When I didn't move, she lifted her hands palms up. "You're looking for someone to share the place with you, right?"

"Oh, right, sorry," I said.

I stepped back, and she entered and began to look around. I smelled the scent of Chanel Nº 5.

"How did you get this location? Who do you know?" she asked.

"A friend of my music teacher in Guildford, England, arranged things for me."

She looked at me and smirked. "It's always who you know in this world, isn't it?"

"I suppose it doesn't hurt," I said.

My father would say it's forty percent, "and you'd better have that sixty percent when the door's opened for you."

"You just came from England?" she asked.

"Last night."

"So how old are you?"

"Eighteen. Just," I added. "What about you?"

"What do you think?"

"Nineteen, twenty?"

She nodded and smiled. "I'll take it."

"The age?" How much older could she be?

"No. I'll share the cost of the pad with you."

"Pad?"

"Apartment. What do you call it in England?"

"A flat. But you haven't seen your bedroom yet."

"What's to see?" she said. She went farther in, glanced at the kitchen, and then looked at what would be her bedroom. "You should see where I just left," she muttered. "So I know the rent. We'll split the utilities. The phone work?"

"Yes. Just today. Mr. Abbot arranged it for me. Here's the number," I said, handing her the slip of paper with it. I had already copied it and pinned it to the wall.

"Great. All right if I move in today? I'm staying with a friend who wants her sofa back."

"Yes, of course."

She looked at me again, this time really looking at me. "You want to be a singer?"

"I am a singer. I came to develop my career on Broadway."

"No kidding." She thought a moment. "You don't

have an agent, too, do you? Your powerful friend of your music teacher get you one?"

"Oh, no. What about you? I think you're a dancer, right?"

"I'm a dancer. I have an agent, but he's not worth more than a subway token. So you have a job at the Last Diner?"

"Yes."

"Another friend of your music teacher?"

"He's the friend, period," I said. "The manager."

"Yeah? I freelance at a burger joint. Maybe you'll help me get some part-time work there if I need it."

"Oh, I don't know. I couldn't promise that. He's doing me so many favors as it is."

"Don't worry about it. When's your first audition?"

"I don't know. I didn't get a copy of *Playbill* yet. I thought I'd settle in first and then—"

"I have one. I'll bring it when I return, and I'll give you my share of the rent."

"Okay."

She had a way of looking at me that made me feel I wasn't authentic.

"You just decided to come here and be on Broadway, huh? Just like that?"

"To try. You never know what you can and can't do until you try. I sang in pubs back home, and I was very popular."

"Pubs. Not exactly training for Broadway, you know."

"Oh, I've been in shows back home."

"I'm Irish, but I've never been to Ireland. I've never been out of New York unless you want to count stepping into Jersey for a party. Don't ask me anything about the Irish, either. I haven't spoken to any relatives there. We can go shopping for some grub when I return."

Like everyone else I had met here, she spoke so quickly, barely taking a breath between sentences.

"Grub?"

"Food. What do you call that in Guildford, England?"

"Food."

She laughed and went to the door. "Teach me some proper English, and I'll teach you some basic steps. Broadway singers have to dance, too."

"Really?"

She raised her eyes the way my father often did when I said something he thought dumb. I didn't mean I didn't know that. I meant really, she'd teach me something? She shook her head like I was someone to be pitied and left.

Not only did most people here speak so quickly, I thought, they did everything so quickly, impulsively. I wished I had spent a little more time getting to know her, even though I was predisposed to say yes simply because I was worried about my funds. She didn't exactly have a letter of reference when she came to my door. Should I have hesitated, done some sort of checking? Had I made another mistake to place at the foot of my innocence? How many mistakes could I make before I'd be sent home?

Then again, Piper Hurley didn't seem to care to know much about me, either, before she had decided to move in with me. I could be some sort of young serial killer or something. Did I look that desperate and innocent? It hadn't taken me long to realize that if I did, it wasn't a good thing here.

"Fools rush in where angels fear to tread," my father would warn. But I was fleeing from all that reasonableness and logic, wasn't I?

Just get used to it all. Get used to the speed. The world could easily pass you by if you are too cautious, I told myself, and returned to cleaning the kitchen to at least get it vaguely to my mother's standards.

Living up to the pace of things here, Piper returned in a little less than an hour. She saw the surprise on my face when I heard her at the door.

"Didn't think I'd come back?" she asked.

"No. I'm just surprised at how quickly you did. Your friend lives close by?"

"No, but I shot a wad on a taxi," she said. She had two suitcases and a large sack of bedding and other linen.

"Wad?"

"Forget it."

I reached for one of her suitcases, and we brought her things to the second bedroom.

"Have you been in shows?" I asked.

"A few regional and three off-Broadway productions that died a quick death," she said, and threw her sack on the floor. She sat and bounced on the mattress. "Nice to have a bed after two months of sofa."

"I'll help you put your things away, if you like."

"Naw, it's okay. Plenty of time." She took a pink pillow out of her sack and put it against the headboard. Then she lay back. "I'm from upstate New York, small town the size of one of these city blocks, if that. What about you?"

"Guildford's not a big city, but it's bigger than a city block, and there are nice houses and apartments outside of High Street." Catching myself, I quickly added, "I mean the main street."

Piper kicked off her boots. "Cozy," she said, looking around. "You don't know how lucky you are getting a place like this in this location."

"Oh, I think I do, but you'd love my family's home if you think this is the bee's knees."

"Whose knees?"

"It means something fabulous."

"Dumb. If you ever got stung, you'd know it's nothing fabulous. Leave a boyfriend behind?"

"No," I said.

There was a silence that I think she interpreted as my waiting for money. "I checked my bank account before I returned. My agent hasn't sent in my money for the last job yet. Should be this week."

"It's okay. We paid for this month."

"So Grandpa won't evict us?"

"No," I said, smiling, but with a little nervousness.

She closed her eyes. "Great. Give me a moment or two. I need to catch my breath," she said. "I packed and got out of there as if the place was on fire. Outlived my welcome, if you know what I mean."

"Fish and visitors smell in three days."

"What?"

"A saying by your Benjamin Franklin."

"The only Benjamin Franklin I'd like to be mine is on a hundred-dollar bill." She closed her eyes.

"Don't you want to make up your bed so you can be comfortable?"

She didn't answer. I shrugged and went out to clean the kitchen and make a list of basic foods. She was so quiet I imagined she had fallen asleep. *There's a difference already*, I thought, recalling how hard it had been for me to fall asleep. Then I looked at my watch and paused.

How did she know the money wasn't in her account yet? Weren't the banks closed? If I asked her, she'd think I didn't trust her, and she might leave.

When I saw my face reflected in the windowpane, it quickly changed to my father's.

He was nodding, his mouth tight, his eyes narrowed.

FOUR

Twenty minutes after she had closed her eyes for a nap, Piper came into the living room. "Sorry I passed out on you. My girlfriend had a party last night, so I didn't get to sleep on her couch until three in the morning."

"Oh, that's all right. I knew you must be tired doing so much so quickly."

"Anyway, I didn't forget." She handed me the most recent edition of *Playbill*.

"Thank you."

"I saw that there's an open call the end of the week for a new musical. They're looking for some supporting roles that require a little solo work. I circled the audition for you. I know this producer. I mean, I know of him. He's always looking to make a discovery. Who knows? Maybe you're it."

"What about dancers? Shouldn't you be going, too?"

"Different audition time. If they did it all together, they'd have a line of candidates that would go over the George Washington Bridge and back into Jersey. Anyway, I'm sorry about the money for the rent. I'm going to my agent's office in the morning and get a check right from his agency."

"That's okay. I haven't set up a bank account yet. I'll do that tomorrow at the bank closest by."

"Perfect. I'll meet you there, and you can deposit the check right away."

Relief washed over me. I would have hated to have made a second mistake in just over forty-eight hours. If I had taken in a deadbeat as a roommate, that certainly would be a classic error. Instead of my name on the directory downstairs, I would have had to post my father's name for financially ignorant people: *Balloon*.

"I've got enough money on me for what we need for some basic food," she said. "I live on a special diet. I'm cheap, a vegetarian. I rarely drink anything alcoholic unless I'm at a party. But I'll pay half of anything we need together."

"Okay. That sounds fine."

"Cleaning, huh?" she said, gazing at the kitchen. "I'm not so good at that, but tell me what you think we need done, and I'll pitch in and do the best I can. My mother stopped asking me to help her years ago. Said I just made her job harder because she had to go over everything I did."

"Oh, don't worry. There's not much more we can do right now. I was surprised to find we had what we would need to hoover. I already did your bedroom, too."

"To hoover? What the hell is that?"

"Oh, that's right, you call it vacuuming here. Just get yourself settled in. We'll work on what's left to do later. I'd like to whitewash the baseboards. I'll speak to Mr. Abbot and see if they permit it."

"Whitewash? You mean paint them?" she asked. She didn't look astonished as much as frightened.

"Yes," I said. "Don't worry. I can do it all."

"They won't pay for the paint," she warned. "I can tell you that. I mean, I didn't expect I'd be sharing that kind of expense. Why fix it up for someone else, anyway? You're not going to live here forever, right?"

"Let's not worry about it now. You're probably right. I've always been accused of being too ambitious about everything."

"Good." She stretched. "We should shop first before it gets too late for either of us," Piper said. "I can put my things away and do my room after we shop. I'll get my jacket, okay?"

"Okay. I wasn't going to do much more tonight, anyway." I paused and smiled at her.

"What?"

"I just thought of something. You're a vegetarian, but you work in a burger place?"

"Oh, I can touch it; I just don't eat it. Speaking of which, we can get something to eat for dinner at the market. They have ready-made stuff. There's even a little area to sit and eat."

"Dinner? That's right. I've been so busy that I forgot I didn't have dinner."

"I never get that busy. I agree with my father when it comes to that. 'You can call me anything you want, but just don't call me late for dinner.' He said that so many times that I hear it in my sleep."

We both laughed. I was feeling a lot better because I had a roommate who was at least close to my age. I was confident we'd have a lot in common, even though there were obviously bridges to cross when it came to becoming close friends.

"So you did have boyfriends, though, right?" she asked as we left. "Someone you left behind, a heart you broke?"

"Not really. Not how you are thinking of a boyfriend. Only good friends, acquaintances."

She raised her eyebrows. When we reached the bottom of the steps, she took my arm and leaned into me.

"Not that I care, but are you a dyke?"

"What? No," I said. For a moment, I thought she looked disappointed. "I went out on dates, with guys, but none of them ever became anything serious."

"Sure," she said, her eyes still full of suspicion.

Leo Abbot opened his door and peered out at us. "Everything good?" he asked, mostly of me.

"Yes," I said. "We're settling in, getting food, and getting to know each other."

"People who share apartments get to know each other real well, real fast," he said. "Dirty habits and all," he added, and then closed the door softly.

"He's a bird," Piper said, smiling.

"Bird? In England, that's slang for a young, sexy girl."

"It's slang here, too, but not for a sexy girl," she said, and walked out, holding the door for me. "Has to do with drugs," she whispered.

I shook my head. Sometimes, I wondered if American was a different language, but I was sure Americans wondered the same about us.

At the market, I ate something close to a shepherd's pie. She had a salad, and we each paid for our own. Afterward, Piper paid for food she said was special and shared what she called the basics. She paid that right to the penny. Despite all I had done today, feeling better about her helped me regain some energy. When we returned, we went about setting up her room and putting away and hanging up her clothes, during which she told me more about herself.

Like me, she had performed in shows throughout her high school years and claimed she was so encouraged by her music teacher that she had decided to pursue dancing as a career. I wondered if that was true. After many things I said I didn't like and liked, she said, "Me, too."

However, unlike me, she came from a broken family. Her parents had gotten a divorce when she was twelve. She said she favored her father more, although, like mine, he wasn't enthusiastic about her trying to make a living in show business. In fact, between the lines, I thought she was saying he wasn't in favor of her making a living at all. He was in favor of her getting married. She called him old-fashioned, stuck in the past. I thought I could say the same for my father, but I didn't. I sensed there were differences between our fathers that would stretch for miles.

Anyway, once Piper started to talk about herself, she didn't want to stop or ask me more about myself. She reminded me of a girl in my class, Violet

Murphy, who was said to be interested in only one subject: herself. I was tired, but I didn't want to be impolite the first day we were together.

"I was supposed to go to college," she said, "but I wasn't much of a student. My mother was on my back all the time because I had barely passing grades. Hated homework. There should be a law against assigning students homework over the weekend. Think about it. Most people who work five days a week get the weekend off from that work. Why aren't we off from schoolwork? I got into trouble more than once groaning too loudly when a teacher assigned something over the weekend. Well, maybe it was more than a groan. I think I said something like 'Fuck no,' and it was like I had set off a firecracker."

She paused. I was never good at hiding surprise or shock.

"I bet you've never been suspended from school, huh?"

"Suspended? No. I was more afraid of my father's reaction to my misbehaving than I was of my teachers. No matter what you do, you have to come home, right?"

"I didn't. Once, anyway. After I got suspended for smoking in the girls' room, I ran away for a week with this guy who worked at a garage. He left school when he was sixteen and got a job as a mechanic."

"Ran away? Where did you go?"

She laughed. "Not far. To his grandmother's house. She had a bit of dementia and didn't even realize we were there nearly a week. I got into more trouble, and he almost lost his job because of it, but that's the way he was."

"Do you still see him?"

"No. Not long after, he was arrested for something and moved on. It was then that my mother decided to take my dancing seriously. Everyone raved about me at the dance clubs, and I guess she thought it was easier than fighting me all the time. It looked like that was all I cared about, anyway. For her, anything that would get me out of the house was gold. In fact, she bought me the bus ticket to New York City. She said, 'I would call it a graduation present, but you didn't graduate.'"

"You didn't graduate?"

"Missed too many classes. No big deal. They don't ask for your graduation certificate at auditions."

I listened as she rattled on about her parents and helped make her bed, even though I thought her sheets could use a wash. The more she told me about herself, the more amazed I was that she had gotten even this far. Mr. Wollard once told me that people start from all different places to get themselves onstage. Sometimes, he said, the harder they struggle to do it, the better they are when they do. I knew he meant that as some form of encouragement, but listening to Piper, I realized I couldn't claim any other struggle to get here besides my father's disapproval. I had so much encouragement from strangers and my teacher. I had earned my compliments. Ironically, after listening to Piper, I wondered if I was really tough enough for the pursuit. She shed disappointments like a snake slithered out of its skin. Maybe that was the real reason my father was so against it for me. He knew I took everything to heart, especially unhappiness.

Thinking this way didn't discourage me, however. It simply suggested I try harder. I vowed to myself that I would master the work at the Last Diner. I would get as crusty as a New Yorker, and nobody would take advantage of me again. I'd make Piper look like a Girl Scout.

"I don't know about you, but I'm exhausted," she said, and fell like an axed tree facedown on her bed as soon as I tucked in her sheets.

"Good idea. Good night," I said.

She groaned something in reply.

Knowing there was someone else with me, someone as tough as she seemed to be, helped me fall asleep a lot sooner than the previous night. I didn't even notice the noise and the lights.

She was still sleeping when I rose. I didn't want to wake her, so I made a pot of coffee and had some toast and jelly. She still hadn't awoken by the time I was ready to leave. I left her a note with the bank's address, looked in on her a final time, and then slipped out quietly.

However, the moment I stepped away from the apartment house, I was feeling skeptical again about her promise to come up with her share of the rent. "You don't want promises in this life," my father would say. "You want guarantees, written guarantees."

It worried me all morning, but she lived up to her word and met me with her check at the nearest bank during my lunch break. She was actually there ahead of me, waiting. I deposited her check, and then I returned to the restaurant. I told Marge about her, or as much about her as I knew. I hadn't wanted to say anything until she had paid the rent.

"Roommates are a tricky business," she said. "Even if you get along real good at the start, the paint has a way of rubbing off. One is always trying to get the other to be more like her. Keep your eyes on the prize, Emma Corey," she warned. "You're not here to make friends, especially ones who will be in and out of your life in the blink of an eye."

I had gotten advice from teachers, from my father, of course, and from older people all my life, but for reasons I couldn't explain, the advice of this hardworking, basically single mother who hadn't had much of a formal education was increasingly the most important to me.

On Friday, I went to the open audition advertised in *Playbill*. Some of the other girls were there hours earlier, apparently. I counted at least sixty ahead of me, and at least that many came after me, all trying out for the same part. I felt funny standing out on a sidewalk in this long line with people who walked by gawking at us. A few of the other girls apparently knew one another from previous auditions. I listened to them talk, realizing a couple of them had been auditioning for years without getting any roles. Why weren't they discouraged? What made them continue? Would it make me? Did I really have what it took to keep trying for years as these girls had been doing? With every passing month, I'd hear my father say, "You could have been well along with your teacher's certificate or in a good bank job."

I couldn't imagine how so many of us could be

auditioned like this, but when it finally came my turn to go in and perform before the producer and his assistants, I realized why it was possible. They gave me barely thirty seconds to sing a song of my choice a cappella. I sang "Smile," a song with music written by Charlie Chaplin. It was a song that always garnered me great applause in the pubs and even brought some of the toughest-looking men to tears. I was almost through the first seven lines when someone interrupted with a curt "Thank you."

For a moment, I didn't move, shocked at how little they had wanted to hear from me; and then I was told to leave my name and contact number. I thought that meant something good, until I learned from others who were leaving that everyone who had sung was told to do the same thing. When I heard nothing after four days, I mentioned that to Piper at dinner one of the few nights she ate with me the first week. She always seemed to have somewhere to go and someone to see. One night, she didn't even come home.

"Welcome to reality, where you're just another number in an audition line," she said.

"It's not my reality. I'm not and never will be just another number," I shot back, with a hint of anger at the mere suggestion.

Her eyes widened. "I hope not. But remember, Emma, the higher you dream in this world, the harder you fall." I was sure that was a line that had been recited to her, maybe often, by her parents or someone who wanted her to do something more substantial with her life.

My father couldn't have said it any better himself.

"Or the higher you soar," I replied. It might be true for her, I thought, but not for me.

She laughed and then leaned forward to whisper, even though there was no one else in the apartment but me, "You're probably wondering where I've been some nights this week."

"I'm sure you have lots of friends," I said.

"No, as a matter of fact, I don't. However," she said, smiling, "I met someone, someone who even my mother would call substantial."

"Really? Who is he? I mean, what's substantial mean?"

"He earns a very good salary as a radio engineer at WVOS AM, a station here in Manhattan. He's not terribly handsome, but he treats me as if I was a princess. Polite as an undertaker. Lives in Queens. After last night, he gave me this," she said, and pulled the necklace up and out of her shirt to show me a black cameo. "Said it was his grandmother's."

"It's beautiful. It looks like a valuable antique. He gave you that after only a few days?"

"Like I said," she replied with a shrug, tucking the necklace back under her shirt, "he's not terribly handsome, so having someone like me on his arm lights up his bulbs."

"If you don't find him attractive, how—"

"Here's a secret a girlfriend of mine in high school taught me. You pick out a guy you'd die to sleep with and picture him when you make love to any other guy. If he's worth it, of course. Jerome is worth it. I call him my backstop."

"What's that?"

"You know, someone you can depend on if you

fail. It's kind of like putting money in the bank. When you need it, you take it out. Didn't your father ever tell you that?"

"Not in that sense, no," I said. "It sounds like you're using someone."

"Duh? Everybody uses everybody. Don't look so shocked, Emma. You and I are using each other, aren't we?"

"What do you mean?"

"I'm paying half of this place so you can live here, and you're paying half so I can. It's not a sin; it's life," she said. "I'm trying out for something tomorrow," she added, maybe to get off the subject because I was questioning her too closely. "It's off-Broadway, kind of a spoof of the cancan. You know what that is, right?"

"Yes."

"Jerome knew someone who knew someone involved with the production, so I have a good shot. See what I mean about using someone? You'd better get into it if you want to survive here," she added.

I'm certain my reflexive look of disapproval was annoying to her.

"I'm not comfortable taking advantage of someone's generosity. My father always said, 'Accepting someone's generosity without giving back something of equal value is the same as accumulating debt.'"

"Oh, brother. No wonder you ran away from home."

"I didn't run away. I came here to pursue my career."

She shrugged. "Whatever. I'm going to spend the

weekend with Jerome. I need some new clothes, and he promised to take me to a mall."

"You mean you'll have him buy you new clothes?"

"I won't make him. He wants to. Never stop a man from rushing into a jewelry store," she said, with a grin my father would say could make Satan jealous.

She stopped smiling when I didn't.

"You're so serious, Emma," she said. "Especially for someone your age. Are all English girls like you?"

"No," I said. Although I thought it, I didn't add, *Nor like you*.

She shrugged and then brightened. "The latest *Playbill* is out tomorrow. I hear there are at least a half dozen open calls this week and next. Maybe you'll get into a chorus. Girls get discovered when they're in choruses, too, so don't knock it."

"I wouldn't. I don't expect to be a star overnight."

"I did." She thought, and laughed. "Still do."

We heard the door buzzer.

"Expecting someone?" she asked.

"No. Are you?" I was thinking it might be her Jerome.

"No. It's probably someone selling something for sure. Get rid of him."

I went to the speaker and pressed the call button. "Yes?"

"Hi. It's Jon Morales. I was passing by and thought I'd stop by to see how you were doing."

Jon Morales? I thought for a moment and then remembered.

"Oh. I'm fine. Thank you."

"Would you like to go for a coffee?"

I looked at Piper, who was standing beside me now, listening with interest.

"We're just finishing dinner. I mean, we haven't done the dishes yet. But thank you," I said. Then I whispered to Piper, "It's just someone I met quickly at a supermarket. He helped me in a small way the first night I arrived."

"Quickly's good. Invite him up," she said. "I'll look him over for you."

"So you have a roommate?" he asked, probably because he heard her voice in the background.

"Yes, she does," Piper said before I could. "Come on up. We'll let you wash a dish."

She pressed the button to open the front door before I could object.

"You shouldn't have done that. I really don't know him."

"Don't worry about it. If he's a loser, I'll get rid of him for you."

"It's not that so much. My first impression is he's far from a loser, but between work and pursuing my career, I don't have time to invest in anyone. I didn't come here for that."

"We all come here for that, unless you're a nun. I keep telling you. Don't take everything so seriously," she said. "Especially men."

This way of treating people like disposable goods was annoying me. I retreated silently to the kitchen and began to clear off the dishes while she went to the bathroom to put on lipstick and fix her hair. Moments later, the apartment door buzzer sounded.

"I'll get it," she said, and moved quickly to let

him in. "Hi. I'm Piper," she announced as soon as she opened the door. "Emma's new roommate."

"Hi," Jon said, and walked in when she stepped back with a pirouette that made him laugh.

"Yes, I'm a dancer," she said.

Jon came farther in and smiled at me. "Hi. I didn't mean to interrupt anything. I haven't had a chance to stop by the restaurant again to see how you were doing. Had a heavy week."

"You're not interrupting anything we don't want interrupted," Piper said. "Cleanup. Would you like a cup of coffee here instead of paying a week's salary for one?" She winked at me. "We were going to have coffee, weren't we, Emma?"

I hesitated just long enough for him to take a step back.

"Oh, no, no," he said. "I didn't mean to intrude."

"Why not?" Piper asked, and he smiled. He looked at me to rescue him. Actually, I wanted to rescue myself. "I'd like to hear all about how you helped Emma her first night in America."

"I didn't do much more than explain the word 'pinched,'" he said, smiling.

The look on her face finally brought a smile to mine. She looked from me to him.

"Pinched? You have to explain that? I think I know what pinched means. I've had my rear pinched many times."

"You know," I said to Jon, ignoring her. "I think I'll take you up on that walk you promised the last time we spoke." I put the dish towel down. "I think it's Piper's turn to clean up, anyway. Right, Piper?"

She looked dumbfounded for a moment and

then smiled. “I don’t think we have to worry about Emma. She knows how to take care of herself now.”

I reached for my light jacket on the hook by the door. He sensed the urgency and opened it quickly.

“Nice to meet you, Piper,” he said. “Nice pirouette, too,” he added.

I stepped out, and he closed the door before Piper could say anything or, worse, invite herself.

“Did she come with the apartment?” he asked as we descended. “Something in the closet, maybe?”

“No, but I’m thinking she does come with New York,” I said.

He laughed, and we headed out.

I had no idea where we would go. I simply wanted to get him away from Piper.

“Let’s walk toward Times Square,” he said. “I know a great frozen-custard kiosk. How is the work going? Are you waiting on customers yet?”

“Monday,” I said. “Just in time. My funds are getting low, but there are also a number of open auditions. I’ll be busy day and night, because I have to make up the time I spend on auditions,” I added, my voice full of warning that spelled out, *Don’t try to develop a relationship with me, not now.*

“I think it’s great that you’re so determined,” he said. “People who discourage easily aren’t meant for careers like the one you’re pursuing.”

Even though I was fighting off admiring anything about him, I liked how softly he spoke, especially in the midst of all the noise and activity around us. He had a comforting calmness. There was a special energy in New York that seemed to come right out of the ground beneath your feet and then swirl around you.

Tourists, many who were obviously here for the first time, were like children brought to their first fun fair or circus. I had felt excitement when I was on our school trip to the West End in London, but it didn't seem to be as explosive as this. People here were shouting to each other even though they were inches away from each other. They walked very quickly, so quickly it seemed the sidewalk was flowing. When I gazed around, it looked like a mass of humanity weaving in and out, and across each other, eyes captured by the bright marquees announcing shows, while giant billboards flashed faces and products. Grand lights washed out the possibility of seeing the stars. An underlying fear streamed beneath my own excitement: it was easy to drown here, to disappear faster than you ever imagined.

"My music teacher used to say people who were successful in entertainment of any kind, including writers and poets, had to have at minimum sixty percent perseverance and forty percent talent," I said. "There are lots of people with talent they just don't develop. For them, the talent is more of a burden."

"Why a burden?"

"It haunts, wants to know why you left it stranded."

He laughed. "You're quite remarkable for someone your age. I sensed that almost immediately."

I shrugged. Compliments like that were dangerous, I thought. They'd get me off my purpose.

I wouldn't dare fall in love. I wouldn't even fall in like that much. There were already too many distractions, too many things tempting you to lose your concentration. Surely, he would sense the reluctance in me soon.

"How does your family feel about your doing this?"

"Not good. My father was so furious about it that he told me if I left, I'd be disowned. He even said he'd burn any letters I sent home."

"Really? That's severe."

"Sometimes, we're like oil and water," I said, recalling how Mummy put it. "He thinks I'm messing up my life. I'll succeed just to show him he's wrong. I dread ever giving him the satisfaction he was right."

"Don't worry. You won't fail, not with that level of determination. Here's the custard," he said, gently turning me to a kiosk. "What flavor?"

"Vanilla, thank you," I said.

He bought us both cones, and we sat on a nearby bench.

"It's fun just sitting and watching people. Trying to guess where they're from or where they're going."

"How long have you been here?" I had tried to fight back asking him questions about himself. It was dangerous, like putting yourself in the path of deeper feelings. Along with that would come guilt for ignoring him or pushing him out of my mind so that I could concentrate on my career. It would be painful to hurt someone as nice as he was, I thought. I didn't want to be put in the position of having to do it. Without my being too cold, perhaps he would get the idea after tonight.

"A couple of years into my job, but I've been to New York many times. Each time I returned, it was like I had first arrived. It has that way of putting on a fresh face. You'll see," he said. "It surprises."

The silence that shortly followed made me uncomfortable, and I rushed to fill it.

"I'd better get back. I need a good night's sleep. I'm going to do ten hours tomorrow at the restaurant. Marge might give me a table or two before Monday, too."

"Marge?" he asked as we stood.

"She's the one training me. She's very nice."

"So what's with this roommate you got so quickly?" he asked as we started back.

"She's trying to be a dancer, but I don't think she's half as serious about it as I am about singing."

"I know you won't let her mess things up for you, but sometimes people get you to do things you don't want to do."

"Not me," I said.

He smiled and nodded, but he still looked concerned.

When we reached my apartment building, he and I paused at the foot of the stairway. He took out one of his business cards.

"I wrote my personal number on the back. If there's any night in the near future when you're free to go to dinner, just let me know. All I need is a couple of hours' notice."

"You have no other obligations?" What I really meant was *no other girlfriends?*

"None that I wouldn't cancel to see you," he said. "Good luck on the auditions and the work. I'm sure you'll do well."

"Thank you, and thanks for the custard."

"My pleasure."

He wanted to kiss me good night. His eyes were as good as tiny windows to his thoughts. A part of me wanted to let him, even encourage him to do it, but my ambition growled warnings. I offered only a smile and started up the stairs.

When I turned at the door, he was still standing there.

I'd be a liar if I told myself I wished he wasn't, but if this was all that happened to me after coming to New York, I would be forever disappointed. I'd even resent him perhaps for stepping in my way. What sort of a future together would that bring? Perhaps it was terrible to think it, but for many girls my age who had dreams to fulfill, marriage loomed like a cage. For the most part, this wasn't true for men, which was why I believed my father, with all his wisdom, was blind.

Was it arrogant of me to think I was wiser?

And yet Jon Morales personified such an easy way out and perhaps an easy way to go back home. I could just imagine the look on my father's face when I announced my engagement to someone in finance.

He'd be lost for words. It was tempting.

Be careful, Emma, I told myself. *You're alone and very vulnerable*.

Falling in love is too easy for someone desperate to be recognized.

FIVE

When I looked through *Playbill*, I saw that Piper was right about the number of open auditions coming up over the next few weeks. However, two were scheduled on the same day and very close in time, so I had to decide which one I'd try. As early as I got to any, there were always dozens and dozens of other girls waiting to try out. I knew I'd spend hours in line, even in the rain. And it wasn't easy making up the time at the restaurant. Some days I was working more like fourteen hours than eleven or twelve.

I didn't want to ask Piper for advice to help me make my choice. The more we spoke, the more I was convinced that she really didn't know all that much about Broadway theater, or any theater for that matter. I even had doubts about the performances she claimed to have done in high school. She was unable to describe the shows in any sort of detail, and with some, she couldn't remember the story. Of course, people made things up to help themselves look better and seem more experienced, but I was coming to believe she wasn't as determined to succeed in show business as she claimed she was.

There were auditions she should have gone to that I went to. Dancers were needed in those shows, too, but she always came up with some sort of an excuse for why she couldn't go. Usually, it was either she had to work at the burger place or the show didn't have that much opportunity for dancers. Once she complained about muscle strain in her legs. Supposedly, she had dance lessons twice a week in a school managed by a famous Broadway dancing star who was close to eighty years old, someone she said was a "slave driver."

She didn't get the dancing part she had auditioned for off-Broadway, but when I listened to her explanation, I began to wonder if she had even really tried out for it. Everything she had failed at, dancing or otherwise, was always someone else's fault. Was this what happened to performers who failed to get a foothold? I worried that I might become like her eventually. My father always said that rationalization was poison. "In the end, it kills your ambition and work ethic." You might find ways to avoid the truth at the moment, but eventually there was no way around it.

I tried not to let her be a bad influence on me. She was like the bad angel sitting on one shoulder, whispering in your ear.

"As you've said a few times, Piper, a lot of it is luck," I told her, mainly to get her to stop cursing out the casting director and his assistants, who were all "too stupid" to be in executive positions. I wasn't used to a woman, especially one close to my age, using such raw language about the anatomy of people who had passed judgment on her talents. According to her, all the men had small penises and the women had their vaginas sewn shut. And that was just the beginning of her rant.

Getting her to accept bad luck as an excuse at least got her off the topic. Luck, after all, was random and had little to do with a decision about your talent, even whether there was any there. That helped her feel less terrible about being rejected, not that she ever took it as hard as I did. She would rather talk about her social life, anyway, which was still built around her patron of the arts, as she called Jerome, after I had explained what that was. She was more intent on not missing any parties than she was on not missing auditions. Over the next few weeks, she continually tried to get me to go to some, even directly from work, but I repeated how I was here for a career, not a social life. Besides, I was really tired and wondered why she wasn't.

"You can have both, you know," she said. "A professional life and a social life."

"Not me, not yet. First, I want to get a foothold on my singing career."

"You're wasting your youth," she warned. "Won't be long before men stop looking at you. I saw it happen to my mother, but that's not going to happen to me."

She paused a moment, thought, and smiled.

"Don't disappoint that Jon Morales, or if you

want, send him my way. I could give up Jerome for him in a heartbeat, even if he isn't a patron of the arts."

She laughed. I ignored her whenever she mentioned Jon, always assuring me that Puerto Rican men were great lovers. She said she'd had a few and spoke from experience, experience I didn't care to hear described. If anything, I thought she was behaving as if she and I were at some college, living in some dorm with our real lives out there yet to be begun. Maybe I came off snobby or boring, but most of the time, I felt I was the older of the two.

I was certainly more responsible when it came to caring for our apartment. Her room always looked like wild boars had charged through it: clothes strewn about over chairs and tables, and some even left on the floor, including panties! She rarely made her bed, and if she did, it looked like it was made by a four-year-old. When she wasn't home, I ended up straightening it a bit, especially to pick up any food she had left on the night table or even in her bed. I had to do the same in our living room and kitchen. It worried me. Mice or maybe even rats were probably shopping these tenements looking for a banquet.

However, despite fighting it, I did think about Jon Morales occasionally, maybe more than occasionally. Whenever a young man in a jacket and tie entered the Last Diner, I would pause, expecting it might be he. Marge, who had made me a personal cause, caught my interest and started to tease me a little.

"Waiting for someone?" she'd ask, smiling.

Of course, I assured her I wasn't, even though I knew I was revealing some disappointment that it wasn't Jon, a feeling of disappointment that surprised and disturbed me. I was still very determined not to permit anyone, especially a man, to distract me from my goal. But it increasingly seemed like I had to remind myself more often than I would have thought necessary.

After a while, I convinced myself that I was relieved he wasn't pursuing a relationship with me. I knew that other girls my age would spend more time wondering why and thinking perhaps that they were lacking in some respect. Maybe they could make themselves more attractive or more pleasant to be with, or maybe they could flirt just a little more. I had heard girls back in England talk like this when they were pursuing one boy or another. I thought I was strong enough to put all that aside for now.

However, Jon eventually called, ostensibly to see how my work as a waitress was going. I knew I hadn't left him with much hope. Perhaps he had thought that the passing of time would have softened me.

"I'm coming to the Last Diner with some of my associates for lunch on Thursday. Are you working then?"

"Yes, I am. I'm working extra hours to make up for new auditions. They take hours and hours for thirty seconds to a minute of performance. I barely have time to eat and sleep these days."

He laughed. "It won't take you long to become an experienced thespian," he said. Because I had mentioned eating, I was expecting him to bring up our potential dinner date, but he didn't. Anyway, if he had, I was determined to refuse. However, because he was so nice, I asked him for his advice on choosing which open audition to try between the two that were happening almost simultaneously on Friday.

"I'm not that familiar with either of the productions, but I'll do some research for you. I know some people who follow theater. I'll get back to you and get some information for you to make a wise choice."

"Thank you, Jon."

"I'll tell you on Thursday," he said. There was a pause. Here comes the dinner-date invitation, I thought, but he surprised me. "How's everything else that's going on in your life, your apartment, etcetera?"

I knew he was referring to Piper.

"I'm surviving," I said. "I'm on what they call a learning curve."

He laughed. "In New York, just realizing you have lots to learn about people is way more than half the battle. See you Thursday."

"Yes," I said, without much enthusiasm. "See you Thursday."

I didn't like being unappreciative and cold to someone who had been kind to me. Jon wasn't the only one who had shown some concern for me, and I knew I should show everyone more gratitude. From the way Piper described her own initial experiences in New York and things I overheard other waiters and waitresses say at the restaurant, I realized I had been lucky to meet people who were considerate and took to watching out for my welfare.

Leo Abbot was always asking me how things were whenever he saw me, sometimes giving me the feeling he was waiting at his window to spot me coming home. Marge was more like an older sister now, and Donald Manning gave me every break he could. All the short-order cooks were treating me like their younger sister, too. I knew some of the other waitresses were jealous over the attention I was receiving. All this kindness made me homesick.

Twice during the week, I called home hoping Mummy would pick up. I called early enough so that both my father and Julia would be at work, but she didn't answer. I was afraid to leave a message that my father might hear first and that would send him into some tirade that would bring my mother to more tears. I did write a letter, addressing it to "The Corey Family." I described my start at work and the few auditions I had attended, making it all sound as perfect as I could. In the letter, I put my telephone number and some suggested times they could call.

But considering work, going to the auditions, and the time difference, my chances to receive a call or even make one were quite diminished. From Julia's description, I could only imagine how troubled Mummy still was. If she did answer and hear my voice, I was sure she would only start crying, and I would not only make things worse for myself, I'd make them worse for her. Better to wait for either Julia or her to call me after they had received my letter, I thought. Or hopefully, when something positive happened and I could get them to see I was doing the right thing. It was the only chance I had to turn my father toward accepting what I had done. Even though I knew that if he did, it would be reluctantly. To get him to that point would be as difficult as pulling an elephant backward.

Meanwhile, each of the auditions I attended was similar to the first. For the first two new ones, the line seemed to be twice as long. For the third, we were all given a minute or so to read a song sheet for one of the numbers in the musical. Many of the girls trying out couldn't read music. I thought, *Finally, finally, I have a big advantage*.

Apparently, I did. I received a callback. Piper was very impressed when I cried out joyfully after hanging up the following day.

"What was that?" she asked, rushing out of her room. "Someone die?"

"No. It's good. I received a callback."

"Really? It's only your fourth try," she said, a little bitterly, I thought. "I've had fifteen in a row without a callback." She was really whining.

"I'm sorry," I said, even though I had my doubts she had gone to as many as fifteen auditions.

She looked like she might cry. Then she smiled. "But you're right . . . it's got a lot to do with luck," she declared, and returned to her room.

Now I wanted to think otherwise: that whether I received a callback had more to do with my talent. The problem, I realized, was that the callback was the same day as the other two competing auditions. The scheduling was even more complicated when I tried to figure in my work hours at the Last Diner. I saw no way not to miss the entire workday. I'd either have to take on some late-evening hours or see if someone wanted to take some time off.

The two simultaneous auditions were starting earlier than my callback. I thought of getting to one ridiculously early so I could be one of the first to perform. I wasn't sure which of the two was worth the extra effort, and if for some reason I was delayed, I'd have to leave. Getting there early would have been an entire waste of time, time I had to make up at the restaurant. I thought about it all the following day, and when I came home, I decided I couldn't wait for Thursday. I called Jon for his advice. Maybe he had spoken to his friend familiar with the theater.

"Should I try to work in two?"

"No, Emma. Put everything you have, every spare minute, into the callback," he said without hesitation. "Forget about the other open auditions. Who was it who said 'A bird in the hand is worth two in the bush'?"

"It's an old English proverb. Our neighbor in Guildford uses it often."

"Proverbs are tried-and-true wisdom," he said, and I laughed, thinking he really was so sweet.

I'm slipping, I thought suddenly. Was I now looking forward to dinner with him and quietly regretting that he hadn't brought it up again?

"Thank you, Jon."

"Thank you for calling and thinking enough of me to ask my advice," he said.

"Will I see you for lunch tomorrow?"

"Absolutely. Until then," he said.

"Will I see you for lunch tomorrow?" What am I doing? I thought after I hung up. *I came here to*

build my career, and instead, I'm thinking I might have a relationship and fall in love. Then what? I give up all my dreams and do what my father was always predicting I would: marry and have kids and throw away my dreams like wedding rice as I rode off into the sunset? Get hold of yourself, Emma Corey. You can have a friend, but a lover? Not now. Get a grip.

Because of this, I was actually nervous about seeing him the next day. As he promised, he came in with two associates, both about his age. I knew what he was doing by introducing me to them. He wanted their approval, and from the way they were looking at me, he was getting it.

Marge was all smiles when I started for the counter to bring their orders to Buck.

"Special customer?" she teased.

"He's just a friend," I said, passing her in the aisle.

"Does he know that?" she asked. "You could be a heartbreaker, Em."

It gave me pause. I looked back at him and saw how he was watching me. Was I doing something horrible by leading him on, only to turn him away firmly in the end? What did you have to do not to lead a man on? Be nasty or indifferent right from the start? I thought I had been indifferent enough, but apparently not. When does friendship start to slip into romance? I had always been quite good about seeing the difference, but right now, my mind was clouded by so many things.

"Wishing you good luck tomorrow," Jon said when I brought them their food.

"Thank you."

"Are you going home afterward or coming here to work?" he asked. The other two were watching me closely for my reaction to his question.

"I'm coming to work," I said. "So much time to make up."

"I hope you'll call me if you get good news."

"Oh, if I get good news, I'll ring up everyone in the city," I said, and his friends laughed.

"Don't be discouraged if you don't," he warned.

"Discouraged? That word isn't even in my vocabulary," I replied. His friends laughed again. When I looked back at the three of them, they were talking and laughing and nodding my way.

"No matter what, you'll get a good tip there," Marge said.

"It's all I want right now," I insisted.

She looked impressed.

"Hey," Buck said to me when I came to the counter to pick up food for another table. "If you get a free night or two, I've got a friend who says he can get you a tryout at Danny's Hideaway. They're looking for a lounge singer for weekends. Some quick money."

"Oh, thank you. I have Saturday night free. I'm working right after my audition. Is Saturday too late?"

"I don't think so. I'll get back to you," he said. "Might be perfect to sing a few on a Saturday night. They'll see audience reaction."

"Thank you, Buck."

"My pleasure, Emma." I thought his eyes were twinkling.

"Careful," Marge whispered. "He's broken more hearts than eggs for omelets."

I laughed, but all this sudden male attention was making me very nervous.

When Jon and his friends were done and leaving, he cut away from them to speak to me as I headed back to the counter with a new order for another table.

"Any chance I can take you to dinner tomorrow night?" he asked. "Either to cheer you up or to celebrate."

"Oh, thank you, but I have to work after the audition."

"Oh, right. You said that." His face brightened. "How about Saturday night?"

"I think I'm having another audition."

"Saturday night?" Skepticism seeped into his smile. Was I brushing him off?

"At a club," I said. He pulled his head back as if I had revealed I worked as a prostitute or something.

"You wanna do that?"

"Singing is what I do, what I live to do. It's the most important thing to me right now."

"Right. Well, good luck. Seems like things are coming your way," he said, but he didn't sound overjoyed. "Give me a call when you know something."

He joined his friends. I watched them leave and thought he surely had bragged to them and was now trying to explain why things weren't moving rapidly ahead with me. For a moment, I felt guiltier than I had when I told my father my singing was more important than anything he could suggest I do.

That evening after work, I was too tired even to bother straightening up the apartment. I had eaten something at the restaurant before I left. Now I wanted to concentrate only on the song sheet for the callback in the morning. I lay down and sang it to myself.

My concentration was interrupted when I heard voices in the hall, lots of voices. Suddenly, the door was thrown open, and Piper, leading four other people, entered, a bottle of red wine in each of her hands.

"Emma!" she cried. "I want you to meet Jerome and some of my friends, our friends. We're all here to celebrate your first callback. We have food, more wine, and a luscious dessert."

I said nothing. I stared blankly at them. Why would I want to celebrate with people I didn't know?

"Say hello, Jerome," she commanded a short, heavy, light-brown-curly-haired man who had a rather thick nose and a small mouth with soft, almost feminine lips. There was little doubt in my mind that Piper was the prettiest girl he had even been with long enough to claim as a girl-friend.

"Hey," he said. When he smiled, his lips seemed to enlarge as if air flowed down and into them from his cheeks. He was carrying two more bottles of wine.

"Hello," I said, and turned to Piper. "I can't party. I have to get up early tomorrow for the audition and then go to work to make up the hours."

"Oh, we're just having a short get-together," she replied. "Some of us work, too, and hafta get up in the morning, right, Jerome?"

"I'm afternoon and evening tomorrow," Jerome

said. She gave him a look of reprimand. "I'm just saying," he added quickly.

"Well, Shirley works in the morning, don't you, Shirley?" Piper asked a very thin-looking girl with the worst dyed red hair with bluish streaks I had ever seen. It was cheap and artificial. The strands looked like straw. All the coloring did was highlight her pale, almost translucent complexion. She looked fragile enough to break if one of the more aggressive New York pedestrians I had confronted bumped into her.

"That's true if I get up," she replied, and laughed. "I work for my father. He has a paper-bag factory in Brooklyn. He wants to fire me because I'm a bad example for his other workers, but my mother won't let him."

The other girl and a dark-brown-haired man standing beside her laughed. They were both carrying bags of take-out Chinese.

"I'm Toni," the girl said. She was the prettiest, I thought, with wavy pecan-shaded hair and a shapely figure highlighted by her tight light-blue mid-calf skirt. She wore a darker blue light-cotton tight sweater. "That's short for Antoinette."

"Let 'em eat cake, huh, Toni?" The man with her looked at me. "Marie . . ."

"I know," I said. "Marie Antoinette."

"Who's that?" Piper asked.

"Toni's great-great-great-grandmother," he said, smiling and winking at me.

"Very funny. Toni works as a bar waitress at the Hot-cha Club in the Village," Piper said. "And Michael," she added, referring to the man who had made the joke, "is part owner."

"Very small part," he said. "I'm more assistant manager."

"I told him you'd sing for us. Maybe he'll get you a gig," Piper said.

"A gig?"

"A job singing one night."

"Oh. I have a possible audition for that sort of thing Saturday night."

"You do?" she practically screamed. "Where?"

I looked at her friends. "It's only possible. It might not happen," I said. I didn't want to reveal the place and have her make negative comments to discourage me.

"Yeah, well, enlighten me when it does," she said. She laughed and then led them all into the living room.

"Emma, you'll have to heat up our food," she called back to me. "We don't have a microwave," she told her friends. "The manager, Grandpa Abbot, is supposed to see about getting us one, but so far he hasn't. We should hold back on the next rent payment," she told me.

"It's not part of our arrangement," I said. I had told her if he did get it for us, it would be more of a favor. "He's not obligated to get one."

"Whatever. I don't know which pot to use and how to work the oven," she told the others. "Emma's been doing all our cooking."

Reluctantly, I told Toni and Michael to bring the food into the kitchen. Piper immediately turned on her radio in the living room. She sent Jerome in to get some glasses for the wine he and she had brought. I began to heat up their food and put out some plates and silverware.

"This is nice of you," Jerome said. "I told Piper it might not be right to bust in on you like this."

"It's not," I said, feeling my father standing right beside me, whispering, *Always be honest. Better to set people straight from the start than stumble around doing it later.*

"Oh," Jerome said, and made a quick retreat to the living room. Whatever he told Piper only made her laugh and turn up the music.

You know what this is, I told myself. *Jealousy and spite*.

Piper had them all dancing and drinking the wine. Michael and Toni were smoking, which was something Piper and I had decided neither of us would do nor permit anyone else to do in the apartment.

"The radio is too loud, Piper. There'll be complaints, and we agreed that no one is supposed to smoke in the apartment."

"It's only tonight," she said. "Don't be so . . . English. The English are so proper," she told her friends.

Everyone laughed.

I didn't.

"Your food is hot," I said, and went into my bedroom and closed the door.

She didn't lower the music. I had to throw my window up to get more fresh air, because the odor of the cigarette smoke was seeping in under the door. For a while, I just lay on my bed, sulking. A few minutes later, I heard what sounded like someone knocking on our door quite vehemently and rose just as Piper opened it. Leo Abbot was standing there.

"Your music's too loud," he said. "It's bothering the other tenant on this floor, as well as the one directly below. We have a time cutoff for loud noises. You were told," he said. He saw me come out of my bedroom and realized from the look on my face that I had nothing to do with it.

"We'll lower it right now, Mr. Abbot. I'm sorry," I said, eyeing Piper.

She smirked and shouted to Jerome to turn down the radio.

"We're just trying to have some fun," she said.

"Have all you want," Leo Abbot said. "Just don't do it at someone else's expense, and please, follow our rules for noise."

He turned and went down the stairs. Piper stuck out her tongue and closed the door.

"There's an old lady across the hall who hasn't been told she's dead," Piper told her friends. Everyone smiled and returned to their food. Piper looked at me. "Why don't you join us and be sociable? It's not that late, Emma."

"It is for me, Piper. Please keep the noise down as Leo asked, and stop the smoking. I hope you'll clean up, too," I said, and returned to my bedroom.

Leo Abbot's complaint and my attitude apparently were enough to discourage them. A little less than an hour later, I heard them all leave, their voices and laughter quite loud, Piper the loudest. I stepped out when they were gone and discovered no one had cleaned up anything. I decided to leave it to see what she would do when she returned.

She didn't come back before I had to leave in the morning, although looking into her bedroom, it was difficult to tell whether it had been used the night before, anyway. It always looked used. I cleared away what I could but left the dishes and glasses to be washed. It was going to be a big day for me. I didn't want to concentrate on any of this or let it dampen my enthusiasm.

My second surprise came when I arrived at my callback audition. There were close to seventy-five candidates who had received the same invitation. All of them could read music.

Overhearing those nearest to me talk, I learned these four had gone to Juilliard. Every one of them was accomplished on some instrument as well. The producers gave each of us a little longer to perform, and I noticed there were different people listening and judging. At the end, everyone was told the same thing: "Thank you. We'll let you know very soon."

I returned to work wondering if I should have tried to make at least one of those conflicting auditions. I was sure the line was still out in the street, but I couldn't drum up the energy to go through another the same day, even though I knew Mr. Manning would have permitted it. I'd just owe more time.

Before I had come to New York, even before I had made specific plans and saved my money, I continually told myself that I was embarking on a very difficult journey, one that for well over ninety percent usually resulted in disappointment. I convinced myself that no matter how hard it would be, I would not let myself get disheartened. When I told that to Jon and his friends, I was as confident of that as I had been before I arrived in New York. Yet here I was with not even a half dozen attempts to get noticed, and I was already feeling despondent and lost. All that had happened at the apartment the night before didn't help alleviate this mood, either; it enhanced it.

Marge was the first to notice something different about me when I arrived at the restaurant. She thought I had already learned I had been rejected at the audition.

"No. It will take a little longer to fail," I said, hating myself for sounding as whiny as Piper usually did.

"Okay. But don't forget to smile here," she said. "People like to feel welcome and needed."

"Right. Sorry."

"Don't be sorry for me, Emma, be sorry for yourself. It impacts on tips."

I did the best I could, and none of my customers seemed especially dissatisfied. When Buck could stop for a moment, he hurried back to me.

"You have the audition," he said. "I'll write the address for you. Get there at eight. The man you want to meet is Curly Becker."

"Curly? Doesn't anyone have a normal name in America anymore?"

He laughed. "If I get out early enough, I'll pop over to give you some support."

"Thank you, Buck," I said. It cheered me a little, but I still didn't have my usual energy.

Marge was watching and pounced when she could. "So, what's wrong?" she asked when we had a short break in the activity.

Where do I begin? I wondered, and also wondered if I should. I really hadn't been here long enough to feel sorry for myself.

"The shine, if there was one, has worn off my roommate, as you predicted." I had dropped hints about Piper all week.

She nodded. "Don't give an inch. She sounds like someone who will take a mile."

"I don't mind that what I've set out to do is difficult. I expected it to be so. I'm just having some early worries about it all."

"I'd worry about you if you didn't. You'll know when to give up if that's what you have to do, Emma. Remember what I said about most people having to do something else in their lives. I had ambitions, too. Although I didn't have half the grit you do."

"I'm far from the point where I would give up," I said. "Although it would please my father. He'd run my life from first morning breath to closing my eyes at night if I went home defeated."

"Have you spoken to your parents yet?"

"Not yet."

"Your father will ease up. Time and distance put out flames," she said.

"My father doesn't have flames; he has hot coals."

She laughed.

Because of my extended hours, she left way before I did. When I got to the apartment, Piper was sprawled on the sofa, a box with leftover pizza on the floor beside her. She opened her eyes.

"Jerome just left," she said. "He wanted to do something to please you so he bought all this pizza. He suffers guilt, which makes him easy to exploit."

"That's terrible." I looked around. "I see you haven't done much to clean up after your party."

"I'd hardly call it a party, being we were forced

to keep so quiet and stifle our fun." She sat up and rubbed her eyes. "I left a message for you by the phone."

"Message? From whom?"

"Whom? The casting director at the audition you attended." She shrugged. "She said thank you, but they've filled the role."

"Oh." I was tired, exhausted, but the news, especially coming from her, seemed to drain me of my last bit of energy.

She saw it, too, and put it in terms I wouldn't think she was capable of expressing. "You look like a kite after the wind dies down and it floats back to earth."

"The wind always comes back," I practically spit back at her.

She smiled. "Maybe."

"Clean up this place," I snapped, then scooped up the message she had scribbled and went to my room.

For a few moments, I just stood there.

And then it happened.

I had my first real cry.

SIX

She knocked softly on my door. I ignored it, but she knocked harder.

"Hey, Emma. Can I come in?"

I wiped away my tears quickly. She wasn't someone I'd ever want to see me cry.

"Come in."

"Hey, I'm sorry about your not getting the role. Don't take it so hard. I'm sure you'll get one soon."

Coming from her, a prediction involving my future in the theater wasn't worth the effort it took to hear it.

"Okay. Thanks."

She lingered. I could feel what was coming. Often in life, you realize something significant and unpleasant about someone you've met and nevertheless in some way have to be involved with or need. The tendency at first is to ignore what you know instinctively. Avoiding the truth that's staring you in the face is what you choose to do, but if you're honest with yourself, you know that eventually you will regret it. Truth is a stubborn thing. It's like a bubble in a balloon. You can push it down, but it will pop up somewhere else in the balloon. It will never go away.

Even though I was anticipating the bad news, her deft pause sent rumbles of thunder down my spine. In the short time I'd known her, I realized she was quite expert at smoothing over her own failures or coming up with excuses.

"What is it, Piper?"

"Don't get upset, but I'm a little short on funds. They cut me back on work this month."

"Did they cut you back, or did you miss it because of your partying?" I asked, fixing my gaze sternly on her. "I was wondering how you can sleep late so many mornings and how you can be at Jerome's place so much when you were supposedly working."

I paused when it came to me. It wasn't exactly an epiphany, but it was surely a logical realization.

"They didn't cut you back. They fired you, didn't they?"

"Don't bust my chops. Just tell Grandpa we'll be a little late. He'll let it slide."

She started to turn to leave, as if what she had declared was a fait accompli.

"I won't do that," I said, turning her back around. "You never paid your half of the deposit, just the first month's rent. I let you get away with that, Piper, but you have to live up to your responsibility for the rent."

"Well, I don't have the money. You going to throw me out?" she snapped.

"If I pay everything, I won't have that much left. I make most of the money I have now on tips. I don't make much by the hour. You know that. But I've missed a lot of time at work going to open auditions."

"So that's your problem, not mine."

"How can you say that? It is your problem if you don't pay your fair share. I can pay my fair share."

She stared a moment and then lost her attitude and smiled with a shrug. "So don't pay the whole rent tomorrow. Just give him your half, and blame it on me. I'll get it in a week or so."

"That's not right, and 'or so' is describing it too vaguely."

"Vaguely? I speak vague?"

"Mock it and call it what you want. You knew what our obligations were, and you accepted them. A responsible adult lives up to her obligations."

"Oh, please," she said. "Give me a break. You sound like you're fifty, not eighteen. Don't rattle off some lecture or another. I've had enough of that in my life."

"I bet you have, and deservedly so."

She stared at me, all calmness and restraint leaving her face. "You know what, your royal high ass, I think I'll just pick up my things and move in with Jerome. How's that sound?"

"Right now, it sounds terrific," I said dryly. Her eyes widened at my defiance.

"You won't last here, Princess Emma Corey," she said. "You should have listened to your father and stayed home."

I felt my face redden. I was sorry I had confided anything personal to her. Satisfied with herself, she turned and walked out, closing my door sharply behind her. There was no question Piper could come up with nasty things to say, but nothing would reach as deeply and sting as much as that.

I took a deep breath and turned over, but I didn't go to sleep. I lay there staring at the windows and the lights flickering outside. It was at times like this when I needed to hear a friendly voice, a loving voice, but it was too early in the morning in England to call. Actually, I was glad it was. I was afraid of calling in the mood I was in right now. My mother would surely hear it in my voice and cry, begging me to come home. I might just give in if she did that.

But that would mean I was turning over my life to my father, who would carve me neatly into the woman he wanted me to be. Years from now, I would wake up every morning and just break out in tears. Whoever I was with would not understand, and I would feel like someone who had gotten married under false pretenses, mouthing "I do," like some puppet whose strings were curled tightly in my father's fingers.

I would be so hollow inside that my thoughts would echo.

I swore to myself that I would never go back like this and let him revel in my failure. Never. I'd be like a cowering puppy whimpering. My mother would cry, my sister would look smug and correct, and my father would demand even more obedience. My neck would ache because of how low I constantly kept my head.

Just before I started to doze off, I heard the door of the apartment slam. All became very quiet. I rose slowly and looked out and then checked her bedroom. She and most of her things were gone. If I was truthful with myself, I'd admit that I never had doubts that this moment would come. I was simply, perhaps foolishly, hoping that I would be better prepared for it mentally and financially. Whether I liked it or not, tomorrow I now had to ask Mr. Abbot to give me a little more time to pay the rent. The utility bills had to be paid, too, and now entirely by me. I'd be left with a little under fifty dollars.

There was no question that Leo Abbot didn't like Piper from the start and probably would be happy to hear she was gone. He might be understanding, but I didn't like falling into debt. In my father's eyes and burned deeply into my mind was the idea that owing people money you didn't have and wouldn't immediately have was practically a cardinal sin. It was beyond mere embarrassment. It diminished you. In one of his Zeus-like pronouncements, he declared that debt darkens your very soul and puts you at the mercy of someone who might very well be inferior in many ways.

"It's a lesson I always try to impress upon those I turn down for a loan," he had told me and Julia. "Unfortunately, few heed my words. I'd never lend money to someone who was happy to be obligated. A personal loan is a burden, and you're born with too many as it is. No need to add to them if you don't have to. Exhaust every other possibility first."

After that fatherly advice, I felt guilty permitting a friend to buy me an ice cream cone, and that was just pennies. Sleep was not going to have a comforting embrace tonight. My conscience would keep it barking at the door. Sure enough, I did toss and turn all night, trying to come up with a solution. Any idea I considered just involved borrowing from someone else. I thought about asking Mr. Manning for something of an advance, but I was afraid of letting him know how close to complete failure I was. There was no choice. The following morning, I waited nervously for it to be late enough for me to go knocking on Leo Abbot's door.

When I did, he took one look at my face, lost his smile, and asked, "What's wrong, Emma?"

"My roommate deserted me. She left last night. We had a fight because she told me she didn't have her share of the rent to pay today."

He nodded. "I expected it. Did she ever compensate you for half the deposit?"

I shook my head. "I can give you all the rent due," I said quickly. Now that I was facing him, I couldn't get myself to ask for more time or tell him I'd only give him my half. The words got stuck in my throat.

"But it will clean you out if you pay it all right now?"

"Almost," I admitted. "I don't want to disappoint you, Mr. Abbot. I'll pay it, and I'll advertise for another roommate today."

He nodded, thinking. "Let's let it go another week. I can let it slide that long," he said. "I don't like you scraping the bottom. Maybe you'll get a new roommate before then and get her to pay half the deposit as well as her share of the rent."

"Thank you, Mr. Abbot."

"Leo," he said, smiling. "Anything interesting happening with your singing?"

"I might get a part-time job in a club to make extra money. I audition tonight."

"Okay. See? You're definitely determined. I'd call you a good bet. Good luck."

"Thank you," I said, and hurried off to the restaurant.

Marge was glad to hear Piper had left me, despite the financial strain it had put on me. She told Mr. Manning, who immediately posted another notice on the restaurant's bulletin board. Everyone, even the other waitresses who I knew were often jealous of me, were sympathetic and supportive. When I left after seven to rush home to freshen up and prepare for my club audition, I felt hopeful and revived, despite the hours and hours of being on my feet at work. Buck had been off today, but I remembered he said he would be there to support me.

Tonight would be my first ride on a New York subway, and I was almost as nervous about that as I was about auditioning. Danny's Hideaway was located in what was known as the East Village. Studying the map I had, I could see that it was only a few minutes' walk from the station.

At first, I thought it might have gone out of business when I arrived, because the front windows were so dark, but when I entered, I saw it was quite lively. In fact, it was probably at least three times as large and as crowded as the Three Bears tavern, if not more so. It had a long bar and tables spread throughout, with a small stage area where the piano player was playing. His music sounded to me more like the music of a player piano. I thought he was racing through songs. People talked and even shouted above the music.

Buck popped up from the bar on my left. For a moment, because he was wearing a jacket and tie and had his hair recently trimmed, I didn't recognize him.

"Hey, don't look so nervous," he said, thinking that was why I looked a little shocked. "This isn't Lincoln Center. C'mon. I'll introduce you to Curly."

He took my hand and led me between tables on the right to a corner table close to the piano. A short, heavyset bald man was sitting with another man, taller, tie-less but dressed in a dark-blue suit. He had light-brown hair, but it wasn't curly. To my surprise, Buck turned to the bald-headed man.

"This is Emma, Curly."

He gazed at me and nodded without smiling. "You're pretty enough, but how old are you?"

"Eighteen."

He looked skeptically at Buck.

"She is. I told you, Manning hired her. You know we serve alcohol. Manning's not someone who plays with the rules, Curly."

"Yeah, well, me neither."

He looked at the other man at the table, who shrugged.

"Buck says you sang in bars in England."

"Taverns, mostly in one in our city, the Three Bears."

"Was Goldilocks there?" the other man joked. Both he and Curly laughed.

"What kind of music did you sing?" Curly asked.

"Songs sung by Jewel, Barbra Streisand, Mariah Carey. Show tunes and famous ballads, even some Irish songs. What would you like to hear?"

Curly looked at me a moment, at his patrons, and then shrugged.

"You choose what you think they'd like. They're who you got to please," he said. "The piano player's name is Bruce. He probably knows something you know."

He signaled to the piano player, who nodded and closed his eyes at the smoke from the cigarette he held between his lips. His black hair was slicked and shone under the lights.

"Go ahead," Buck said. "Show 'em what a real singer can do, Emma."

I gazed about at the buzzing crowd. At least the patrons of the Three Bears came in expecting to be entertained when I was advertised to be there. Surprising this audience was going to take a lot more energy, I thought, but if I could do it, I'd surely be hired.

"Hey," Bruce said when I approached him. I thought he looked tired and bored and wondered how long he had been playing today. But when I looked closer and smelled the smoke, I could see he wasn't just puffing on a cigarette. He was smoking pot. He looked relaxed enough to melt on the piano stool. "What's your poison?"

"Do you know anything Jewel sings?"

He smirked. "Jewel? Who's Jewel?"

"What about Mariah Carey?"

He sat back and took a better look at me. "Don't you know this is a jazz joint?"

"What?"

"How about a standard oldie but goodie?"

He started to play some melody. I racked my brain but couldn't recall it. He paused, grimacing.

"'My Baby Just Cares for Me.' Nina Simone," he said, and I shook my head. "How old are you?"

"I'm eighteen."

"You gotta know Sinatra, right?"

"Yes."

"Can you do 'Fly Me to the Moon'?"

I nodded. I had sung it a few times, but it wasn't a top number in my repertoire. He started to play and then nodded at the microphone.

Hope I remember all the words, I thought, and began.

Some of the patrons stopped talking. Some looked my way a moment and then went back to their conversation.

"Slip into 'One for My Baby,'" Bruce said, and just transitioned into the melody, but I didn't know it. He played a little and muttered, "'Mack the Knife'?" I shook my head. He stopped. "What, then?"

"'Memories'?"

He grimaced. "'Memories.' Streisand?"

"Yes."

He shook his head. "Go for it," he said with obvious disinterest, and began playing.

I sang with everything I had, drawing on visions of the patrons at the Three Bears when I had sung it. Again, some people paused, but most kept talking. Also, he was rushing the song.

"You got to light a fire under this crowd," Bruce said when I ended. "Come back when you learn some livelier stuff."

"I can sing livelier songs."

He looked at Curly, who was shaking his head.

"Go talk to Curly," he said. "See if he wants you to keep going."

"Thanks, honey," Curly said, even before I reached his table. "We're looking for a different sound here." He turned to Buck. "Get her a burger or somethin' on the house, Buck." He turned to the other man to continue their conversation.

I hadn't felt this dismissed even at the open theater auditions. It made me feel so diminished and unimportant.

"I'm sorry," Buck said as we started away. "I shoulda asked you more about what kind of singing you did at that tavern in England. This gets to be a rowdy crowd some nights."

"It's all right. Thanks," I said, heading for the door.

"Hey, let's get something to eat."

"I'm fine, actually a little tired. Thanks, Buck. I know you meant to do something good for me. I really appreciate it," I said. I kissed him on the cheek and then practically ran out of the restaurant and toward the subway station. I could feel the tears flying off my cheeks.

On the subway train, I sat with my chin in my hands, my fingers around my face, and stared down at the floor. I didn't want to look at anyone. In my mind, I imagined even complete strangers looking at me and shaking their heads to commiserate. My head was an echo chamber filled with my father's warnings. I could certainly imagine Julia shaking her head and waving her teacher forefinger at me, back and forth, like a metronome on a piano with the words *I told you so* chanted to the beat: *I told you so. I told you so.*

A few minutes later, when I emerged from my station and began walking toward my apartment building, the troubles and work of the whole day rained down over me. I felt fifty years older and more lost than ever. I had known it would be difficult; I had known that failure was the currency I had to live with until I had my lucky break, but there was no bounce back in my gait. I was walking like someone approaching her own funeral.

As I was turning my key in the door lock, I heard the phone ringing inside. It was Jon.

"I hope it's not too late to call," he said. "I called a little earlier, actually about ten minutes, so I assumed . . ."

"No, it's fine. You didn't wake me up. I'm just coming in."

"I wanted to see how your audition went tonight. You'll have me going all over the city with friends to see you perform, I'm sure."

"It did not go well, Jon. You don't have to worry about following my nightclub career."

"Oh, I'm sorry. I was just kidding, of course."

"American bars are different from British taverns, I guess. I was foolish to think I could simply put on another dress."

"Oh, you'll find success. How about I cheer you up with dinner tomorrow night?"

"I'm afraid I'm going to be working a lot more hours for a while, Jon. Thank you, however."

"Why more hours? You work quite a bit already, don't you?"

"Piper deserted me. I'm advertising for a new roommate, but until then . . ."

"Oh, sorry." He was silent and then quickly said, "Actually, think of it as having a silver lining. You could be better off with her out of your life."

"That's correct. I could be better off," I said. "We'll see. I must apologize, but I need to get some sleep. Thank you again for calling."

"Sure," he said, his voice drifting away even before I hung up the phone.

Every time you meet someone new in your life, you can't help but wonder if you'll ever see him or her again, if that will even matter. I certainly liked Jon. I didn't know him long, and I'm sure there was lots more to learn about him, but, perhaps because of the way I was feeling, I wasn't concerned. Maybe that was selfish and unappreciative, but right now, I was soaking in too much self-pity to worry about someone else's feelings.

Once, Mr. Wollard had warned me, "You'll have disappointments on the way up, Emma. Be kind to those who care. Sympathy isn't always pity."

I'd had no idea what he meant until now. When I said I was on a learning curve in New York, I had no idea how true that was. Marge once said, "This is a city in which sharks swim freely and eat people's dreams for lunch, but if you're successful, there ain't no city where you're celebrated as much."

So far, more wisdom flowed in the restaurant where I worked than anywhere else I went.

Buck was very apologetic in the morning. I tried my best to look undisturbed and make him feel better about it and assure him I didn't blame him. I was grateful to him for finding me an opportunity. One thing I didn't want to see was everyone else pitying me. Marge obviously knew about it. She said nothing, but I could feel her watching me closely to see how it had affected me. As difficult as it was, I put on the expected happy face for my customers, but every quiet moment I had was jammed with concerns, now mostly financial.

No one had yet answered the advertisement for a roommate. I didn't want to appear desperate when someone did. *This time*, I told myself, *I'll be far more discerning. I'll ask more questions, and I'll do just what Leo Abbot told me to do, demand half of the deposit*. I might suddenly have become a beggar, but I would not give up being a chooser.

Before the end of the week, I gave Mr. Abbot the full rent. The extra hours and some good tables that I suspected Marge had sent my way resulted in a little more money than I had anticipated. It wasn't enough to carry me through another month, but I assured him I had enough funds to provide for my utilities and immediate needs. However, he had learned how to read my face too well. There was no way to hide the concern that if I didn't get a new roommate soon, I'd be faced with the same crisis when the next month's rent came due.

In the meantime, the following week, there were three new auditions for smaller productions off-Broadway. When I went to them, I saw that the size of the production didn't seem to matter, however. There were just as many girls trying out for the same roles as there were for larger, far more expensive musicals. And the pay for these smaller productions made it almost financially dumb for me to take a role if offered one. I'd have to give up too much time at the restaurant and essentially lose that job, earning less money. I was at the point where I was trying out just to see if I could get a role that I would then turn down. If it happened, it would be enough to restore my confidence, however.

None came my way.

The second day into the start of the following week, I was finally lucky, however. Another young woman contacted me about sharing the apartment, and she was far more mature than Piper, not only because she was four years older at twenty-six, but she had a stable position at an insurance firm. Her name was Clara Denning, and she was surprisingly forthcoming.

"I'm looking for a new apartment because I've just broken up with my boyfriend, Curtis," she said. "We broke up just before he left for a sales conference in Houston, Texas. Being that sharing your apartment can be immediate, I'd like to come over to see it. You're two stops away from my company. I was ready to just take a hotel room for a while."

I invited her over whenever she wanted to come, and she replied, "I'll be there in twenty minutes."

You can never tell what people look like from the sound of their voices on a telephone. On the other hand, my father used to swear that he could tell if a prospective borrower was someone substantial or not from the way he or she phrased sentences or from the vocabulary he or she employed. He claimed "first impressions are rarely mistaken." But I thought you had to have a certain amount of arrogance to believe that, something that was beyond self-confidence. I never doubted that was what my father had.

Maybe more of him than I wanted was emerging in me, but to me Clara even sounded like someone substantial. She spoke in clear, sharp, authoritative tones and did not giggle or laugh nervously after something she had said. Later, when I got to know her, I had no doubt she would realize her ambition to become the private secretary of the company's president. My fear was she wouldn't think the apartment was good enough and after a while would decide she had to look for something more fitting for a top executive secretary. After all, it still needed quite a bit of touching up and renovation. Piper hadn't been interested, and I didn't have the money to do anything, anyway.

The woman at my door twenty minutes later was shorter and thinner than I had envisioned. She wasn't pretty, yet she wasn't unattractive by any means. Her dark-brown hair was done in a neat pageboy style, but nothing about her hazel eyes and diminutive features particularly stood out. Her smile was friendly although firm. She wore a little lipstick. The shade was conservative, simply correct for her hair and complexion. I guess the best way to describe her was she was someone completely under control. I imagined there were times when her eyes looked a great deal brighter with excitement, but it wasn't going to be now. She was too serious to pretend anything just to please me.

I had removed any trace of Piper from the apartment, throwing out anything she had left behind, fearing she had somehow contaminated it. I still waited anxiously as Clara inspected the bedroom, the kitchen, the living room, and the bathroom.

"I think it will do," she concluded.

I told her the rent and the deposit and showed her the only utility bills I had.

"Very good." She sat at the kitchen table and crossed her legs. "Now, tell me about yourself. I don't want to move in with some Mary Ann Cotton," she said.

I laughed, but I was impressed. "You know who Mary Ann Cotton was?"

"One of your country's most infamous female serial killers, a sort of black widow, right?"

"They believe she killed three of four husbands, yes."

She finally smiled. I sat and told her more about myself in a half hour than I had told Piper the whole time we were together. She then took out her checkbook and wrote the total amount needed to move in with me.

"Most everything I have is already packed," she said. "I have a car service to help bring my things over here." She looked at her watch. "Let's say by five?"

"That's fine." I fetched Piper's key from the shelf by the door and handed it to her. "I have to be at the restaurant, but you can do whatever you have to and check the food in the cupboard and fridge to see what you want. I'll be home at eleven tonight."

"Very good, Emma. Thank you."

Oh, no, thank you, I wanted to say, but I was determined not to sound desperate. She left, and when I was ready to go to work, I stopped at Mr.

Abbot's and told him about Clara and how she had written out the check for half the deposit as well as her month's share of the rent.

"Knock again when you deposit the check into your account and it goes all right," he cautioned.

New Yorkers, I thought. They were born with distrust and probably eyed their mothers with caution.

But even after the short time I had been here, I couldn't really blame them. It just wasn't who I was when I had arrived. I couldn't help but wonder if it would soon be who I was when and if I left. Failure can change you in ways you least expect. For other reasons, I might be afraid to look in the mirror. *Why and when?* I wondered.

I knew the answer would come flying at me. I just didn't realize how quickly.

SEVEN

Fall came, and the number of auditions diminished significantly as New York theater started its full-blown season. Even auditions for the smaller productions off-Broadway were few and far between, but that didn't result in my getting to know my new roommate better. Because of our work schedules, mainly mine, Clara and I didn't spend all that much time together. She had weekends off. I envied her for that, but more than ever now, I wanted to work seven days a week, because I had to earn the money for more than rent, utilities, food, and other basic necessities. I needed new clothes and nice shoes. How do you walk past all the wonderful department-store showcases and not think of something new and pretty for yourself?

New York had an earlier snowfall than usual that year, too. Colder weather was on the horizon. I needed even warmer clothes and boot shoes to walk the streets. All the other waitresses were coming to work in their fall and winter things, and I was still wearing clothes I had brought with me from England. One girl, Lillian Thomas, even offered me some of her clothes she was replacing. I could feel my face burn with embarrassment.

"Thank you. I just haven't had the time to shop," I told her. "I will soon."

Whenever Clara and I did spend time together, I could see it was on the tip of her tongue to ask me why I wasn't wearing warmer things, different articles of clothing. I suspected she had gone into my room and inspected my wardrobe one day or evening when I was at work. Yet she said nothing that might embarrass me.

One late afternoon when I returned from work, I found a package at the door. It had no return address or any stamps to give away its origin. "EMMA" had been typed on a label pasted to the front of it. I took it in, went to my room, and sat on my bed, staring at it in my lap. I tore it open and found a pair of fur-lined leather gloves. My first suspicion went to Leo Abbot, and then I thought it was also possible Clara had done it. Deep in my heart, I had harbored the hope that it had come from England, even if it had come without my father's blessings, but who would have taken it out of the package that revealed its origin? No, it simply had to have been left here at the door.

I went downstairs and knocked on Leo's door. He looked like I had just woken him but rubbed his cheeks vigorously and said hello.

"What's up, Emma? Something wrong in the apartment?"

"No. I wanted to know if you had bought these for me and left them at the door."

I showed him the gloves. He took them and looked at them, pretty clearly revealing he had never seen them.

He shook his head. "Expensive. You have a secret admirer?"

"Very secret, apparently."

"Well, as I've said before, never look—"

"A gift horse in the mouth. I know. Thank you," I said, smiling.

He scratched his head. "Any news other than that?"

"I'm afraid not," I said.

He nodded. Then he shrugged. "Well, don't worry yourself about it. We all need a little Santa Claus from time to time."

I thanked him and went up to wait for Clara. I prepared some dinner, a pasta and cheese dish and some salad, and waited to see if she would arrive in time to eat with me. We didn't alert each other to our schedules; however, what I did notice about Clara was that she didn't have that many close friends. She rarely mentioned anyone beyond someone else who worked at her company. Some weekends she went home to visit with her family in Islip, Long Island. As I anticipated, however, she was very responsible when it came to taking care of the apartment, even addressing some of the issues like the need for better lighting in both her room and the living room.

She didn't come home in time for dinner. I put what was left over in the refrigerator and went into my room to read. When I heard her enter the apartment hours later, I quickly rose to greet her.

"Oh, hi," she said, like someone who had been caught sneaking in.

"I don't know if you ate, but I made some pasta and cheese, and there's some salad and—"

"Oh, I had dinner, thank you. How are you?"

"I'm okay," I said. "I had a surprise waiting for me today."

"Oh?" She took off her grape-colored above-knee-length quilted coat with its furry dark-blue collar and hung it on the hook by the door next to the raincoat I had been using. "What was it?"

"This," I said, showing her the gloves.

She took them and looked at them. "Beautiful. Who gave them to you?"

"I don't know. Only my name was on the package."

She handed them back and smiled and then stopped smiling. "You thought it might have been me?"

"I thought . . . I didn't know what to think."

"Someone's trying to say hello in a very nice way," she said. She looked wistful. "It's nice to have someone care." She started toward her room. "Anyway, perfect timing. I hear we're getting near-freezing temperatures next week." She nodded at my raincoat. "That won't be enough."

"I know. I'm going to do some shopping."

I waited to see if she would offer to go with me, but she simply smiled and entered her bedroom.

The next day, I did manage to get a warmer coat, in a thrift shop one of the other waitresses had mentioned. I suspected the gloves might have come from Jon Morales, but he didn't call right before I found them, and he didn't call afterward, either. For a while, I thought it might have been

Buck, but he didn't do anything to indicate it, nor did he show any special interest in me. Nevertheless, I seriously considered him and even wondered if it might have been Donald Manning, who very well could have told Mr. Wollard how desperate I seemed to be. Mr. Wollard might have sent them. No one came forward to claim giving the gift, and after a while, I stopped wondering about it.

The reason was simple. It was painful to realize that nothing like it, nothing loving and full of concern, had come from my parents and Julia. Perhaps my father had declared, "Let her suffer and therefore learn how wrong she was." Maybe Mummy especially was hoping he was right, and I'd be forced to come running home. They called it "tough love" here. However, as far as I knew, they had little information, if any, about me and how I was really doing. Nothing I would say would be believed if they could hear or read me say it, anyway, I thought.

You're as good as an orphan, Emma Corey, I told myself. I could blame my father to help myself feel better about it, but in the end, there was no other conclusion, nothing that would make the realization land softly.

In February, there was another open audition. This one was for a musical that would start in the spring. It was to have a sizable chorus, so I thought that it could be a real possibility for me. Since it was so cold, I didn't anticipate as many candidates would attend, but once again, by the time I had arrived, the line was out the door and nearly a city block up the sidewalk. Girls were getting one another hot drinks. Many were wearing hats with earmuffs. When anyone spoke, her breath looked like a little puff of smoke. The line of us resembled an old steam engine barely moving. I thought I might very well get frostbitten toes, but no one left the line because of the weather. By the time I got in, I thought my teeth were chattering too much for me to sing. Nevertheless, I gave it all I could.

I didn't even make the chorus.

Shortly afterward, I finally did have a conversation with Mummy. She didn't cry when she heard my voice, as I had anticipated she would. A part of me wanted her to cry. I wanted to be terribly missed, but I felt like I was talking with someone who had begun to get over the loss of a loved one. Time had diminished sadness. She seemed resolved to face the reality that I wasn't going to come running back. True, with Clara's contribution and my steady work, I was able to make ends meet, but I was able to do little more.

She didn't mention my father; perhaps he had forbidden her to do so. She told me Julia had been dating another teacher at the school, a man seven years older, which was about how much older my father was than my mother. She didn't ask me a single question about my effort to develop a singing career or what my life was like in New York. Instead, she ended the conversation by telling me she had to prepare tea, even though it wasn't very late in the day there. Tea for us meant the evening meal. I was depressed about my conversation or lack of it with Mummy for days afterward but kept myself as busy as I could so as not to think about it.

And then, one night when I had dragged myself home after a particularly grueling ten straight hours on my feet, made more stressful by the failure of two of the other waiters to show up for work, I entered the apartment later than usual and was surprised to find Clara sitting up and waiting for me. Usually, she went to sleep at ten like clockwork, because she was up at six to prepare herself for work, have a good breakfast, and leave. She had told me she was closing in on being the top candidate for the private secretary position, and by doing extra work, coming in earlier than necessary, she thought she was becoming just that.

Until now, we had talked surprisingly little about our love lives or, more accurately, the absence of any. Thanks to Buck again, I had worked two gigs at two different clubs, but neither was interested in making me a regular. Twice I had gone to dinner with Buck, mostly because I felt indebted to him, but he realized that I didn't have any romantic interest and stopped asking me out. He was still quite friendly and concerned enough about me to keep looking for other singing opportunities.

Jon hadn't called me or returned to the restaurant since that last phone call. From time to time, I was tempted to call him but quickly snuffed out the spark. To some of the other waitresses and even Marge, I seemed to be an all-around failure when it came to men, not that a romance had become any sort of priority for me. I still believed that any serious relationship would only hinder my pursuit of any sort of singing career, not that

I could claim an iota of real progress. No one had discovered me.

Except for managing to keep up an apartment, with Clara's help, of course, I had little to show for my adventurous and determined effort to become the next Barbra Streisand. Julia's mocking of my dreams was becoming less something to hate her for and more something to thank her for. And I loathed just the thought of my being forced to come to that conclusion.

Clara was in her robe and slippers, obviously sitting there and waiting for me.

"Hi," I said, entering the living room.

"I couldn't remember your schedule today. For some reason, though, I thought you were coming home earlier."

"That was my intention, but Doug Martin, the head waiter, didn't show up and didn't even call to say he wasn't coming in. Mr. Manning is going to fire him if he hasn't already found a different job, which is what he suspects. Very deceitful. Also, Terry Longstreet called in sick with the flu. She and I share half the left side of the restaurant. Marge had to leave early because her mother wasn't feeling well, so I agreed to stay longer and take on three more tables than my usual load. For some reason, we got busier than ever, too."

I plopped onto the small sofa, took off my socks, and began rubbing my feet.

"I think I need thicker socks."

"I bet you wish we had a fireplace," Clara said, smiling. "Once, when I was in England, in Salisbury, I stayed in a quaint bed-and-breakfast that had a wonderful fireplace. It was only September, but the nights were already that cool."

"Somehow, to me, it seems colder in New York than in England."

"I imagine where you don't have the ocean air, you don't feel winter as much as we do here."

"So how are things with you?" I asked. I was really looking forward to some hot ginger tea and curling up in bed, but I also sensed she had something important to tell me.

"Well, I think overall quite improved," she said.

"I can sense you're happy about something," I said. I really didn't. If anything, I was feeling just the opposite. "What's new?"

She took a deep breath and said, "Today I learned that I'm getting the private secretary position."

A big smile filled my face. "Cheers, Clara. I'm so happy for you."

"Thank you. There's more," she said. She sat forward. "I haven't been totally forthcoming, but we haven't seen each other that much, especially to sit and have a long conversation."

"Forthcoming? About what?"

"The past four weekends, I didn't go to visit my family. I've been seeing Curtis on and off. Yesterday, he met me for lunch and gave me this," she said, and extended her left arm to show me the engagement ring on her finger. She had kept her hand tucked against her thigh until she was ready to display her ring.

For a moment, all the air in my lungs evaporated. I could recall my father saying, "The future has a way of surprising you no matter how prepared you think you are. And remember, there are never enough parachutes to go around."

"Oh. Well, congratulations, Clara. That's a beautiful ring."

"It's a full carat petite solitaire. More than I wanted him to spend, but he's determined to show me how committed to our relationship he is now to make up for our splitting up."

"If it's what you want, I'm very happy for you."

She sat back, her smile sinking back into her face. "Maybe you won't be. I'm moving back in with him until the wedding."

My smile sank away, too. "I see. Well, that's not unexpected. When, exactly?"

"I've paid for our new month's rent here."

"Yes," I said slowly.

Was she going to ask for the money back?

"And I've discussed the situation with Curtis. He thinks it would be fair for me to leave the half deposit, since I'm moving out so quickly and you have to find another roommate so quickly. Although I can't imagine your having difficulty finding someone new."

Finding someone wasn't the problem, I wanted to say. Finding someone suitable was the problem.

"When are you moving out?" I asked again.

"Tomorrow," she said. "There would be no point to my putting it off, and I would be staying at Curtis's apartment every night, anyway. He's a little farther from the company, but these days I'm getting there earlier, and now I won't have to."

When I didn't say anything, she added, "I'm sorry."

"No, no," I said. I hadn't even realized I'd gone

so silent. "You have your life to live any way you choose. I was lucky to have you share expenses this long. You have no reason to feel sorry."

She rose. "You're a very sweet person, Emma. I don't mean to hurt you in any way, and I'm cheering for your success."

My success, I thought. Suddenly, what I was doing seemed so fantastical, especially compared to what she was doing. Where would I be six years from now? How settled, how successful, how happy?

"Thank you," I said. "I might have bitten off more than I can chew, as you Americans say."

"Stay here much longer, and you'll be saying and doing more American things than you dreamed." The way she said it made it sound like a terrible danger, something infectious.

"I'm not leaving," I said firmly. She nodded. "I once told someone that 'failure' wasn't in my vocabulary. It still isn't."

She smiled. "One way or another, you'll find satisfaction, I'm sure," she said.

I thought it was quite the political thing to say, *satisfaction*. That could mean almost anything. She had found satisfaction in her romantic life and her job. I had neither yet and wondered if one would overtake the other. I could end up becoming a professional waitress like Marge. That might be all that came out of my coming to America. I could have been that back home.

"Oh," she said, turning back on her way to her bedroom. "I'm leaving one hundred dollars to cover any utility bills for the month. It's run about that for everything. Is that okay?"

"Yes, thank you."

"Someday in the near future, I'll let you know our wedding date. Love you to attend," she said.

"Me, too."

"'Night."

"Good night, Clara, and once again, congratulations on all the wonderful things happening in your life."

She smiled and went into her room.

I sat there for a while. I wasn't sure if I was more exhausted or more stunned. Despite how long I had been here, whenever I turned a street corner in New York, I anticipated some surprise. Were there more of them here than in any other city? There were certainly way more than there were back in Guildford. Was I a small-town girl after all? Had I put on a pair of shoes too big?

More than once, I had dreamed the same nightmare. I was going home, desperate and defeated, and when I got to the door, my father opened it before I could and stood there looking out at me with an expression of cold satisfaction, that biting wry smile of his.

"You can come in," he would say, "but you will be who I said you would be and nothing else, nothing more. No more pipe dreams. No more balloons."

Behind me, the tinkle of the piano at the Three Bears stopped. The silence was like a crown of thorns. He stepped back, and I entered, my head low, cowering like a frightened child.

I anticipated a repeat of the dream this evening, but I think I was simply too tired to dream. Clara was already gone by the time I had awoken in the morning. She often was, but the silence this morning was sharper, pounding in the reality. I rose, dressed, and had some breakfast even though I had no appetite. I didn't have to leave yet, but suddenly, I couldn't stand being there. Keeping an apartment was always going to be a burden, a lead chain around my neck, demanding and sucking up all my energy and meager finances. I never foresaw how much of a slave to rent I'd be in New York City. My father's smiling *I told you so* face was flashing on every wall, even the windows.

On my way out of the apartment building, I stopped to inform Mr. Abbot about Clara's engagement and departure.

"So you're at it again," he said. "Come in. Let's have a chat. I don't admit it much, but I often have what you call a cuppa."

I was hesitant. In my heart of hearts, I was afraid of the older, wiser man's or woman's advice right now. I didn't want to hear logic and good reasoning. The conclusion would be obvious. *This is too hard for you. You're all alone in the world here. You're trying to climb a mountain barefoot. Rethink what you are doing.*

"Thank you, Leo, but I have to get to work. I'll have Mr. Manning post a new advertisement for someone to share the rent. I'm sure my fellow employees will keep me in mind and recommend that anyone they know coming to the city or anyone looking for a new place to live get in touch with me. I'll be fine," I said. "I will," I added, just as much for my benefit as his.

He nodded, his face awash in skepticism. "Okay, Emma. You come see me if anything changes and you're in any sort of difficulty."

"I will," I promised, and left.

I didn't really have to get to work yet. Instead, I did something I rarely did. I walked aimlessly about the city. I didn't even notice the cold. It was nearly totally overcast, and the air smelled like snow. People rushed by me with more speed in their steps. They all looked more like people being chased. I felt like I was moving in another dimension, slowly, looking at everything through a wall of haze, almost a true London fog.

Marge once told me that it was dangerous to look directly into the face of another pedestrian here, anyway. New Yorkers were generally suspicious of someone's sudden interest in them. The person who did that was usually someone looking for a sucker to sell something to or a panhandler.

"They read you like a billboard. For that reason, you'll notice that people rarely give each other a friendly smile, something I'm sure you are used to seeing back in your smaller city. Terrible that hello has become dangerous, but it is especially true for a young girl like you, Emma. Be cautious, always cautious."

I knew she wanted to give me this advice because of what had happened to me the first night here. I often overheard her describe me as a "sweet, innocent thing," despite how long I had been here and how streetwise I had become. The person she was speaking to either said it loudly enough for me to hear or said it with his or her facial expression when he or she gazed at me: "New York devours sweet, innocent things."

Was there anything left of the original me?

My whole rhythm was off at the restaurant when

I went into work later. I couldn't get myself to tell anyone that I once again needed a roommate. I thought I had time for that. I'd look too pathetic asking for everyone's help so soon again. I had been so confident in Clara. She was supposed to be a long-term solution that would make my continual pursuit of singing credible.

Because my mind wasn't on my work, I made mistakes, brought the wrong food, forgot to go back to my customers to see if they needed any refills, and even made two errors with the billing that so angered my customers that they stiffed me. Soon after that, I fumbled a bowl of soup, rushing to get it served and on to another table. It shattered, the soup splattering onto the trousers of a man in a gray suit. I could have dropped a bomb and had less of an effect. Mr. Manning rushed to the scene and immediately offered to pay for the man's dry cleaning. I was practically in tears, apologizing. I was also at a disadvantage not having Marge there to help defend me. It was her day off.

Mr. Manning called me into his office as soon as I had a break.

"What's up, Emma? You're having a helluva bad day," he said pointedly.

I sat staring down at the floor.

"Well?"

"My new roommate is leaving. She made up with her boyfriend, and they got engaged," I said. "She's leaving today."

"I see. There you go again. And you're still not getting along with your parents? No help from them?"

"Oh, no. My father is probably champing at the

bit waiting for me to go rushing back to beg his forgiveness."

"I'm sure he's in pain about it, too."

"Not in the way you think, Mr. Manning, not my father. Sometimes he leads me to believe I had borrowed my life from him and would be in endless debt."

He took a deep breath. "I've been giving Billy monthly reports about you. You haven't written or called him?"

"No, I have nothing good yet to tell him, and I don't want to disappoint him."

"He's pretty cool with it all, Emma. He's been through it."

"Failure, you mean."

He held up his hands. "I'm not calling you a failure. You might want to step back and take stock, however. Maybe return to England for a while. Billy thinks you can get work singing there or go to music school anytime you want."

"I'm not giving up," I said. I tried to sound as firm about it as I could.

"Okay. But I'd like you to take a day or so off and rest up a bit. You're driving yourself too hard."

"I need the money, Mr. Manning, more than ever now. I'll be more careful. I promise," I said. My voice resonated with pleading.

"I'm giving you a little bonus you can use to compensate for the two days."

"Why?"

"You're my hardest worker. You deserve it."

I couldn't help being suspicious. "Is this a bonus or a handout?"

He laughed. "Handout? Didn't take you long to become a New Yorker. It's a bonus. See? I had it in here just waiting for the right moment. Just don't announce it out there."

He reached into his top drawer and took out an envelope.

"Go on. Take it and rest up. See you for the morning shift in two days."

I took it and got up. At the door, I turned and looked back at him. "This didn't come from Mr. Wollard, did it?"

"Don't insult me," he said, but I didn't believe him. "I'll post your apartment again. Go on."

"Thank you," I said, and left. Despite what he had claimed about the money, I still felt like the recipient of charity, and just the vision of my father's expression made me feel like some of or maybe all the homeless people I saw in the streets surely felt, diminished, less than human.

Leo Abbot was either waiting for me or saw me coming home earlier than usual and didn't wait for me at his doorway, either. He was there at the main entrance to greet me. I had a suspicion that Donald Manning might have called him, too.

"Aren't you feeling well?" he asked immediately.

"I'm fine," I said. "It just wasn't turning out to be a good day for me. Thank you." I was not in the mood to do much talking, but he wasn't stepping out of my way.

"You should go home, Emma," he said. "There's no shame in it. You gave it as big an effort as anyone could."

"Oh, no, Leo. I've just gotten started," I said, but

not with the enthusiasm I would have felt when I had first arrived.

"You could go home and get rejuvenated and then come back in the spring and give it another try, Emma."

"But I'd lose the apartment. You'd have to rent it."

"There are other apartments, ones not so expensive, in the Bronx or Queens. Now that you know the city better, you don't have to be so close to the restaurant."

"Who says I'd still have that job?"

"Go home. Rethink it all. It's best to be around people who love you and those you love when you're making big decisions about your life."

I shook my head. "Did you ever hear of a novel titled *You Can't Go Home Again*?"

"No, but I'm not that much of a reader. I should be. What happens in it?"

"People back home believe you think less of them because you've left to go to places that are more exciting and promising. They realize you think you can't be satisfied the way they were. It's not exactly what happens, but it's the way things often are. There's a resentment and a pleasure in seeing you so desperate. Besides, Leo, I could tolerate living homeless more than living under my father's ego now."

"It's that bad, is it?"

"For me, it is. I'll make the rent. Don't worry."

"You hurt me when you say it like that, Emma. I'm thinking more of you."

"I'm sorry, Leo. This isn't my day for doing things right, even saying them right. I need some sleep," I said, and headed up.

He remained there looking up at me.

I had a little dinner, read some to keep my mind off things, and went to sleep early. I had yet to do anything that was fun in New York, so the next day I decided to be a tourist for the day and even went to the top of the Empire State Building. It was cold but clear, and at least for a few minutes, I could feel like I was on top of the world.

I had a call from a prospective new roommate the following morning and met her at the café on our corner an hour later. She looked to be younger than I was and had her shoulder-length hair dyed red, green, and yellow. Her name was Marla Green, and she said she was in New York working in a tattoo parlor, learning the art. When I described the costs, including one month's rent in advance, something I had decided I had to have now, she started to negotiate, telling me she could get that after two months or so.

I hated those two words: *or so*.

At the moment, she was living with her sister and brother-in-law. She complained about her sister's two children. I told her to call me later that afternoon. When I returned to the apartment building, Leo was working with an electrician in the lobby and again invited me to have a cup of tea. This time, I accepted. I wanted his opinion on my prospective new roommate.

"Sounds like you're buying into trouble," he said. "Wait for a bigger fish."

When Marla called later, I told her I had found someone who could pay everything immediately, and I was sorry but that's what I needed.

"Sure," she said, and hung up abruptly.

I did eventually get a more qualified roommate, a twenty-year-old woman who was studying at the Fashion Institute. Her name was Jennifer Richards. She was quite serious about her work, but as before with Clara, my schedule and hers rarely coincided, so we could not do much together. Jennifer had her own cadre of friends, too. After five months, she informed me she was moving in with one of them who had a place closer to the Institute.

By spring, I had sung two additional gigs in two other clubs, again making extra money but not gaining any real employment. I thought I came very close at one of the open auditions, because they asked me to remain and sing again after dozens of other girls had tried out. They were nice enough to call to let me know I didn't get the part, but they were keeping me in mind, whatever that meant.

My tea time with Leo became more regular. He was becoming more like a grandfather to me, carrying me when I didn't have the full rent and telling me more and more about his own life and his own family, never failing to remind me not to lose mine. I knew he wanted me to return to England, but after a while, he stopped suggesting it.

"You really are a determined young lady," he concluded. "But I'm not sure that's always good."

For a while afterward, he didn't appear when I returned home from work, and he stopped inviting me in for tea or just to talk. I thought he was giving up on me, too. I had gone through another roommate and was once again in debt. Actually, I was in the most debt since I had arrived. I imagined he was getting up the courage to tell me I had to leave, find a place less expensive.

And then, one late afternoon after I had worked a long morning shift and lunch, he opened the door to his apartment when I entered the building and looked out at me.

"I have something for you," he said, "to consider."

"What could that be?"

"Something that will keep you from going home with your tail between your legs and stake you well enough to pursue a singing career until your voice gives out," he said. "Interested?"

"Is the pope Catholic?" I replied. It was something he would say.

He smiled and stepped back.

I entered his apartment.

And changed my whole life.

EIGHT

When Leo Abbot first offered me his suggestion for solving my immediate problems, I thought the worst of him, worse than I could think of any man his age. Thinking that all the concern and affection he had shown me was a façade, I nearly jumped up and ran out of his apartment before he could explain further. The expression on my face should have been enough to shatter his bones.

"Just listen," he said firmly when I started to rise. "I never told you much about my wife. She died twice, as far as I was concerned."

"Twice?" I lowered myself back to the chair. What did this have to do with what he had just said? Had he gone mad? Was he a closet alcoholic?

"She had heart failure, and she was almost misdiagnosed, and at a big hospital here, too. But a young doctor detected her problem after they had used those paddles and gotten her heart beating again. He was already considered a talented heart surgeon. He told me she needed a heart-valve replacement. My wife was so impressed with him that she didn't hesitate to say yes, even though it was quite a risky operation back then.

"We kept in touch with this young doctor even after he moved to his hometown of Hillsborough to become the head of the cardiac department there. He lives with his young wife in his family mansion on the shores of Lake Wyndemere, a five-mile-long lake on the border between New York and Massachusetts."

What a beautiful story, I thought. The way he described it made it sound more like a fairy tale. I smiled like a little girl hearing one for sure.

"Whenever he came into New York City to see a show or be at some medical conference, usually where he was a chief speaker, he'd stop by to see us, even before he was married. We went to his wedding, by the way. He took us to dinner many times, too. He was very fond of my wife, Rose. I think he saw her as the mother he wished he had instead of the one he had. You might say he was her surrogate son."

"I love happy endings," I said.

He thought I was getting up and held out his hand.

"Wait. My daughter Toby was always very fond of him. She and her husband don't live too far from Hillsborough, so they see each other often. Toby is especially friendly with Dr. Davenport's young wife, Samantha. She knew her before she married Dr. Davenport, because Toby's husband, Greg, is an executive in Samantha's father's company, the Avery Dental Equipment Company.

"Long story short," he said, sitting back, "is it's Samantha Davenport, not me, who'd like you to consider being pregnant. Of course, she has to meet you first, and Dr. Davenport has to approve. You'd have to undergo some medical examinations, but I guess I've been talking you up so much with my daughter Toby that it was just natural for her to suggest you to Samantha, and since she and the doctor were coming to New York anyway, I figured I'd mention it to you. All of us are more like relatives than just friends, you see."

I stared at him as if he had gone mad.

"Mr. Abbot," I began. I couldn't manage to call him Leo right now. "You want me to have someone else's baby? Someone . . . this doctor's wife, wants me to do this, I assume, with her husband, or doesn't she care who the father is as long as she has a baby? Don't you see what this sounds like? Why doesn't she just adopt one?"

"Whoa . . . whoa . . ." he said, holding up the palms of his hands. "Steady, there. I'm not suggesting any sort of thing like you're thinking. I'm sorry that I'm not explaining it well. I'm just understanding it all myself, and like my wife used to tell me, I have a habit of thinking after the ship has already sailed."

"Understanding it all? It's not really hard to understand unless you're four years old. I'd say five or six, but nowadays not even storks believe in that fairy tale."

"No, no, there's no sex involved here," he said. "I should have started with that."

"Pardon?"

"It's called in vitro fertilization. Everything will

be explained to you in great detail. Best way it was explained to me was you'd carry their baby and give birth to him or her, but the baby is totally made from them."

"You mean like an embryo created in a petri dish in a clinic?"

"Yes, yes," he said excitedly. "I should have realized that you would know something more about it than me."

"I know what it is. I've heard of it, but in heaven's name, why would I do such a thing?" I asked. I was actually feeling nauseous.

"Well, some girl your age or about your age is going to be asked to do it, and they're going to pay you or her a lot of money."

I shook my head. This was all so unreal and out of the blue, especially coming from him. My father was right when he told me that there was no greater mystery than the mind of someone you knew. No matter how friendly you were and how long you had known each other, there were layers and layers of thoughts swirling within him or her, thoughts you never imagined were there. "Just think of your own," he had said. "How often do you surprise yourself with what you're thinking?"

Leo reached for my hand. "Believe me, Emma. The only reason I agreed to mention this to you is you have me convinced that you're determined not to go home. You're struggling something terrible here, and I'm worried about your welfare."

"My welfare? So that's the reason you suggested my name for such a thing?" I asked, pulling my hand back.

"Well, yes. I'm thinking of you, what might help

you. I've observed you. I know you take as good care of yourself as possible. You're not a party girl, by any means. You're far more responsible than most young girls your age, very mature, in fact. Right now, this idea seems somewhat shocking to you, but to the Davenports, it's the most serious decision of their lives. And don't assume anything. Even after all I've told them about you, they still might not choose you.

"On the other hand, if they both like you, Emma, they'll give you seventy-five thousand dollars."

"Seventy-five thousand?" I could feel my eyes widen.

"That's not all. Until you gave birth, you'd live in the Davenport mansion, all your needs and then some paid for. All your debts here would be covered right into the future."

"Future? Meaning?"

"They'd pay to keep the apartment for you so you could come back to it and continue to pursue a singing career in New York, if you like."

"Pay the full rent for the entire time?"

"Yes."

I sat back. "That's a lot of money."

"Well, he makes a lot of money, but he also comes from one of the richest families in the state."

I sat forward like someone with a hearing problem. "And they'd pay me seventy-five thousand dollars?"

He nodded. "With that kind of money, for a while at least, you could do whatever you wanted full-time. You wouldn't need a job. You wouldn't be obligated to anyone." He leaned forward. "These are financially sophisticated people. You wouldn't be paying any income tax."

I sat back, astounded. It was like someone heaving a pail full of gold coins at me. Seventy-five thousand dollars? I would be lucky to make twenty-five thousand all year, and I knew how hard I would work for that.

"Look, I'm very fond of Dr. Davenport and his wife, Samantha. As I said, we've become like family. I'm not only thinking of you. I would never suggest you to them if I didn't know you'd be perfect for it, for their sake as much as for yours. Please don't be angry at me for suggesting it."

I nodded, still feeling stunned, and not because of any religious reason. Every girl thinks about what it would be like to be pregnant. Of course, it was uncomfortable, and giving birth was no walk in the park, but what sugarcoated it was you were going to have your baby, a child of your flesh and blood, conceived, you hoped, out of wondrous love. What Leo was suggesting was all mechanical. You were agreeing to sell your body, in a way, rent it. Why wouldn't it be enough to send me packing? But seventy-five thousand dollars and all these added financial benefits kept me from getting up and running out of his apartment.

Money had been the master in my family home for as long as I could remember. Had I brought that master with me to America? Would he always be beside me? I recalled the shock in Mummy's face when my father once said, "Money is life." When she started to object, he rattled off everything it could do, like end starvation, bring warmth and shelter, keep church doors open, but most of all, provide opportunity to grow and become someone, something of value.

She looked at Julia and me helplessly. We were too young to offer any counterarguments to support her disagreement, and besides, it wasn't only that our father was making another regal decree; despite what we wanted to believe, we both agreed. We were old enough to understand what he meant. The only thing I could think to say to soften it for her and myself was, *It might be true, Mummy, but that doesn't mean we have to like it.*

I could tell myself the same thing now.

"There's one more thing," Leo said. "If you agree to go through with it, that is."

"What?"

"You'd have to keep your participation secret."

"How do I do that? A pregnant woman isn't exactly someone incognito."

"Once you show, you don't leave the house; maybe you don't leave the property from the moment you arrive, except for medical business. You'll sign something promising to keep the secret of your participation, or you can be sued to return the money."

"I don't think it's something I would talk about anyway," I said.

"I don't imagine you would. I'd appreciate your not mentioning this talk with me to anyone at work, even if you should decide against it."

"Of course," I said.

"That's it, then." Leo slapped his knees and sat back. "If you agree to listen, Samantha and her husband can be here to see you as soon as tomorrow."

"Tomorrow?"

"It's quick, I know, but if you want to do it, you could do it in baby steps. Meet with her, listen, meet with the doctor, listen, and if everyone's satisfied, visit their mansion, where you would live for nine months or so, and then make a final decision. That's the way they explained their procedure to me."

"I still don't quite understand this. Has she lost a baby, miscarried, maybe more than once?"

"No. My daughter would know if that had happened, and she would have told me."

"Then why would she want someone else to carry and deliver her baby?" I asked.

He shrugged. "Now you're asking me to explain a woman's mind. I think it's easier to go over Niagara Falls in a barrel."

I didn't laugh, didn't even smile.

"Look, there are other women like Samantha Davenport, women who for one reason or another don't want to be pregnant, don't want to go through it and lose their figures, whatever. Neither my wife nor your mother would think like those women, for sure, but as someone once told me years ago, one person's problem is another person's good luck. I'm sure you'll learn more when you meet her, if you do."

"I don't know what to say, Leo. After hearing this, I feel like I am going over Niagara Falls."

"Yeah, I'm sure. Go sleep on it, and let me know if you want to hear more about it. Seventy-five thousand dollars, all your debts paid, no living expenses for nine months or so, and your apartment kept. I'd tell you to talk it over with family, but I doubt you'll do that," he said.

I nearly laughed at that idea.

And then I thought for a moment and nodded. "Actually, Leo, my father might compliment me on getting a good deal."

He nodded, looking sympathetic. Then he smiled. "Think of it this way, Emma. You've been trying to become an actress, a musical one, for sure. There'll be no orchestra, but you'll be in a different setting, and there'll be a limited audience, but you can imagine yourself playing a part, I suppose."

"The part of a soon-to-be mother?"

"I suppose. With a little more than a nine-month run."

"And casting starts tomorrow?"

"If you want it to," he said. "If not, no problem with me. I'll still be rootin' and tootin' for you, no matter what you do, Emma. Hey, it wasn't as easy as it might seem to you for me to call you in and suggest this, but I kept askin' myself, what if I didn't and you ended up packin' your bag, feelin' like your life was over, and went home with your tail between your legs? I'd feel sicker than a hot dog with no mustard."

I nodded. "Okay," I said. "Thank you."

I rose and left to do just what he had suggested, sleep on it, only I didn't envision getting much rest thinking about it. Meanwhile, as if he somehow had sensed my life in New York had reached another crisis point, Jon Morales called that evening.

"I'm sorry I haven't been to the restaurant, called, or dropped by to see how you were doing," he began. "I was away for a while, visiting my family in Puerto Rico. How are things?"

"Not much different," I said. "No breakthrough, if that's what you mean."

"I'm sorry. You are going to keep trying, aren't you?"

"I'm not sure," I confessed. "I'm giving everything more thought."

"You mean you might return to England?"

"I don't know. I'm not sure about the next hour, much less the next day."

"If I can help in any way . . . if you need someone to bounce ideas off . . ."

Of course, I wouldn't mention my conversation with Leo and the proposal. Despite what I had promised, I could talk it over with Marge, I supposed, but she was working so hard to keep herself and her child safe that the idea of someone having one as if it was just a means to an end, with no real feeling for the child, surely would be off-putting. I was afraid of what her opinion of me would be simply by my suggesting I might do it.

"Do you have any free time this week?" Jon asked.

"I might," I said.

"Saturday night, perhaps?"

"As Marge says, 'Let's pencil it in,'" I replied.

He laughed. "I will. I'll call you on Friday or drop by the restaurant for lunch, maybe. You should know by then, right?"

"Right," I said.

"Hey, everything's going to be fine," he said. His excitement did give me a little relief. "Don't worry."

"Okay. I'll put it on the back burner."

He laughed again. "See you soon."

At least I made one person happier tonight, I thought.

Afterward, I sat by the window and looked out at the street and the lights, watching people hurrying along up and down the sidewalk, most everyone appearing like someone who knew where he or she was going. I envied them, envied people who were so clearly focused on their purposes in life, even their daily routine, as boring or as monotonous as it might seem to others. If they had any fantasies about their futures, those fantasies came with lightning speed, like a flash of their names in lights and then a laugh at how silly that was. No real disappointment lingered. Depression didn't rain down around them in the same way it did for me, as cold and dreary as an English winter's day.

My sister, Julia, whom I had never looked to as a role model or someone I would aspire to be like, suddenly seemed so right in the way she had gone about planning and living her life. She was contented with who she was. Except for what she confronted at work, her daily life had so few serious challenges. Yes, her happiness was limited, her world of satisfaction so much narrower, smaller, in comparison to mine, but so was her world of dissatisfaction. How many weekends since I had been here struggling did she sit with friends and laugh while I obsessed about my failures? She had enjoyed a birthday, Christmas, probably been with fellow teachers on New Year's Eve. She thought about me from time to time, for sure, but her rage at my defiance had kept her from shedding a single tear. She would always take our father's side; she always had. It shielded her from sorrow in ways I now coveted.

None of them, not even my mummy, would fully understand how deep my defeat would go if and when I showed up on our doorstep. Their pity for me would be restrained, if not totally absent. In their way of thinking, it would all be my fault, anyway. Probably the worst thing of all would be how mute I would become. I'd never sing another note in public. No matter what the song, I wouldn't be able to sing it without tears streaming down my face. Go home, I thought, and say good-bye to whatever wonderful feeling blossomed inside me when I saw the appreciation on the faces of my listeners. Good-bye to that as well as the self-satisfaction I once enjoyed. Good-bye to dreams. Accept failure like bitter medicine.

Buy that ticket home and say good-bye to Barbra Streisand. Turn off the music, stop humming, even begin to hate the songbirds. I'd be as good as deaf.

On the street below, I saw a girl who resembled me. She was walking at a good clip, but she paused, almost as if she could feel my eyes on her, and turned to look up at me. She smiled. I'd swear to that, and then she walked on, went around a corner, and disappeared forever. That was the amazing thing about New York City, probably all cities like it: you'd see someone, someone you thought for one reason or another was extraordinary, and then he or she would get into a taxi, board a bus, or go around a corner and disappear forever and ever. It was almost as though this was truly a city of ghosts.

I vowed not to become one of them, even though I was in great danger of becoming one.

I rose to my feet.

Who was I kidding? I didn't have to sleep on it.

I marched myself down the stairway and knocked on Leo's door.

He stood there looking out at me, the answer so clearly written on my face.

"I'll call her first thing," he said. "You'll meet her here in the mornin'. I'll leave you two and find some errands I've been puttin' off for one reason or another."

I turned and walked back up the stairs.

Amazing, I thought. I hadn't spoken a word. It was truly as if all of it was destined to be. Leo and I, and soon Samantha and Dr. Davenport, were players in a performance begun years before we had thought of it. Sometimes, you meet someone, and the connection between the two of you is so strong you both feel like you've known each other for a long time, if not all your life, or maybe even in a previous one. There's that sense of destiny.

I certainly felt that way about Samantha Davenport the following day, and from the look on her face, the delight in her eyes, I sensed she did, too, when we confronted each other. We met at ten in the morning in Leo's apartment, and as he had told me he would after he had introduced us, he left to do some shopping. He had made a pot of coffee and had some nice biscuits on the coffee table in his small, austere, but neat living room. Pictures of his wife, children, and grandchildren surrounded us, a proper setting for the discussion Samantha Davenport and I were about to begin.

Despite her being six years older than I was, she

looked six years younger, her features perfect but childlike, as was her soft smile, full of an innocent trust, her laugh melodic but fragile. I saw immediately that she realized her own beauty and catered to it. Her makeup was subtle, with just enough eyeliner to highlight her soft blue eyes and with just a brush of lipstick on her full, perfectly shaped lips. She had a slight cleft in her chin that looked more like a perfect dimple. If my grandmum had set eyes on her, she would have told her what she had told me often: "Your perfect features should be captured in a cameo."

It wasn't only our dainty features that recommended us to each other. We had similarly willowy figures, our features diminutive but well proportioned. I imagined she was often teased about having no hips, just like I was. I could easily slip into what she was wearing at the moment. I had recognized it immediately as a Versace ruched mesh dress, because I had seen it in a storefront on Fifth Avenue. It was a popular spring-summer dress for those who could afford it.

Samantha had chosen a hairstyle for her light-brown hair that complemented her features. It was shoulder-length, sleekly cut, with layers and mid-length bangs. Her hair hid her modest diamond stud earrings, but her engagement and wedding rings made Clara's look like a pebble.

"Thanks to Leo," she began, "I feel like I've known you forever. I can't wait to hear you sing."

"Apparently, the rest of the world can," I said dryly.

She smiled so softly at my sarcasm that I immediately felt bad sounding bitter.

"Where we live, you can burst into song at any time and let your voice carry over the hills and fields like Julie Andrews in *The Sound of Music*."

That made me laugh. I really liked her, and so quickly, perhaps because I saw my own earlier innocence in her. When you had a life that rivaled our royals', most of the uglier things in life were unseen. Everything was viewed through rose-colored lenses, but what caught my interest and made me feel comfortable was how easily relaxed she was with me, a stranger, despite what we were here to do. I felt no tension, no embarrassment, and no prying eyes. We were like two long-lost friends eager to catch up with each other.

"I can just see my father's reaction to that. Whenever I sang in the back of our house, he was horrified, afraid I would draw the ire of neighbors who wanted nothing more than silence at the end of a day's work."

"Oh, you must tell me everything about your family, your life in England, all of it. We'll talk until we're both hoarse, late into the night. And there must never be secrets between us. My house, Wyndemere, nurtures secrets, pounces on them, and quickly makes them part of the decor. Whispers echo down the long corridors, and the walls capture nasty thoughts like fishermen catch fish with nets. My in-laws can tell stories about the original inhabitants so accurately that you just know they put their ears to the walls and hear those words exactly as when they were spoken decades ago.

"I don't. I don't care to know anything unpleasant. I hate when my mother-in-law describes the dead as if they were standing in the room with us. I walk right out. I won't even listen to the weather report if it doesn't suit me," she added, and laughed.

How nice to live in a world where you could ignore anything that displeased you, I thought. I was intrigued. Would I live this way for the next nine months or so?

"Now, don't ask me specific and technical questions about it all," she said, tightening her face into as serious an expression as she could manage. "I leave that all to the doctor to explain. I'm sure I would get it wrong, anyway. To me, it's simply magic."

She put her fingers over her mouth, as though she had uttered something disgusting or forbidden. Then she smiled.

"My husband hates me to say that about anything medical, because he can tell you in detail why this is that and that is this. I was never good in science. I love poetry and music. I drift; he ponders. We complete each other. It's not good when a husband and wife are too similar, you know. There's no . . . completing."

Brilliant, I thought. *Out of the mouths of babes . . .*

"My mummy and father are certainly quite different," I said.

"'My mummy'? Oh, I love it. You must say all your English expressions whenever you want. We were in London as part of our honeymoon, but Dr. Davenport wouldn't do tourist things, so I missed a lot of it. He had been there many times.

"Am I talking too much? I haven't given you time to ask a single question," she said.

"Why do you want to do this?"

She didn't lose her smile, but there was just a slight tick of surprise. Then her eyes widened and brightened. "I am so glad that was your first question. My fear was that whoever Leo recommended might be interested only in the money she'd be getting."

I nodded slightly. That was most of what I was interested in, but I didn't speak, so she'd know I was waiting for real answers.

She laughed. "The short reply is I'm simply too vain. Now that there is a proven and safe medical way to have your child without going through pregnancy and having the toll it takes on your body, why not do it? That's what came to my mind first. I'm a bit of a coward, too, I suppose. The thing is, my husband doesn't love me any less for my faults, and to be sure, I do admit that they are faults."

She was quiet a moment, her smile gone.

"My mother had a very troubling pregnancy," she continued, as if any silence between us was painful. "She nearly miscarried with me twice; both times involved serious bleeding." She paused and looked more serious than ever. "She never hesitated, nor does she hesitate even now, to tell me how much trouble I was. One result that convinces me what she says is true is the fact that I'm an only child. After going through delivering me, she was determined never to go through it again. My father was disappointed. He wanted a son. What father doesn't?"

Oh, how true about mine, I thought. *He'd have put me on the shelf.*

"My husband is willing to do all this, but he insists on being in full charge of it all, meaning you would have to live with us during the pregnancy. He will have a close friend, another doctor, perform all the necessary tests and monitor you right up to the delivery and for a while after. There is one other thing, which might spook you," she added.

"And that is?"

"As far as the world will know, I will be delivering the child. Some women can go into their seventh month without showing all that much. I will, shall we say, avoid being in public so much, if at all, during the last six weeks. Someone is going to help me look pregnant anyway, and voilà," she said, lifting her hands, "the baby will be born at Wyndemere. No one, except very trusted employees and my in-laws, of course, will know the truth. Once you deliver and you're done, you can bury the experience as deeply as you want. No one, you see, will reveal you did it. I imagine that might please you."

"It was something on my mind, yes, but Leo explained that I had to keep it secret."

"If you want, you can keep it a secret from your own family, especially since they are in England. Less ears, less tears."

"What?" I smiled.

"My mother-in-law's expression. She despises gossip unless it originates from her lips, which works fine for us. But don't worry. We'll do whatever you need done to protect you.

"Now, before we go too much further, I must tell you that you will meet my husband after I report to him. He might want to see you this afternoon, in fact. Not that he doesn't trust my judgment, you understand. He'll be looking at you from an entirely different perspective, a doctor's first, a father's second.

"If it all goes well, we'd like you to leave with us tonight, and he'll arrange for you to be examined by his close friend tomorrow, go through the required tests to be sure of everything, and then enjoy being at Wyndemere with me until the magic is done in the laboratory. Again, don't ask me any questions about it. He'll go into the details. He's very good at explaining complicated things in a way that almost anyone can understand. I suspect, however, that you're brighter than average.

"So. Enough about all this. Tell me about yourself," she said, and finally poured herself a cup of coffee.

"Tonight?" I said, astounded.

"There is success with what he calls stage one. My husband believes time is the enemy. It makes us older and weaker, susceptible to disease, and if there is something that needs to be done, time might get wind of it and speed up, making it too late."

"My father hates wasted time, too, but for a different reason."

"Men think in almost a different language," she said, and smiled.

"But leave tonight?" I said. "It's very quick. I barely have time to give what your husband tells me any deep thought."

"Nothing will happen during the next few days, anyway, except you'll get a free medical exam. I'd hate it, but you could turn around and come back immediately or soon afterward. And you'd be paid something significant for doing just that. But let's not talk about the money. It makes it all so much . . . less than it is, don't you think? Cheapens it, in a way. My mother-in-law does that with so many things. Her first question always is, how much did it cost? Sometimes I feel like putting tags on everything in the house that's mine, describing the cost. I know it sounds funny for me to say that knowing what something costs cheapens it. There are some things you cannot put a money value on, like friendship or love or . . . having a baby."

"Yes. Yes," I added, more emphatically.

It was as if I had found a new argument for my mummy to reject my father's declaration that money was life. There was definitely something more important: self-respect. Money didn't always give someone that. And when he said people respect rich people more, I thought to myself, *Not respected: envied or feared*. There was a big difference. It surprised me that he didn't see that or maybe refused to see it. Samantha appeared to understand, despite her innocence.

Leo returned close to an hour later and found us talking and laughing in his living room. He looked very pleased.

"I'll be taking Emma to lunch," Samantha told him. "She's never been to Fontaine's."

"Me, neither."

"It's all girl-talk time, Leo. I'm sorry."

"It's okay," he said, smiling. "You girls do your thing."

"Dr. Davenport will be here about three, if that's all right with you," Samantha said. "I phoned him a few minutes ago to confirm."

"I'll keep my appointment with the president, then," he replied.

All three of us laughed. Leo looked at me with twinkling eyes. He looked happy he had arranged for all this.

Should *I* be? I wondered.

Was something wrong with me? I was feeling better than I had in months.

A weatherman or woman might say, *There are storms beyond your imagination on the horizon.*

But for now, thinking of the money, all I could see were clearer skies.

NINE

The moment we left for lunch, I felt pangs of panic.

Was I deceiving myself? *I can't go through with this. I will have a baby? Me? Someone who's never had sex? A virgin giving birth? Mother of Jesus? And someone else's baby as well?* Is this what science had created? And just because it was in a clinic run by respected doctors, that didn't make it less weird to me.

I wasn't sure if it was a nightmare or simply foolish fantasy. Samantha either noticed my nervousness now and simply ignored it or was so excited and pleased that I was the one who would carry her baby that she wouldn't let herself notice anything negative. She struck me as the latter, because from the way she described her childhood and life at Wyndemere, it was easy to conclude she was someone who never had spent time looking at the downside of things. There would always be someone holding that net if you fell. Money, which could buy you the best education, could also buy you obliviousness.

Fontaine's reeked of wealth, yet it wasn't overstated and gaudy like some restaurants with expensive menu items. Nevertheless, I sensed that the combined wealth of the patrons having lunch might easily be twice that of most Third World countries. Naturally, I felt underdressed, but Samantha refused to permit me to think that way.

"We don't care what anyone else thinks, anyway," she said when I suggested it. "We don't live to please them. We live to please ourselves." She said it as if she were the queen of selfishness, but she was so innocent and harmless about it I had to smile. It was all in fun. She wasn't being condescending or arrogant.

However, despite how many ways she was listing to conclude that we were so similar, I knew we were as different as two young women might be. We were, after all, brought up in different worlds and not just different countries. Even if my father was as wealthy as hers obviously was and as wealthy as her husband was, he wouldn't have permitted me to demonstrate an iota of blissful indifference when it came to what something cost.

She ordered a bottle of very expensive champagne and then a platter of hors d'oeuvres that included beluga caviar, something I had never had. The most expensive item my father would permit my mother to buy either to prepare at home or have in a restaurant was a prime cut of beef. From the way the waiter at Fontaine's treated us, I had the sense that Samantha had been here many times. I felt like Eliza Doolittle in *My Fair Lady*. There were so many forks and knives, the correct way to drink champagne, and French descriptions of foods and wines. Some I could translate, but many I could not.

Samantha was eager to teach me anything and everything. I had the strange, almost eerie feeling that she was out to mold me into a mirror image of her as quickly as possible. It was important for me to like the things she liked. If I indicated in the slightest way that something wasn't my cup of tea, she suggested substitutes. It was as if she believed the fetus that would live within me could be fooled into thinking it was indeed she who had carried it to its birth.

"You don't have to bring a single thing with you tonight," she said. "We're the same size. You will see that you will have miles of clothing from which to choose. And everything is fashionable. I'm pretty sure we're the same shoe size."

"Seven?"

"Yes," she said, clapping her hands. "Seven. Serendipity. Our guest rooms—there are seventeen bedrooms—are fully stocked with everything any guest would need. My mother-in-law keeps Wyndemere as if it were a first-class hotel, a five-, even six-star. It's been in the Davenport family for decades and decades. It was originally built and owned by the Jameson family, a family with a history full of intrigue, most of it embellished to give the house more character, as my mother-in-law likes to remind us all."

She leaned toward me to whisper.

"Sometimes, just out of spite, I attempt to change

things. I've been after Dr. Davenport to remodel the outside, but my mother-in-law considers it a historical site. I'm lucky to change the color of my own bedroom curtains."

I think she saw me immediately pick up on the word *my*.

"The doctor and I sleep in separate bedrooms because he keeps terrible hours. I'd have my sleep interrupted every time he had an emergency. I'd be wakened in the middle of the night and rise with bags so big under my eyes they could be used for luggage."

I had to laugh at that.

"But that doesn't mean we don't enjoy the pleasure of marriage," she added. "In fact," she said, her eyes twinkling, "it adds romance. I can pretend a strange, handsome, debonair new lover has found his way to my boudoir." She scrunched her nose. "Sometimes, I think he's doing the same thing . . . pretending I'm someone new.

"It's so important to keep romance alive, even after years and years of marriage, don't you think?"

I never thought that about my parents. Could it be true?

"Really?"

"Of course. My in-laws let romance dry up like a peach or something. The only time I saw them kiss each other was on their anniversary, and it was as mechanical as could be. Now, with him being an invalid, they are unable to do anything together again. Sometimes, I get the feeling they had separate bedrooms on their honeymoon, and it wasn't to make it more romantic, either.

"Elizabeth always said he snored so loudly that

he woke the dead, but don't you worry. You'll have privacy. In fact, you'll love Wyndemere. Wait until you see the grounds. There are more than fifteen acres, and the lake is five miles long. We have rowboats and motorboats. It's always been too cold for me, but my husband swims in it.

"The dining room seats twenty, although we haven't had a dinner like that since my father-in-law became a severe diabetic. He has a full-time nurse caring for him now. That doesn't slow down my mother-in-law, however. Elizabeth Davenport attends one charity event after another and always seems to have a lunch date. She still has dinner parties, too. Sometimes I avoid them, claim I have a headache or something, especially when I know the doctor won't be there because of some medical thing or another. No one would bother saying much to me. I don't move in her circles."

She leaned over to whisper again.

"She thinks she looks fifty at most. She's seventy-four but has had so much plastic surgery she's practically opaque. Her true self is buried under surgery. I know she can't close her eyes fully anymore and has to sleep with blinders. But don't give her a second thought. She won't even notice you're in the house. She won't look at anyone who's worth less than three or four million. I 'yes' her to death.

"Frankly, to disagree with her only prolongs the conversation, and she'll always find something wrong with something I'm doing, whether it's the shade of my shoes with a certain dress or the way I sit. Any other daughter-in-law would explode, but I look at the doctor and see the amusement in his eyes and think to myself, *Samantha, just pretend she's one of the ghosts she swears she's heard walking the corridors."*

"Do you always call your husband 'the doctor'?"

She laughed. "He's not terribly fond of his given name, Harrison. He thinks it makes him seem too stuffy, but I do call him Harrison. I just don't refer to him that way when I'm speaking about him with strangers or the servants, of course. But you won't be a stranger. After a while, he'll probably prefer you call him Harrison," she predicted, although not with complete confidence.

"Anyway, when you see the house, how big it is, you'll understand why you don't have to be too concerned about my mother-in-law. You can go days without seeing her. Before my father-in-law became more or less an invalid, he used to tease his wife by telling her one of their houseguests never left.

"Oh. Let's have something to eat," she said. "I'm starving."

I was happy for the short intermission. I was beginning to feel bowled over by one wave after another at high tide. As it turned out, it was the longest lunch I'd had in New York, or anywhere. We were there until almost three, when she suddenly realized the time and signaled the waiter in a panic.

"The doctor is always prompt," she explained. "Remember what I told you about how he feels about time. I think it comes from the tasks he performs during heart surgery. A moment is a life, after all."

"My father believes time is money and money is life," I said.

"Sometimes, I get the feeling my husband hates

money—but don't make him wait. That he hates more."

She was right. We returned to the apartment house just two minutes after three, but her husband was already there, waiting in the living room with Leo. Despite being quite skeptical and undecided about it all, I was surprised at how nervous I was when we entered. I was less nervous auditioning for a Broadway role.

Dr. Davenport was seated in Leo's chair, his legs crossed, leaning back, but sitting perfectly straight, stiffly. He was in a dark-blue suit and matching tie. When we entered, he turned slowly, the way a man who was careful about all his moves might turn. He didn't smile. His sterling-silver-gray eyes focused entirely on me with an intensity that made me feel naked. I thought he was very handsome and quite distinguished-looking. There was firmness in his lips that tightened the muscles in his jaw. His pecan-brown hair looked recently cut, with a slight wave in the front.

"Oh, we had such a good time at lunch, Harrison. I wish you could have been there."

He nodded. "Why don't you return to the hotel, Samantha, and get things organized for our return?" he said. He had the tone of someone whose orders were politely cloaked in the dress of a suggestion but were not to be doubted or opposed. "Our car is waiting for you. Leo will signal him."

"Sure will," Leo said, rising quickly. "I have to check on a plumbin' problem, too."

"Don't frighten her to death, Dr. Davenport," Samantha warned with as much authority as she could muster.

His eyes did soften, as did his lips. I imagined that no one but she could speak to him this way. His love for her was palpable. His face might as well be a marquee advertising it.

She squeezed my hand for support and walked out. Leo rushed after her.

"Please," Dr. Davenport said, nodding at the sofa.

I had a moment of hesitation I would remember for the rest of my life. Half of me was turning to the door to leave. I wasn't even sure I wanted to hear any more, but when I envisioned what awaited me upstairs, the empty apartment, the absence of any potential success, and the suitcase that I would pack for my return to England, I turned to the sofa.

Dr. Davenport finally offered me a warm smile. "I can imagine the fear and hesitation swirling around inside you," he said. "Do you know anything at all about in vitro?"

"I've heard of it. That's about all," I said. "There was something on the BBC once, but I didn't pay enough attention."

He nodded, uncrossed his legs, and sat a little more forward. "I have to ask you some rather personal questions first, and then I'll explain it all. Is that all right?"

"It will have to be, won't it?"

His smile softened even more. "Yes. Are you sexually active?"

"Actually, I was going to ask you a related question right off that would give you the answer. Does it matter that I'm a virgin?"

"No. Matter of fact, there are a number of virginal women involved with in vitro fertilization. They don't want relationships, for one reason or another, but they do want children. I'd like you to understand it as much as possible just in case you discuss it with someone and get incorrect information. There are two kinds of surrogate mothers, traditional and gestational. The traditional is artificially inseminated with the father's sperm. She carries the baby and delivers it and is the baby's biological mother. Gestational surrogates have the egg from the mother and the father's sperm from something known as in vitro fertilization. The egg and the sperm are combined in a laboratory. Once the embryo is formed, it's placed in the uterus of the surrogate mother. That's you."

"Is it painful?"

"Only the pain of natural labor and delivery, but that will be mitigated with some new drug therapies my good friend Dr. Franklin Bliskin will use. He will do all the pretests that are required for someone to become a surrogate mother."

"What are they?"

"First, he'll do a hysteroscopy to determine the clear passage of your fallopian tubes, the size and shape of your uterus. You'll be checked for any signs of any infectious disease. You'll get a Pap smear, and then he'll do what is called a mock cycle. He'll give you estrogen pills three times a day for about eleven days and then do an ultrasound to look at your lining. If everything looks good, you're done with that. There's also something called a trial transfer. Dr. Bliskin will do a better job of explaining that and all the rest."

"How long before . . ."

"Before in vitro? We'll start the process in the

laboratory a day or so after you see Dr. Bliskin so we have viable embryos ready when you're ready. We want you to be comfortable the entire time, and that's why I thought you should come to Wyndemere now, spend some time with Samantha, and be sure you want to do this. I'll pay your debts here and an additional five thousand dollars no matter what, which we'll deduct from the seventy-five. How's that?"

"So it will be a while before I'm actually . . . something is actually . . ."

"Let's plan on two weeks at least. Samantha will keep you busy, I'm sure, the entire time. Another personal question," he said. "Do you now use or have you ever used recreational drugs?"

"No. Before you ask, not even pot," I said.

"Okay. There are ways to tell," he warned. I just stared coldly at him. "Leo told me he gave you an outline of what you'll be paid, what I'll do for you."

"Yes."

"We'll draw up an actual contract between us all. I don't imagine you have an attorney to review it."

"No. And I don't have the money for one, anyway."

"It'll be quite clear, and if you do have questions, I'll have my attorney at your disposal."

"You really want me to go back with you tonight?"

"We're determined to have a child. We'd like to start our family now. Lots to do beforehand," he said. "And from what Leo tells me, there's nothing to keep you here."

"No, nothing," I said.

"Not to say there won't be in the future," he offered with a smile. "I appreciate how big a step this is for you; it's big for us, too. We'll all be on a learning curve, especially with each other. I take it Samantha has clued you in on my parents, the house, some of it."

"Some of it," I said. "Yes. She did tell me about your parents, your father being ill."

He nodded and then looked at his watch. "How's two hours from now? We'll be coming back with my limousine."

This was it. *Say yes or no, Emma.*

"Two hours," I said. We both rose.

"Once, when I stopped in to see a patient before he was going to be wheeled into the OR, I told him we were going to do our best and everything looked good for the preparation. He nodded and said, 'Doc, nothing is until it is.' Simple but true," he added. "I urge you to keep that in mind. I always do."

"Thank you."

"Look. If you get cold feet before I return, here's my car phone number." He handed me a card.

I nodded, took the card, and left. My heart was pounding with anxiety. If I had said any more, I thought, I would just have packed my bag and left for England. I went up, and despite what Samantha had suggested, I organized some of my things to take along, my necessities. When I closed my suitcase, I considered again what I was doing. For a moment, this felt like a whirlpool into which I was dropping myself and spinning. Everything I was about to do would take on another complication, another form of deceit. Was the money really worth it? Did I want to continue my career with such money? Would it affect what I thought of myself forever and ever?

Despite the rosy picture Samantha had painted, this was not going to be easy for me. I was agreeing to become pregnant. I turned and looked at myself in the mirror, imagining being six or seven months along. Like any girl, I'm sure, I had always been intrigued by and a little frightened of the idea. When I was little, the sight of a pregnant woman fascinated me. Would she simply explode one day? I'd look at my mummy and wonder how she could have been this way.

Like hail, the realization of what I was agreeing to do pelted over me. Someone was going to live inside me. My own child would be one thing, but this was going to be a stranger. And once it had begun, there was not a good way to stop it. I couldn't change my mind, no matter how much I regretted doing it. I was going to sign a contract. Being my father's daughter, that meant something very serious. Put your name to an agreement, and you practically taped your soul to it as well.

About a half hour later, there was a knock at my door. It was Leo.

"Hey," he said. "I just wanted to wish you luck. The doc's done what he promised in the meantime. You're paid up and paid for another month, even if you change your mind and return tomorrow."

"Okay."

"I hope I've done the right thing, Emma," he said.

"We all hope that, but I know you're trying to help me, Leo. You've done the right thing when it comes to that. Thank you."

We hugged.

"Good luck," he said. "I'll be right here whenever

you need me. In the meantime, I'll cover for you if anyone comes askin'."

"Oh, no," I said, now that I felt like this was really happening and my feet were on the ground again. "Mr. Manning. What am I going to tell him?"

"I was goin' to tell him you had decided to go home for a while."

"I don't think that will work, Leo. He's friends with Mr. Wollard, remember? He'll know I didn't return."

We both stood there looking at each other.

"I don't like lying to him, but I can't see myself telling the truth about this. I'm not sure of it, and I'm not sure I won't be ashamed if and when I go through with it. And they do want me to keep my participation secret. That's very important to Samantha."

"Okay. Leave it to me," he said. "I won't reveal anythin', but I'll get him to be understandin'."

"Oh, and Marge, and oh, I forgot all about Jon Morales."

"Who?"

I looked at the time. "I'll take care of that," I said. "Thank you."

"Right." He hugged me and left.

How would I tell my parents, if ever? I wondered. In the meantime, what would I say if they called here and never heard back from me for almost a year? I had to come up with some explanation. I was never good at deception. It was always easier to simply not say anything. That, at least, didn't feel like lying. But how could I do that now? At the moment, I saw no other way than to make up some story, perhaps tell them I had a job in a regional theater in Massachusetts.

Was there such a thing as a good lie? Julia used to try to convince me there was, especially if it was to avoid riling up our father. "Words have consequences," she said in her slightly arrogant teacher's voice, even before she became one. "If you can avoid them and not really hurt someone, why not choose the words that prevent trouble? After all, we're only trying to keep Daddy from becoming upset. He could have a heart attack," she'd warn. In the end, although I didn't utter the words, I went along with them, telling myself I was still mostly innocent.

First things first, I thought. I found Jon's number and called.

"Hey, what's up?" he asked. "Free tonight?"

"No. I'm afraid I won't be able to see you, Jon. I'm leaving."

"Leaving? Why? To where?"

"I'm returning to England for a while," I said. "I have to see my family."

I paused to see if my voice had betrayed my falsity. I really did not want to hurt him. If he thought I was making up something just to avoid him . . .

"Oh. Sure. I told you I just saw mine. But you'll call me when you return, right?" he asked. He sounded convinced, but I still felt guilty.

"Yes," I said.

I'll call you, I thought, *but when I return, I might be so different from the girl you knew that you'll be the one to find excuses to avoid any relationship.*

"Well, have a good, safe trip."

"Thank you."

"Send me a postcard if you think of it. I don't think anyone's written me from England."

I heard my buzzer sound.

"Someone's at the door. I think it's my car service. 'Bye, Jon," I said quickly, avoiding any promises. I hung up the phone and pushed the call-box button. "Yes?"

"It's Parker Thompson, Dr. Davenport's driver."

"I'll be right down," I said. I picked up my suitcase, looked about the apartment a moment, and then took a deep breath and stepped out.

Leo waited at the door. There would never be enough good-byes for him, apparently. I could see the concern in his face. It troubled him. For days afterward, he was going to ask himself the same question. Had he made the right decision when he suggested me? I squeezed his arm gently.

"I'll be all right," I whispered. "If not, I'll come back immediately."

Parker Thompson, an African American man of about thirty, tall, with shoulders that filled out his black jacket, took my suitcase.

I walked out after him. He opened the rear door, and I paused. I paused long enough for Samantha to slide over and smile at me. Then I got in. She reached over to take my hand.

"It will all be fine," she said. I was probably wearing my nervousness like a Halloween mask.

Dr. Davenport was up front. He didn't turn back to look at me. I couldn't say from the short time we talked if he was really for this or not. Did he deep down resent his wife for forcing it to happen? Or did he agree because he didn't want his wife losing her figure? Or was he so much the scientist and so much less the husband? Questions seemed to be floating around me like fluffy dandelions, more with every passing moment as we drove out of the city.

I smiled at Samantha and nodded. It wasn't until that moment that I realized how much I was helping her. She was escaping her fears and holding on to her beauty and her youth. She would be a mother, yes, but one with a nanny. The birth of her child would make almost no change in her life. She might even love him or her the way she once loved one of her precious dolls.

Yes, I thought, *despite what you wish, how different we really are*.

Between the two of us, there wasn't a moment of silence for practically the entire trip. Dr. Davenport spoke to Parker but rarely turned around to look at us unless Samantha brought him into the conversation to confirm something she had said about Wyndemere. I thought she was exaggerating with her descriptions. It sounded more like an English castle, but when we were approaching it and the lake, I realized that if anything, she had understated what their home was.

The house itself was a nineteenth-century Gothic Revival. Dr. Davenport confirmed that the house was over fifteen thousand square feet. It had a dark-gray stone face, with louvered vinyl black shutters, towering brick chimneys, and gargoyles like the ones I had seen in pictures of Notre Dame in Paris. There was elaborate outside lighting, but night had fallen, and the hedges and fountains were silhouetted against an inky backdrop. As we turned into the driveway, I could see that the land rolled down toward the lake, a glimmering slice of silver.

"I can't wait until you see it all in daylight," Samantha said. "Right after breakfast, we'll take a walk to the lake."

"No," Dr. Davenport said. "Right after breakfast, Emma will be going with me to see Franklin."

"Oh. Of course. How silly of me," Samantha said. "But there'll be time to take walks later, right, Harrison?"

"She'll take many walks, I'm sure. Franklin will want that."

Samantha grimaced, as if my reason for being here was primarily to be her friend and only as a side purpose was I here to carry her and Dr. Davenport's baby.

Dr. Davenport turned to her and smiled. "Don't overwhelm her, darling. Elizabeth will take care of that," he said.

"Oh, and will she," Samantha said, laughing.

How strange, I thought. *He refers to his mother by her given name*.

We pulled up to the front entrance. Dr. Davenport stepped out, but Samantha didn't move until Parker came around to open her door and then mine. He fetched my suitcase, and we all approached the grand, large wooden front doors with their embossed figurines that depicted two sprawling trees. Dr. Davenport opened the door and stepped back. He glanced at me, to see my reaction to all this, I'm sure.

I had been to castles that had belonged to wealthy noblemen and relatives of the king, but I was still impressed with Wyndemere's elegant beige foyer with a Louis XVI console. The main entrance had an open staircase, molded cornices, and a red-marble fireplace.

"You'll be in the bedroom nearest to ours," Samantha said.

"Why don't you take her there, freshen up, and we'll see about some light dinner?" Dr. Davenport said. "I'll speak to Mrs. Marlene."

"She's our cook," Samantha quickly added. "We can take it from here, Parker." She reached for my suitcase.

"Oh, I can carry that," I said.

"Nonsense. Anyway, it's so small. I can manage."

Then why couldn't I? I wondered. Did she already see me as pregnant? I let her have the small suitcase.

"You should see the suitcases my mother-in-law has with her, even for a few days of travel. Besides, you're a visitor, and we have to treat you in the manner the Davenports treat their guests. For a while, anyway," she added, smiling.

"I'll speak to Mrs. Marlene and then be in my office," Dr. Davenport said.

"That, our bedrooms, and the dining room are practically the only rooms in this mansion he uses, but mainly his office," Samantha said with feigned disapproval. "It's not difficult to find him."

He laughed and started away.

Before we reached the second step on the stairway, a woman I would soon know was Elizabeth Davenport stepped out of the living room. She was in a floral lace high-low cocktail dress with a string of small diamonds around her neck and matching diamond earrings. Her dyed brown hair looked so sprayed that you would need a comb with steel teeth to separate a single strand. Her lips were almost comical to me because of how puffed up they were with some filler her plastic surgeon used. The skin around her chin and over her cheeks resembled a freshly ironed silk blouse.

"Oh, hi, Elizabeth. You look so nice. I remember you wore that dress to the governor's ball. Did we miss something big and important?"

"Dinner with the Ramseys," Elizabeth replied. "It was scheduled two weeks ago."

"I don't know how we missed that. Harrison is always so careful about his calendar."

"Where is my son?"

"He went to speak to Mrs. Marlene about some dinner for us, and then he's off to his office for something or other," Samantha said.

Elizabeth Davenport turned to her right as if moving too quickly might cause a wrinkle and then looked back at us.

"Are the Ramseys still here?" Samantha asked. "We'll have a light dinner soon."

"Still here? Hardly. Dinner has long since come and gone," Elizabeth said. She pulled herself up like a drill sergeant for the queen's royal guard and looked at me with her piercing gray eyes. "Is this she?"

"Oh, yes. This is Emma Corey. Emma, this is my mother-in-law, Elizabeth Davenport."

I had no time to say hello.

"Ridiculous," Elizabeth said, and walked back into the living room.

"She hasn't quite made it into the twentieth century," Samantha said. "Pay no attention. Actually," she whispered, "she's jealous. She wishes in vitro had been perfected when she was my age."

She nodded at the stairway to indicate we should continue up.

I looked back toward the living room and then followed her. When we reached the top, a nurse came out of a room down to our right and headed toward us.

"Oh, Mrs. Cohen, how is my father-in-law tonight?"

"Exhausted," she said. "Your mother-in-law insisted we bring him down to dinner. He didn't last five minutes and was brought back up before her guests had arrived." She looked at me.

"Mrs. Cohen has been with the Davenport family for nearly a decade in one capacity or another," Samantha explained. "She will be assisting us later. She's aware of it all. No secrets from Mrs. Cohen."

"Oh, there are a few still hidden in the corners of this house," Mrs. Cohen said.

Samantha laughed. "Anyway, Mrs. Cohen's quite capable. Her grandmother was a midwife. Isn't that true, Mrs. Cohen?"

"She wasn't exactly that, but there were many times when she oversaw a delivery, yes. Welcome," she said, then flashed a smile at me and continued to the stairway.

"Oh," Samantha called after her, "I forgot to tell you. Her name is Emma."

Mrs. Cohen looked back at me.

"She's from England."

Mrs. Cohen's smile was a little friendlier, actually the smile of someone amused. "Oh? Your baby might be born with an accent, then," she said, and continued down.

"She's joking," Samantha said. "Don't you think?"

She looked a little worried, and I wasn't sure if I should laugh or cry at the moment.

I had been brought to Wyndemere, in which there was a mother-in-law made of ice, who obviously didn't approve of my being here and what her son and daughter-in-law were doing, and a very sick father-in-law, a house so cavernous that echoes from yesterday were still bouncing off the walls. For months and months, this world would be mine, too.

TEN

The bedroom that was to be mine was easily twice as large as the one in my apartment. I recognized the furniture: a dark-oak Churchill five-piece poster bedroom set. Mrs. Taylor had a similar set. This room had a light-blue and ivory area rug that looked like it had just been brought in. The curtains matched. There was a vanity table with an oval mirror on the right, also with a blue frame. On the wall to the left were two paintings of clouds and cherubs with lots of blue sky.

"I ordered some new things for your room in anticipation of your arrival," Samantha said.

My room? I thought. Surely she meant the room of whoever took on this job. Should I call it a job?

"My mother-in-law complained, but Harrison stood up for me. Of course, she thinks when you leave, she'll take out anything at all I bought. She'll restore it to the drab way it was. Do you like it?"

"Yes."

"I thought you would. Why don't I leave you to freshen up? I will, too, and then we'll go down to have some dinner. You should find everything you need, but if you don't, I'm right next door. Just turn left when you walk out and knock."

"Thank you."

She nodded and then burst into a bigger smile. "Harrison tells me that we'll be able to know the sex of our child between the eighteenth and twenty-sixth week. As soon as we do, we'll design the nursery. I hope you will help me do that," she said. "It'll be such fun."

"Oh, I'm not any sort of expert when it comes to designing and decorating."

She nearly lunged forward to take my hands into hers. "Of course you are. I want you to feel as much a part of this as you wish, Emma. Even years afterward, I would hope you would visit to see him or her, not telling him or her who you really are, of course, but I imagine you'll be curious, don't you think?"

She was waiting for my response. I was struggling to find a suitable feeling, a reaction that wouldn't end with my rushing out of the room and down the stairs. She held her smile, anticipating.

"Of course," I said, trying to smile. My whole body seemed to tighten, but she was waiting with obvious anticipation. "How could I not be?"

"Exactly." She let go of my hands. "After all,

you'll be the one who first feels my baby move. And you'll hear his or her first cry. I haven't decided yet whether I will be present during the delivery. Harrison and Franklin, Dr. Bliskin, think I should be. I should be standing there with open arms."

"I imagine you should be," I said.

"We'll see. Now, take a shower, a bubble bath, whatever you like. You'll find some of my clothes hanging in the closet. Choose what you wish to wear. There are shoes to match every dress, skirt, and blouse. The dresser drawers are filled with your underthings and socks. There is a selection of lipsticks in the vanity-table drawer, but I bet I know what you'll choose."

"Oh?"

"And this is my favorite perfume," she said, showing me the bottle. She sprayed it on her wrist and brought it to my nose. "Isn't it wonderful? Makes you think of the first day of spring."

"It is nice. Thank you."

"I'll give you an hour, okay? I'll need an hour. It's been a long day for us both, but a wonderful day, don't you think? It's always wonderful when you meet someone you know you will like."

She hugged me. "Welcome to Wyndemere," she said, and walked out.

I still hadn't taken a step. Her words and enthusiasm, and the speed with which I had been rushed here, were altogether so overwhelming. I felt nailed in place, felt like a pawn on a chessboard played in a game with an outcome known years ago.

Moving like someone sleepwalking, I started to

unpack the few things I had brought. The bathroom was impressive, big, with a full-size tub and a separate shower stall, marble walls, and floors that, although they were clean to the point of sterilization, nevertheless looked like they were still made of the original building materials. The brass fixtures resembled antiques, in fact.

Towels and washcloths, bubble baths and soaps, shampoos, and all sorts of facial creams were neatly organized on the shelves. I had the feeling that everything in this bathroom was a duplicate of what was in Samantha's. After all, from what she had told me, I understood that the control of this room and everything in it had been given over to her.

I showered but didn't wash my hair. Afterward, I sat at the vanity table, wearing the pink silk robe that had been hanging on the bathroom door. I brushed my hair and then looked at the lipsticks. There was a variety of shades of two similar colors, very close to what Samantha had been wearing, which wasn't that much different from what I usually wore. Thus I understood what she had meant when she said she thought she knew what I would choose. How did she know that?

I went to the closet. When she had told me some of her things were in it, I anticipated three or four dresses, a few blouses, and a few skirts, but the closet, which was almost as wide as my apartment living room, had racks with clothing from one side to the other. Shelves to the right were loaded with shoes, shoe boots, and additional slippers. If this was what she called some of her things for my temporary use, how much did she possess?

When I sifted through the garments, I realized one quarter of the rack was devoted to maternity dresses. As soon as I touched the first one, I drew my hand back as if I had grazed a hot stove. My mind had not completely embraced what I was intending to do. This was a splash of reality in my face. I stepped back for a moment to question myself. The answers were the same. *Do it, and continue to pursue the life you dreamed you'd have, or stop now, return to New York, and start your journey home*. For a moment, despite how large this room was, I felt claustrophobic, trapped, and unable to breathe.

I took a moment to calm my thumping heart, sat on the bed, and stared at the closet. Instinctively, I knew I had to embrace everything and at least pretend to be excited and grateful. After all, this was a lot of money. I'd have my independence. Gradually, my breathing became normal, and the wave of heat that had rushed over me dissipated. I rose and returned to sift through the clothes.

I plucked out and held up a navy, yellow, blue, and green floral print that had a low scooped neck. I thought it was beautiful. There was something about it that suggested it wasn't a dress Samantha had long owned. In fact, when I tried it on, I was surprised that it still had a shop tag attached. The price was over twelve hundred dollars.

She had definitely said the closet contained her clothes. Why did she buy something for herself and never wear it? Was this a mistake, perhaps?

It shouldn't have been transferred from her closet to mine? I had no doubt that if I pointed it out to her, she would still insist I wear it. I cut off the tag and gazed at myself in the full-length mirror on the closet door. It couldn't have fit me better if it had been tailored for me, yet I wasn't pleased as much as a little spooked. Everything was just . . . a little too perfect.

I went to the dresser and began looking at what was in the drawers. Everything was my size, including brand-new bras. There wasn't a variety of sizes, either; everything would fit me. It was so odd. I stood thinking about it all. My gaze went to the clock Mrs. Taylor had bought me on my birthday. Placing it on the night table was one of the first things I had done. It didn't strike me then, but I was suddenly aware that it matched the blue in this room, just as it had in Julia's and my bedroom in Guildford. It truly was as if this room and everything in it was put together in anticipation of me, not just anyone.

Of course, that cannot be, I told myself, and shook my head. It was all coincidence. I had to get hold of myself. I was getting a little too paranoid.

Wasn't I?

For a moment, I had the suspicion that Leo Abbot might have told them about me much earlier than he had claimed. For all I knew, the Davenports could have hired a private detective to follow me, take pictures, and report to them about my behavior. Maybe I even had served him in the Last Diner.

After I put on the shoes that matched the dress, shoes that also looked unused, I gazed at myself again in the full-length mirror. On second thought, the size coincidences weren't that astounding. Samantha and I were about the same height and weight. *It happens. Stop making a thing of it*, I told myself. I broke out of my reverie when I heard someone knocking gently.

"Yes?" I said.

I was expecting Samantha, of course, but Dr. Davenport opened the door and stepped in quickly.

"I'm sorry to interrupt, and I'm certainly not here to rush you," he said.

"It's fine. I'm ready. Thank you."

"Yes, I imagine you're hungry. I know I am."

He didn't close the door behind him completely. He had changed his clothes and wore a light-blue jacket, shirt, and slacks with a dark-blue tie. I had been so nervous in Leo's apartment when he and I first met that I really hadn't looked at him. I had a suspicion that he was someone who never totally relaxed in the presence of someone else, especially someone who was yet a stranger, but he looked far less severe right now, his gaze not as stern or as analytical, his lips softer. Yet he didn't lose what I had recognized in my father early on, a posture reeking of self-confidence.

"Although I pride myself on being careful and a bit skeptical of first impressions," he said, "I believe you are very bright and perceptive, especially for someone as young as you are."

"Thank you."

"I don't imagine it will take you long to size up

this family and navigate the waters of Wyndemere successfully, but I want to be sure you understand how delicate and fragile Samantha really is. She floods anyone, especially someone new, with a plethora of distractions, keeping you from seeing just how vulnerable she really is. I hope your life in New York, as short as it has been, hasn't made you too cynical or hardened you."

"No, I don't think so, but I'm not sure if that's a good thing or a bad thing in today's world."

I knew where he was going, but I waited to hear him say it.

"Some cynicism is necessary for survival, of course. But to our issue . . . having a child, children, is very important to us, even though Samantha is apparently tossing overboard what most would agree is the essence of motherhood, carrying and giving birth to one's own child. Dr. Bliskin will tell you that for most women, being pregnant is, at one stage or another, a time when they feel most fulfilled, healthy. Indeed, it seems almost antithetical to a woman's essence to reject natural motherhood."

"I've heard that, yes."

It bothered me, too, I thought, but seventy-five thousand dollars . . .

"From what Leo tells me, you come from quite a traditional family structure. I doubt you've ever come into contact with this sort of thing."

"In vitro?"

"That, and a woman like Samantha," he added, to be sure his point was clear.

"I come from a male-dominated family," I said. "My father oversaw all my social contacts. I can't imagine that you'd appreciate how important my independence is to me now, but please be assured, I am capable of making my own decisions."

"Yes, I believe you are. Leo warned me that you could be very determined."

"In that way, I am my father's daughter," I said.

He finally released one of his precious smiles, precious because when he smiled, his demeanor changed instantly. The warmth that rushed in enhanced his good looks. He was like a man who, for the moment at least, had stepped out of the portrait painted of him.

"However, there's a bit of a reversal here when it comes to what we call a traditional family. You'll find the older generation in this house is female-dominated. My father would never admit it."

"Yes, I met your mother for only a moment or two, but long enough to get an initial impression."

"She won't be any problem for you. As they say, more often than not, her bark is worse than her bite. She tends to ignore what she doesn't approve of rather than truly face it down. But I'm here to talk about Samantha. I know you're still deciding about this. What I want to be sure about is that whatever your final decision, you do not make her feel any less of a woman. I have no doubt that she will love our child more than her own life once he or she is delivered into her arms."

He paused, expecting me to say something either to reinforce that or to challenge it, but I was silent. I could almost feel his eyes searching my face for a clue, but I really wasn't sure how I felt about it. I didn't know her well enough yet to voice any opinion about that. My hesitation stiffened him a bit.

"It's, as you British say, 'early days,' but any derogatory statements or comments of disapproval, criticism, and disparagement of her for wanting to do this will be, could be, devastating for her. If you're already carrying and such a thing happens, I might be forced to house you somewhere else until you've completed your obligation," he concluded, his voice tempered but clearly thick with threat.

"I understand," I said. "I wouldn't take on something I thought was wrong. Being critical of Samantha for wanting to do this would be the same as criticizing myself."

His eyes brightened. I wasn't saying it simply to please him. I really believed that much.

"I was hoping to hear something like that. Well then, let's begin your Wyndemere education by us all having something to eat in the dining room. I don't think you've met Mrs. Marlene yet, right?"

"No."

"She, our estate manager George Stark, my father's private nurse, and Parker are my most trusted help. There are a variety of maids coming and going, going mainly because of something my mother sees them do or not do that upsets her, like forgetting to dust one of the grandfather clocks," he added with a smirk. I couldn't help but wonder how he really did feel about his mother.

The door opened farther, and Samantha looked in at us.

"Oh. Have you come to fetch her, Harrison? That's so sweet. When he's a mind to, Harrison can be a wonderful host, even for his mother's guests," she said, and Dr. Davenport laughed.

Then he did something that really surprised me. He held out his arms.

"Can I escort the two most beautiful women to ever grace the halls of Wyndemere to dinner?"

Samantha took his arm quickly and then looked at me. "That dress looks better on you than it did on me. Doesn't it, Harrison?"

I hesitated to question whether she had ever worn it besides trying it on to buy. Could she have and not noticed the tag?

"Better? It looks very nice," he said, carefully negotiating a diplomatic reply. If he knew she hadn't worn it, he was keeping that to himself.

He continued to hold up his arm for me to take.

I did, and the three of us walked down the long, wide corridor toward the stairway. However, before we reached it, Mrs. Cohen came hurrying toward us from the opposite direction. Dr. Davenport stopped.

"He's had a cardiac event," she said as she drew closer.

Dr. Davenport took his arms away from ours quickly. "You two go down, Samantha. I'll come as soon as I can."

Samantha took my hand. "Don't be frightened," she said.

Coming from the young woman who was supposed to be quite a bit more delicate than I was, her words of comfort during what was obviously a family crisis nearly brought a smile to my face.

We started down the stairs. I looked back.

"He's had a number of those episodes lately. Harrison wanted him taken to the cardiac ICU, but his mother insisted his father could have just as good care here. She hates going to the hospital and vows she will die in her own bed, so her husband should, too. There are all sorts of medical equipment and things in his room, and there's a specialty nurse around the clock. Someone comes in later to relieve Mrs. Cohen."

"So he's very, very sick," I said. *Fatally ill* was what I really meant.

"Oh, I think so. I really don't know any details aside from his being diagnosed as a severe diabetic. Harrison is like a police detective," she said when we reached the bottom of the stairway and paused, now both of us looking back up.

"A police detective?"

"You know. Someone who doesn't want to bring the ugliness of his work home to his family."

But this is your family, I thought.

"I don't hear about a patient of his dying until weeks afterward or when I read it in the newspaper, if I do. I don't like reading the obituary section, do you?"

"Come to think of it, I don't recall ever reading it, even in England."

"See? We think alike," she said, smiling. "Let's see what light dinner Mrs. Marlene has made for us."

She led us down the hallway to the dining

room. It was grand, with its high ceilings and large chandelier centered over the long, elegant dark maple-wood table with its floral-patterned cushioned chairs. It did indeed seat twenty. The wall to the left was almost all windows, which provided a view of the lake below the grounds as they sloped toward it. The lights of some homes surrounding the lake twinkled like falling stars. Now the water itself was a dark silver splashed like an immense tablespoon of tungsten on this picture-postcard view of the valley and the mountains.

On the opposite dining-room wall hung a large oil painting of what was obviously Wyndemere. It was done in a romantic style, with the background dark, the night sky light, and the figures of a man and a woman in a horse-drawn carriage being brought to the front. The contrast and texture in the painting highlighted them. The picture was quite big, leaving barely a foot or so on each side of the wall.

"That's very beautiful in an almost mysterious sort of way," I said.

"Supposedly, the people in the carriage are ancestors of the original family. The artist wasn't someone important. The story is he was the son of the Jamesons' best friends, a man who died before he was twenty-five. He had tuberculosis and lived in the attic of his family home. Most of the scenes he painted were born in his imagination. He could see like a psychic. Supposedly, he lived here while he did that painting. There are so many stories and legends about this house and the people and things in it that if you listened to them all, your head would spin."

"Legends and fables are my favorite stories, especially about mysterious things."

"Really? I don't read as much as I should. Perhaps you'll suggest some. Wait until I show you the library. My mother-in-law brags that there are over three thousand volumes, not that she reads anything but the social column. We'll have nothing but time on our hands soon enough. I'm not a big television person, are you?"

"Not since I've been here. Had no time for it."

"Oh, how dreadful. Everyone should have some time to relax."

I looked at the table. The platters of salad, shrimp, and what was surely pieces of lobster were set before three prepared seating places, all facing the windows. There was bread, at least three different kinds, butter pats, and goblets of water. On a table this large, with two chairs at the ends with arms and a bit taller than the others, the food, although plentiful, looked diminished.

"I hope you love shrimp and lobster."

"Yes," I said. "Although my father usually frowned on the expense."

"Is your mother a good cook?"

"Not a gourmet cook," I said.

"Mrs. Marlene is. She doesn't live in the house. She's been with us only a year, but she is as dedicated to my husband as anyone can be. He did something that saved her husband's life, although he's been put on disability or something, which is why she has to work. She's like you, only she's Irish," she said.

I had to laugh. "She's like me? Don't tell the Irish that."

"Don't tell the Irish what, now?" we heard, as Mrs. Marlene, a tall, attractive woman with reddish-brown hair and true kelly-green eyes, came in from the adjoining kitchen. She carried a platter of fresh fruit.

Instead of answering, Samantha laughed and nodded at me. "This is Emma Corey from England."

"Oh, you're from England. No one told me so," she said, standing back after she put the platter on the table. "How long have you been here?"

"Not even a year," Samantha answered for me.

"Is that so, now?" She smiled and looked at Samantha. "If you study on it, Mrs. Davenport, you'll find the English have been here quite a while. Where is your hometown?"

"Guildford."

"Yes, I know it. I have a nephew who attended the University of Surrey. He teaches dramatic arts in Cork now."

"Emma is a singer," Samantha said, and then looked at me. "Did you attend that university?"

"No," I said, smiling. Didn't she realize how old I was? "I came to America right after secondary school."

"What school is that?"

"What you call high school here."

"Well, you'll have a lot to discover between you," Mrs. Marlene said. "Is there anything else you might want?"

"We don't, do we, Emma?"

"No, this is wonderful."

"My husband is looking after his father. There was some sort of cardiac thing, so we'll start," Samantha said, indicating we should sit. "Thank you for doing this after working what I'm sure were two tours of the kitchen for my mother-in-law's guests."

Mrs. Marlene nodded but didn't smile. She gave me a long, hard look and then left.

"She likes you," Samantha said immediately.

"Really? How can you tell that so quickly?"

"I can," she said. "Let's eat, and then, if Harrison says it's all right, I'll show you his office and, of course, the library and the rest of the house. Go on, take what you want."

I looked toward the doorway. It sounded like someone had entered Wyndemere and was hurrying up the stairs. I thought there were at least two or three people talking.

"What's going on?" I asked.

"Something," she said. "But nothing that will disturb us. Harrison will see to it."

How protective, I thought. My father believed that love was compromise, but in my heart of hearts, I believed love was nurtured for a woman most when the man she loved wanted to do nothing more than keep her safe and satisfied. Maybe that was selfish. Maybe it was simply a reaction to my father's insurmountable arrogance. He was truly lord of the manor, even if he had nothing like a manor, nothing like this.

I looked at Samantha as she chose what she would eat, the delight in her eyes, the simplicity in her smile. There was a grace and innocence about her that I was sure had stolen Harrison Davenport's heart. Perhaps he saw in her everything he had wished was in his mother. I didn't have to be here long to sense that Samantha Davenport floated through this mansion like an independent spirit, with the power to make herself deaf and blind whenever she thought something might shatter the soft smile of pleasure that was as necessary to her existence as oxygen.

The noise increased in the hallway. Suddenly, Mrs. Marlene came out of the kitchen and walked quickly through the dining room, a look of absolute terror on her face.

"Something's going on? Should we go see?" I asked.

"No," she said. "Harrison will tell us if it's important."

I was sure I heard a scream. Samantha ate and kept facing forward, but I detected a trembling starting in her body.

"Was that your mother-in-law?"

She didn't answer. I turned to the dining-room doorway when I heard footsteps approaching. Dr. Davenport appeared.

"I'm afraid my father has passed," he said.

"Oh!" Samantha cried, dropping her fork. She looked like she might topple.

Dr. Davenport came in quickly to embrace her and turned to me. "I knew his heart muscle was weakening. Diabetes can lead to heart issues. My father was not one who would pay attention to the dietary issues, and he thought exercise was a waste of time."

"I'm so sorry," I said.

Samantha was sobbing almost in silence.

He caressed her shoulders and kissed her cheek. "There's nothing for you to do, sweetheart. Finish your dinner. I'm working on the arrangements. I've given my mother a sedative. She'll remain in her room. Mrs. Cohen is attending to her."

Samantha wiped the tears from her cheeks with her napkin and looked up at him. "What will we do?" she asked, nodding toward me.

"There's no reason not to continue with our plans," he said, which brought a soft smile to her lips. "The arrangements are in place, Emma. Samantha can accompany you to Dr. Bliskin's office in the morning. I'm going back to see about my father," he said. "The medical examiner will be here shortly."

"Aren't you a medical examiner?" Samantha asked.

"I'm the son. We have to have him to confirm cause of death. No worries, darling."

"Can I show Emma your office?"

"Of course."

He kissed her again and left.

She smiled. "Well, you heard him. There's nothing we can do," she said. "I feel so helpless at times like this. The best thing for us to do is stay out of everyone's way. Harrison will have everything under control. He has that calmness, that control a heart surgeon must have, don't you think?"

"Yes, but I'm sure he's quite upset," I said. "It's his *father*." I looked at my food. My appetite had collapsed.

"Oh, finish your dinner," she said. "You heard Harrison. There's nothing for us to do, and everything is still set. I'm sorry it happened the first night you're here," she added, and reached for some grapes. "Honestly," she said, "I don't eat this much."

She leaned in to whisper.

"Someone might think I was pregnant."

ELEVEN

I had been to funerals with my family, but I had never been in a house in which someone had just died, the corpse still there. Even though this was such a large house, the empty rooms and dark shadows seemed like a garden for flowers of gloom. Perhaps chased by similar feelings, Samantha moved me through the hallway quickly to her husband's office. There was still some commotion behind us: the nurse hurrying up and down the stairs, Mrs. Marlene bringing something up on a tray, and Parker rushing in to get some orders from Dr. Davenport. In the background, we could hear an ambulance arriving, but Samantha didn't look back to see what was happening, and from the way she was clinging to my hand, tugging me forward, it was clear she didn't want me to, either.

Her voice was thin, on the verge of cracking, as she rushed her words as well as her steps.

"You will have the whole house to use, except Harrison's office and my mother-in-law's rooms, of course. She doesn't like anyone but the maid in her bedroom. Even Harrison's father rarely goes in there," she said, as if nothing unusual was occurring at the moment.

When I glanced at her, I saw there were tears in her eyes, but to me they were tears of panic.

"We have a game room and an entertainment center, but I'm sure Dr. Bliskin is going to want you to take nice walks every day that it's not raining. I'll walk with you, of course. We'll walk to the lake and back. During the early months, we can walk part of the path that goes for miles and miles and circles the lake. Harrison runs, you know. I think he's run completely around the lake."

Best to ask no questions, I thought. Best to follow her lead.

"He looks like he keeps fit."

"Oh, yes, he does. Speaking of that, Mrs. Marlene may be a little upset, but I've discussed another idea with Harrison."

"What idea?"

"Bringing in a nutritionist to design the right things for you to eat. You don't want to get too heavy, but you do want to eat everything that will help us have a very healthy baby. Right?" she asked as she opened the door to Dr. Davenport's office.

"Yes, of course."

"I'll follow the same diet so you don't feel strange eating what no one else eats."

I looked at her to see if she was joking, but she was dead serious.

We entered an immaculate large office that so far looked to me to be the most modern in furnishing and fixtures in the house. It was dominated by the large dark-oak desk before us, the top of which was clear except for a long yellow pad, a telephone, a pen stand, and some framed pictures. There was a tall black leather chair and a small desk lamp. Behind the desk were bay windows creating a small nook.

To the right were shelves of books, many looking leather-bound, and the wall on the left was dominated by a beautifully framed large picture of Samantha in her wedding gown. In her hands she held a bridal bouquet of coral peonies paired with ranunculus, garden roses, and Queen Anne's lace. My mummy loved all those flowers.

The floor of the office was a charcoal-colored tile. At the right front of the desk was a comfortable-looking cushioned metal chair, and on the left, under the framed portrait, was a black leather settee with a small glass-surfaced coffee table, also silver metal. There were some medical magazines on it in a neat pile.

"That's a beautiful picture of you," I said. "And a simply magnificent bouquet."

"Thank you. Elizabeth was in charge of all the floral arrangements. Give the devil her due. We had our wedding here at Wyndemere. I wish you could have seen it. Simon, Harrison's father, had a dance floor built on the lawn, and there was a gazebo with an arch decorated with arrangements of the same flowers. We had two hundred and fifty guests and a full orchestra." She stared up at herself. "My mother hired a designer for that dress, someone from New York City whom Elizabeth Davenport had recommended. I don't want to tell you how much it cost. Probably equal to half my wardrobe.

"The Davenports insisted on contributing to the wedding because they wanted to invite an additional one hundred guests. Elizabeth claimed the event was equal to the budget of some states in the union." She laughed. "Harrison was a little embarrassed by it all, but he put up with everything to please me more than to please his mother."

"That's lace pearl, isn't it?"

"Yes, a one-of-a-kind design."

"It's a beautiful dress."

"Thank you. I put it on sometimes just to relive that day. Harrison enjoys that. My mother-in-law thinks it's ridiculous. She had her own wedding dress redone to create a gown she could wear at some charity ball."

"Really? Most women keep their wedding dress sacrosanct."

"Most women are not my mother-in-law," she said. Then she paused, her expression finally reflecting what was happening in the house. "I shouldn't speak ill of her right now. I'm sure she's in a bad way. Despite how much she does by herself, she's been married for nearly fifty years. Now she's a queen without a king. When you see the rest of Wyndemere, you will see many portraits of them together, many framed photographs of them at important events with powerful politicians and celebrities. They were a very important social couple. And Simon was very good friends with my father. They did some business venture together, actually, before Harrison and I were married. My father looked up to Harrison's as a sort of mentor.

"My own father passed two years ago," she quickly added. "He died from complications during an operation to remove a cancerous tumor on one of his lungs. Harrison wasn't his doctor, of course. My father was a heavy smoker. He went from cigarettes during the day to cigars at night in his office."

"I'm sorry. What about your mother?"

"She lives with her sister now. She sold her house and moved to Hudson, New York. My aunt lost her husband years before." She looked at me like she'd remembered some unspoken instruction. "You haven't told me much about your own family. How many brothers and sisters do you have?"

"Just an older sister, Julia. She's a grade-school teacher."

"Oh. Are you close? I'm an only child."

"We were, but we drifted apart as we grew older. She saw herself as my second mum or something."

"How trying," she said with a sigh. "Is she married?"

"No."

"Is she as pretty as you?"

"We have different looks," I said.

She smiled. "That's one thing I noticed about you from the start."

"What?"

"Your modesty. Harrison teases me and tells me I need lessons. I know I'm spoiled, but I love it," she confessed sotto voce. "I think that happens when you're an only child. I didn't ask to be spoiled."

"Interesting how you and Dr. Davenport are both only children," I said.

She shook her head. "Oh, no. Harrison wasn't always an only child. He had a sister, Holly. She died very young. She had a heart defect. I think that was what drove him to specialize in cardiac medicine."

"Oh. I'm sorry. I didn't know."

"How could you? There aren't any pictures displayed of her in the main part of the house, only in my in-laws' rooms and Harrison's bedroom. She died when she was six. He was nine and quite devoted to her. He has a picture of her here on his desk."

She stepped up to it and held the picture out to me.

"What a beautiful little girl," I said.

"Yes." She took it back quickly, giving me the feeling that Dr. Davenport didn't want anyone seeing it, much less touching it. She set it exactly where it had been.

"We don't mention her. It resurrects deep sadness. Of course," she said, gazing back at the doorway, "we're back in the well of sorrow now, aren't we? The house will be so dreary, but don't worry. We'll brighten things up when we can. Let's go look at the library and the rest of the house, if you're not too tired."

"I'm fine."

We left the office. I gazed down the dark hallway on my left. There were no lights on, but I could see it continued for some distance.

"What's down there?"

"Oh, that leads to what was sort of the help's quarters, but right now no one lives there."

Dr. Davenport was descending the stairway, talking to a much older man. He looked toward us, but Samantha turned us quickly into the library. It was quite large. She hadn't been exaggerating about the number of books, either. I perused the bindings of some and rattled off which I had read. She had read none but vowed she would start reading now.

"We'll have so much time on our hands waiting for your test results and, of course, months and months afterward. Most afternoons, we'll sit in here, have tea and Mrs. Marlene's crumpets, if Dr. Bliskin says you can, and read for hours and hours."

I had the eerie impression that she would hover over me every moment of every day, and not simply to have companionship. I would become a ship carrying her precious cargo. She would watch anything and everything I put in my mouth and keep aware of everything I did that could even slightly jeopardize the pregnancy. I supposed I couldn't blame her.

"Harrison has come up with a wonderful plan to convince people I was the one who gave birth to our child."

"Oh?"

"When I start to show, which I hope won't be until the seventh month, I'm going to leave to visit a college friend of mine in Switzerland." She leaned toward me. "That's who you'll be if anyone sees us these first two weeks. That makes it logical. I'll leave, but I won't stay away for two months. I'll return secretly when you're close to delivery. Isn't that all brilliant?"

"What do you mean when you say 'when I start to show'?"

"Oh. Well, I'll have to mimic you, won't I? Whatever you experience, I'll experience, or pretend to, I mean. I've got to think like a pregnant woman, so when Harrison and I go out, people who meet us will be convinced I have a baby on the way."

"Where did you go to college? In case someone asks me."

"Bennington in Vermont. I know. We were in plays together," she added.

"Plays?" I smiled to myself.

"Does that upset you?"

"No. I was just remembering how Leo characterized all this as my being in a play. Actually, you're the one who will be in the play. You're the one who will be acting the part. I'll be living it."

It was only after I said that last part that I realized what I'd done. Suddenly, she looked a little upset, even a little insulted.

"I'll live it, too. It won't be just sympathy pains or something. It will be important for me to be mentally tied to my child."

"Yes, I guess it will. Of course," I said. "That's very wise."

She smiled. "I thought so. Nevertheless, I don't want to think of you as simply someone in a mirror, someone to model myself after and imitate. I want to know as much about you as an individual as quickly as I can." She sat on one of the two settees that faced each other. "And you're always free to ask me anything about myself. We've got to become best friends quickly, almost lifelong best friends, so we can carry our story credibly. Do you mind?"

"Absolutely not. I haven't had a best friend for some time," I said.

Her smile warmed.

She nodded for me to sit. She looked at the closed door when we could hear people in the entryway and on the stairs, not subduing their voices as much. Her face took on a look of abject fear. I thought she was having this conversation simply to do all she could to avoid confronting what was happening in the mansion, but when she turned back to me, I could see that she was sincerely curious about my upbringing and life in England.

Surprisingly, as I described it, answering one question after another, I felt a little more homesick than I had when I was in the city. Perhaps that was because I was so busy then, my every hour seemingly taken up with work and solving problems as well as chasing my dream. Here, it would be the filling of time, almost like an inmate in a prison counting days and hours, despite all that the mansion and its grounds had to offer. I was still confined, and what I had surmised as to how it would be looked to be accurate. The implication was clear that when I began to show, I was going to be practically incarcerated so her secret could be kept intact. No contact with anyone but some of the trusted staff and Samantha, my every movement supervised, and every morsel I ate carefully prepared and served were what loomed before me. The isolation and the pregnancy would justify every penny they gave me.

I asked her questions about her college life, and from her answers, I had the distinct impression she was never serious about finding a career. For her, it seemed more like a giant sorority. She had met Dr. Davenport during her spring break when she was a senior, and by the time she had graduated, they were engaged.

"We were . . . how would you say . . . smitten with each other."

"Yes," I said. For a moment, thinking about my frustrations in New York, I was envious, but I fought that back, shaking the hope for such a destiny out of my mind.

"Let's go look at the rest of the house," she said when the house became silent. We had been talking nearly an hour.

We went to every remaining room, even visiting the kitchen. Mrs. Marlene was gone, but Samantha wanted me to see how modern it was and how big their pantry was. According to her, Elizabeth Davenport would have a fit if something she wanted had not been properly stored.

"She once had a tantrum because there were no Ritz crackers for her wine-and-cheese late-afternoon time. Parker had to rush into Hillsborough, the village, to get a box, and Mrs. Marlene was nearly brought to tears.

"Harrison is constantly warning her about her high blood pressure. He says she's a perfect example of someone being her own worst enemy, but she's stubborn. What good is it to have a specialist for a son if you don't listen to him?"

She gave me a clear look of warning. I had better listen to him and my maternity doctor.

"Like my father, she's probably cemented into her ways," I offered. "My mother likes to say, 'You can't teach an old dog new tricks.' Of course, she won't say it in front of him."

"Oh, if I ever called Elizabeth Davenport an old dog . . . I'd have to leave the country, not just Wyndemere," she said, her eyes bright. She giggled as if we were already conspirators.

After she ended the tour of Wyndemere, we both agreed we were tired enough now to go to sleep. Dr. Davenport came quickly down the hallway when he heard us walking toward our bedrooms.

"You two going to sleep?"

"Yes, we are, Harrison. It's been a long and trying day, and so sad now, too," Samantha said. She took his hand, and he hugged and kissed her. "Are you all right?"

"Yes," he said, releasing her and turning to me.

"Parker will be taking you to the hospital and then Dr. Bliskin's office at nine in the morning," he said.

"And me, too," Samantha said.

"Yes, of course. I'll be in touch throughout. He's going to expedite all the tests we need."

"How's Elizabeth?" Samantha asked.

"She's asleep. My mother puts on a good act, but she's a bit more vulnerable than she'd like to be. In a way, it's better for the two of you to be busy tomorrow."

"What about the funeral?" Samantha asked.

"I'll get the details to you tomorrow." He looked at me. "I'm sorry that this is your introduction to Wyndemere. However, I'll be taking time off now, and I'll do what I can to make everything run smoothly."

"I can return to New York and come back," I suggested.

"Oh, no!" Samantha cried. "We have everything planned, down to the month our child should be born, or close to it."

"It's not always that specific, Samantha. Things might take a while," Dr. Davenport said softly.

"I don't think so, Harrison." She looked at me. "Everything is too perfect. You'll see."

He smiled. "You might be right," he said, touching her cheek.

I had no doubt that to keep her happy, he would move heaven and earth to make it so. I wondered if I would ever find a man who looked at me the way he looked at her. It was as if she was the sun, the very source of his health and happiness.

However, this man hadn't even had a moment to mourn, I thought. He was hiding his sadness to avoid making her sad.

He turned to me. "Are you all right? It's been something of a whirlwind for you. I didn't anticipate all this so soon."

"Yes, I'm fine, but I am tired."

"Of course. Have a good night's rest," he said.

"I'll wake you," Samantha promised after she hugged me. "We'll have breakfast in the little alcove off the kitchen. It gets the morning sun. It's not going to rain tomorrow, is it, Harrison?" she asked, practically demanded.

"I don't think so."

She looked down the hall. "Is he . . ."

"No, he's been taken to the funeral parlor."

"Good," she said. "Oh. I didn't mean *good*."

"I know, sweetheart," he said. He glanced at me.

It was obvious she meant that she didn't want to think about what had happened, but I didn't believe it was because she was unfeeling. Death frightened her because it had visited this house, a place I easily understood to be her fortress. The grounds, the servants, and her doting husband all provided her with the walls that kept her safe from the tensions and turmoil of the outside world.

"Maybe you should give me something to help me sleep," she said, "like you did for your mother."

"We'll see," he said. "Good night, Emma."

"Yes, good night," Samantha said.

I watched him walk her down to her room and go in with her before I entered mine. The bedding smelled brand-new. With the oversized, exceedingly soft pillows, I easily imagined I was going to sleep on a cloud. Despite what had happened and how strange I still felt being here, the emotional turmoil inside me and the traveling pushed me to near exhaustion. I think I fell asleep seconds after closing my eyes.

But I didn't sleep through the night. The sound of someone sobbing woke me. When I listened harder, I thought I heard voices. I rose and went to my door. Peering out toward the sound of sobbing and voices, I saw Elizabeth Davenport in a robe. Dr. Davenport, also in a robe, was embracing her and trying to get her to go back to her bedroom.

I glanced toward Samantha's room, but all was quiet. When I looked back at Dr. Davenport and his mother, I thought he looked in my direction. I closed the door softly and returned to bed. I really didn't know these people. What was happening wasn't my business. Their grief was still quite raw. Samantha had welcomed me to her world with open arms, almost the way someone might welcome a long-lost close and loved relative, but I was still a stranger, someone feeling more like I was imposing on their grief instead of sharing it.

When I closed my eyes again, I started to think about my parents and Julia. The Davenport family was seriously diminished; mine was in a state of limbo. Tomorrow, when the time difference permitted it, I would have to call. If my father answered, I would plead with him not to immediately hang up. If Julia or my mother answered, I would tell the "good lie" and say I had a role in a regional theater show. Hopefully, they would believe me, and I could call them periodically until I had delivered the Davenports' baby and returned to New York.

With so much money, I could afford a quick trip back to England and try to win back my father's affection and convince him to approve of my efforts to develop my career. Time can heal. Despite how angry he was, it surely had cooled to the point where he might regret being so furious as to cut me out of his and my mother's lives. My absence hopefully kept him awake at night, too. If people who were meant to love each other couldn't forgive each other, who could?

I fell back to sleep and slept so deeply that Samantha indeed had to wake me in the morning. I felt her shake my shoulder and opened my eyes to see her standing there in the exact same silk robe I had.

"Harrison said I should wake you. After breakfast, we're going right to the hospital to get your blood tests and . . . let me remember . . . something called an EKG and a chest X-ray. Then we'll go to Dr. Bliskin's offices for the important tests a candidate for surrogate mother must take." She recited it all like something she had just memorized.

I sat up and looked at the clock. I might be able to reach my mother, I thought.

"I have to call home. They might try to reach me in New York and not understand why I'm never there now."

"Oh. Of course. Call them. I'll come back in an hour," she said.

"How is your mother-in-law this morning?"

"I don't know," she said. "Harrison didn't say before he left, and she's shut up in her room."

Her relationship with her mother-in-law must have been cool even before this, I thought. Why wouldn't she want to offer her sympathy and companionship?

She opened the closet. "You should probably wear something like this." She reached in and took out a short-sleeved multicolored T-shirt dress. "It's easy to get in and out of when you're at the hospital and the doctor's office. I'll wear one just like it. These sandals are perfect, too."

She laid the dress over a chair and the sandals at the foot of it even though I didn't say I would wear it. Then she started out, pausing at the door before opening it.

"I don't like talking about it too much. I don't want to think my baby will be any different from any other, but Dr. Bliskin had prescribed a fertility drug for me so I could produce more eggs, and I did. Don't you hate thinking of it as eggs inside you? I haven't eaten any since.

"Anyway, just like normally, Harrison's sperm has to fertilize successfully. If all goes well with you this morning, the embryo will be transferred to your uterus as soon as five days after we get your results, maybe even three. We can declare you're pregnant with our baby soon after that. I'm sure you want to get it all started as soon as possible, right?"

"Yes," I said. I was thinking, however, that even after all the tests I took, I still had to make the final decision. Dr. Davenport had left that possibility open. Samantha would be devastated if I backed out. She wasn't even going to consider the possibility.

"Harrison was going to find time to explain this timetable to you before we left for the hospital, but I told him it would be more comfortable for you if I did. He's too . . . scientific when he talks to people. I told Dr. Bliskin that, and do you know what he said? He said that's Harrison's way of avoiding being too emotional. He can be very emotional, despite the act he's putting on for you and the act he puts on for his patients," she said. "Late last night, he returned to my bedroom for me to comfort him."

Probably after he dealt with his mother, I thought, but didn't say.

"He was closer to his father than he is to his mother. Anyway, forget about all that. Let's have a good breakfast. I already decided that after all your tests and your doctor's visit, we will go to one of the best restaurants in Hillsborough for lunch."

She opened the door and paused again. "You're all right, right?"

She had rattled off everything with barely taking a breath and hardly looking directly at me the whole time. It was truly as if she had rehearsed her speech in this room many times. Surely, she had in her own mind.

"Yes, I'm fine," I said. I know I sounded unsure, because I was, but she ignored it, smiled, and left.

As soon as I rose, I called home. The phone rang so long I was sure it would go to the answering machine.

However, just before it would have, Mummy said, "Hello."

"Mummy, how are you?" I quickly asked, happy it was she who had answered.

"Oh, Emma. Are you calling to tell us you're coming home?"

I could probably count on the fingers of one hand how many times I had lied to my mummy, if they even qualified as lies. Most of them were half-truths. It was always easier for me to live with my father's disappointment in me than it was to live with my mummy's. His reactions were solely crusted in anger; hers were layered with pain. When she discovered I hadn't told the whole truth, she acted as if I had stuck a needle in her finger. Rather than shout and bawl me out, she looked like she would cry, and then I would feel so terrible that I would cry.

I couldn't see her face right now, but I could easily envision it.

"No, Mummy. I have a part in a show outside of New York City."

I knew this was weird, but in my mind I was treating it that way.

"I'm letting you know I won't be at my apartment and my telephone number."

"Oh," she said.

"If the show's successful, I'll be in it for months and months, maybe close to a year. It's a big opportunity. Important people come to see these shows."

"Months and months," she repeated, as if she had to stuff the words into her ear. Then she took a breath and said, "Mrs. Taylor was taken to hospital yesterday. She had a bad fall and was nearly unconscious."

"I'm sorry. Is she going to be all right?"

"Your father says she won't be able to live alone anymore. He spoke with her son. They'll be putting her place up for sale. Your father hates the idea of new people next door. You know how he gets used to things," she rambled on. "He hates changes."

"I know."

"So you're not coming home," she said, as if she was confirming it with herself.

"Not for a while, as I said. It's why I came here," I added. I knew I was rationalizing, committing one of my father's declared deadly sins, but I was still convincing myself what I was doing was still part of my plan.

"He's not been himself," she added, seemingly out of the blue. "He's never forgetful, but everything annoys him more these days, and he gets distracted. Julia's not seeing that man anymore. I don't know why. She won't say. I don't think your father liked him."

"That's why," I said quickly.

"Poor Mrs. Taylor," she said. "She'll wither like an apple on the branch. Dreary days, dreary days."

She was wandering from topic to topic to avoid discussing what I had told her. The silence that fell between us was painful.

"I'll call you again, very soon, Mummy," I said, swallowing down my tears.

"I won't tell him you did," she said.

I waited a moment to see if she would ask any questions about my show, causing me to embellish my lie, but she didn't, perhaps because she was too frightened to ask.

"Mind yourself," she said, and hung up.

I stood there for almost a minute, holding the receiver. A part of me was screaming to get my clothes on, ask to be taken back to New York, and arrange to return to England. I was on the verge, tottering. Then I looked at the dress Samantha had chosen for me, again thought about the money and the opportunity doing this would give me, and went to shower and dress.

Close to an hour later, Samantha returned. For a moment, I was speechless. She wasn't just wearing the same kind of dress; she was wearing the exact color and the same sandals.

"We'll look like twin sisters," she said.

"Why did you buy two exactly the same?"

"Oh, often I do when I really like something, two pairs of the same shoes, two of the same hats, and yes, two of the same dress. I hate when I can't wear something because it needs cleaning or has a tear. Whatever." She laughed. "I'm so spoiled, and now, for a while, so will you be."

Would I? Did I want to be?

We went down to breakfast. Mrs. Marlene looked like she had been up all night. While Samantha rattled on about what we would do once we were free after the medical exams, Mrs. Marlene continually glanced at me. Our eyes often met and we exchanged knowing glances. I thought and felt Mrs. Marlene agreed that Samantha's exuberance was coming from her nervousness and her desire to ignore what had happened at Wyndemere.

I couldn't help but wonder if Mrs. Marlene fully understood why I was here and what I was about to do. How much had Samantha and Dr. Davenport actually shared with her? Did she approve? Disapprove? Would she ever tell me? I had no doubt she would worry about losing her position if she said anything negative about it to Samantha. Dr. Davenport had made it clear I was not to do so.

When it was time for us to leave, Samantha lingered beside me until Mrs. Marlene left the room. I had the feeling she didn't want me to talk to Mrs. Marlene or Mrs. Marlene to talk to me without her present. Was it always going to be like this? Or was she just going to be this worried about me talking to anyone until I had completely agreed and had the embryo transfer? Even if that were true, would I be any different if it was I and not she who was having this done? Probably not, but I couldn't see myself doing it unless it was the only way I could have a child.

Parker was waiting for us. All the way to the hospital, Samantha was obviously filled with more trepidation than I was. In a real sense, she was going to be having these tests, too. If I failed, she failed, at least for now.

When we arrived at the hospital, it was clear that Dr. Davenport was something of a hero there.

Everyone moved quickly to get me processed. At times, I felt like this was more of an emergency than a routine examination. Even Parker looked surprised when we emerged much sooner than he had anticipated. We got back into the limousine to be brought to Dr. Bliskin's office.

"There was one book I confess I read from cover to cover," Samantha said as we drove on. "Once Harrison and I decided we wanted a child now."

"What was that?"

"It's called *My Mommy Brain*. You don't have to read it, though—I can tell you everything," she said. "And I'll be right by your side should you have any of the symptoms."

"What symptoms?"

"Nothing to be afraid of. A woman's personality has to change a little if she's pregnant, don't you think? For you, it's only going to be nine months. For me, it's the rest of my life."

Didn't she think I might have a baby of my own someday?

"I'd like to read that book, too," I said. "Who gave it to you?"

"My husband." She thought for a few moments and then nodded. "Okay. I'll give it to you after you're pregnant."

I wondered about it.

"Did your husband give it to you before or after you decided to do this?"

She smiled. "I really don't remember," she said, but I thought she said it just a little too quickly.

Something in that book might have frightened her. After all, how many women were going to deliberately seek out a surrogate to carry their own child? Surely, this was not Dr. Davenport's intent when he gave the book to her. Perhaps he felt responsible, however. If my theory was right, he was the one to introduce her to all the medical possibilities because he feared he had ruined their chances to have a child.

When I thought about this, the part of my father in me wondered if I should have asked for more money. Chances were that I would have gotten it. But as strange as my father might find it, I would have felt guilty afterward, and certainly after meeting Samantha. "You be quiet," I told the Daddy inside me. "Not everything in this life is measured in a profit-and-loss statement."

TWELVE

Dr. Bliskin had his offices in a beautiful, new modern building off the main street of Hillsborough. The lobby was paneled in a pretty Wedgwood blue with slightly darker blue marble tiles. The room was softened by a half dozen cheerful paintings of idyllic country scenes. There was an array of cushioned chairs and two matching settees. Magazines, most about motherhood and childbearing, were stacked neatly on a center table. The receptionist was behind a glass panel that she slid open the moment we stepped into the lobby. Before we even reached her, she was smiling and informed Samantha we should go right in. Two pregnant women, one quite a bit further along than the other, looked up, curious and annoyed.

Samantha opened the door, and we were immediately greeted by Dr. Bliskin's nurse, a woman who looked no more than forty, if that, with short light-brown hair. "Mrs. Topper, RN," was on her breast label.

"Dr. Bliskin wants to start with you in his office, Mrs. Davenport," she said.

For a moment, it felt as if I were the one accompanying her. Mrs. Topper barely acknowledged me with a glance. We followed her to the first door on the left and entered an office with a desk upon which were a number of framed photographs of very young children.

"He'll be right in," Mrs. Topper said. She finally smiled at me to acknowledge my presence. "Just make yourself comfortable." She nodded at the chairs in front of the desk. "We're all very excited for you," she told Samantha, who thanked her.

Did she think Samantha was having her own child? Did she think I was some servant or friend accompanying her and nothing more?

"She's very sweet," Samantha said after Mrs. Topper left. "She's been with Franklin ever since he started his own practice here. Oh, these children are his triplets." She picked up one of the framed photos that had all three, not looking much more than six or seven months old. "They were all born prematurely. Touch and go for about a week, but they all survived."

"Does Mrs. Topper know anything about our potential arrangement?"

"Whatever Franklin told her," she replied, and sat, her face frozen in anticipation.

Moments later, Dr. Bliskin entered. "Ladies," he said.

Dr. Bliskin looked to be about six feet tall,

with dark-brown hair that was a shade lighter than black. He had hazel eyes and a dark complexion, the complexion of someone who had just returned from a restful vacation in the Caribbean. Unlike Dr. Davenport's, his face was not as well chiseled. His cheeks were fuller and his forehead wider, but he had a strong-looking mouth and a firm jaw. When he looked at me, his smile deepened with a pleasant surprise. There was a delight in his eyes that immediately relaxed me.

"And you must be Emma Corey," he said. He extended his hand and then looked at Samantha and nodded, as if confirming something she had told him. "So," he said, walking quickly behind his desk. "Everything I have so far from the hospital is A-plus."

"Results already?" I asked.

"I know somebody who knows somebody," he joked. There was a very youthful glint in his eyes. He turned to Samantha. "Do you have any questions, Samantha?"

"No," she said. "I've explained to Emma how much confidence we have in you, Franklin."

"Thank you. Well then, why don't you give me a couple of hours with Emma?" He looked at his watch. "Come back about twelve thirty."

"Oh, no. I want to wait here," she said firmly.

He nodded and turned to me. "I understand Dr. Davenport gave you a heads-up on what we'll do here today?"

"Somewhat, yes," I said.

"I'll explain it more as we go along. Feeling okay?

Even going to a hospital for routine tests can exhaust you."

I took a deep breath. I could sense Samantha's eyes were intensely focused on me. This was another moment of decision, another chance to spin around and head home. There would be one more, but after that . . .

"I'm okay," I said. "Everyone's been very considerate."

"Good to hear. Okay, then, why don't we get right to it?" He rose. As if she could see through the walls or perhaps had her ear to the door, Mrs. Topper opened the door.

"Mrs. Topper will get you all set," he said. "Samantha, you're welcome to stay in my office if you like."

I could almost feel it. She wanted to be right beside me just as she practically was at the hospital. She looked at Dr. Bliskin, who sensed what she wanted and shook his head slightly.

"We'll be fine," he said.

I started out.

"Emma," she called. I turned to her. "Don't be frightened."

"Why should she be?" Dr. Bliskin answered for me.

"I would be," Samantha replied.

He smiled at me, and in his smile, I saw he understood everything. It was hard to explain it, but I could feel his self-confidence just as I could feel Dr. Davenport's, only his had something extra. There was warmth attached.

Later, at lunch, Samantha wanted me to describe everything. I could see she was still annoyed that she wasn't right there, practically lying beside me, experiencing everything I had. I wasn't about to tell her some of the things Dr. Bliskin had said, either. Throughout it all, his questions revealed how surprised he was that I had agreed to be a surrogate, even knowing how much money I was offered.

"I don't know as I can describe the tests accurately," I said. "While it was going on, I closed my eyes and tried to mentally transport myself to a park. He was very gentle and considerate of my feelings the whole time. I think any woman would be comfortable with him."

And then, the first time I directly challenged what she was doing and paying to have me do, I added, "I'm sure he could alleviate any woman's fears about her own pregnancy. She would have no regrets."

"If he assures us you're in perfect health for what has to be done, he's alleviated mine," she said, smiling. Either she didn't get what I was implying or she chose to ignore it. "Anyway, there's nothing left to do but wait, which will hopefully be shorter than we expect."

When it came time to leave to return to Wyndemere, she hesitated before we walked to the limousine.

"I wish I could take you away until this was over, but I should be at Harrison's side during this troubled time."

"I'll help as much as I can," I offered.

"That's so sweet. I wonder if I would be the same if the shoe was on the other foot, but you're not expected to do anything."

When we arrived at Wyndemere, we saw half a dozen cars.

"Harrison's medical associates paying their respects, I'm sure," she said.

"What do I do?" I asked. What I meant was, *How are you going to explain me? And how are you going to explain not being there before they arrived?* Would she be out shopping at a time like this?

"Nothing. You simply showed up at an unfortunate time. Remember. You're my college friend. We had some things that had to be done. No one will question us. Just relax."

"Okay," I said, and we entered.

We could hear soft conversation in the living room. When we stepped into the doorway, everyone stopped talking. Dr. Davenport was on the larger settee, two younger men in jackets and ties sitting beside him and two older men and a gray-haired woman in a jacket, skirt, and blouse outfit sitting on the other settee. Two more older men, who looked like they would probably be Dr. Davenport's father's friends, were standing.

"How's Mother?" Samantha asked without waiting for me to be introduced. I thought it was interesting how in front of others, she would refer to Elizabeth Davenport as "Mother." It implied a far warmer relationship than the one I had witnessed so far.

"Calmer," Dr. Davenport said. He nodded at one of the men across from him. "Marvin is looking after her for me. You remember Dr. Wasserman, Samantha."

"Of course," Samantha said.

Everyone was waiting for her to introduce me, but she seemed stricken with a case of stage fright.

"This is Samantha's friend from college, Emma Corey," Dr. Davenport said.

"Oh, yes, sorry," Samantha followed. "Emma was an exchange student from England who unfortunately has arrived to visit me at a difficult time."

Everyone nodded at me, everyone but the older lady, who stared with skepticism.

"Exchange student?"

"Yes. Of course, she wanted to go home, but I assured her Harrison would appreciate her staying as long as she likes."

"Where are you from in England?" the older lady asked.

"Guildford."

"Yes, I know it well. I did some work at the Imperial College in London and took a few weekends there, but that was quite a while ago," she said wistfully. She looked at the others, who nodded and smiled.

"This is Dr. Durring," Dr. Davenport said. "She's the head of our pulmonary department."

"Hello," I said.

"Friday," Dr. Davenport told Samantha, as if he wanted to avoid the word *funeral*. "At eleven. St. Christopher's."

"I can't get it through my mind," Samantha said, her lips trembling.

No one spoke.

I took her hand. "Perhaps we should go rest," I suggested.

She nodded quickly. "I'm sorry," she told Dr. Davenport's friends.

We turned and hurried to the stairs.

"You don't have to go to the funeral, of course," she said as we started up. "We'll just tell them you left."

"Oh. Well, I . . ."

"I'd rather you didn't go," she said firmly. "More explaining to do. There'll be so many people there."

"But, afterward . . . you'll surely have people come here and . . ."

"No one will come up to your room. I'll make sure you have everything you need. You must be very tired. I am. Tests take something out of you, right?"

"Yes," I said, but she hadn't had the tests. I had.

She hugged me at my bedroom door. "Thank you," she said. "You're absolutely perfect."

I watched her hurry away and went in to take a nap. There was no doubt in my mind that she was going to do the same. I ended up sleeping for hours. When I awoke, it was dark, and I saw I had slept past six. The house was very quiet. I was a little surprised that Samantha hadn't woken me. I rose, washed my face to really wake up, and then stepped out. I wondered if any more people had arrived, but I didn't hear any voices, so I went to Samantha's bedroom door and knocked softly. There was no response. I thought perhaps she was waiting for me downstairs, so I started for the stairway. Before I got there, I heard a door open and close and saw Mrs. Cohen walking toward me.

"How did it go for you today?" she asked as she approached.

"I think well, but I'm on some hormones, and we have to wait."

"Yes, I know." She seemed to be studying me. "This is quite the commitment for someone so young to make. Your reasons are none of my business, but I would assume primarily money."

"What other reason could there possibly be?"

She nodded. "If everything goes forward, I'll do my best to make sure you're comfortable."

"Thank you. How is Mrs. Davenport?"

"She's not a well woman. All the concentration these past few years has been on Mr. Davenport, but she has some serious medical issues. She does a good job of covering them up, keeping herself busy, but as long as I've been employed here, I've known her to be in some pain. It's probably what makes her appear so irritable at times." She nodded at the stairway. "Going down?"

"Yes."

She followed closely behind me and then went directly into the kitchen. I looked into the living room. No one was there, so I had started for the dining room when I saw Dr. Davenport coming down the stairs. He moved quicker when he spotted me.

"Samantha's still asleep," he said. "She doesn't show it, but this is a very emotionally exhausting thing. Hungry?"

"A little."

"Me, too."

We headed into the dining room. There was a setting at the head of the table and two on both sides of it. He moved quickly ahead and pulled out my chair.

"Samantha will be down in a while," he said when Mrs. Marlene looked in on us. "What's the menu tonight?"

"Grilled salmon."

He looked at me.

"That's fine," I said.

She disappeared, and he sat.

"I've heard from Dr. Bliskin. You're batting a thousand so far. I think we can get you started sooner rather than later. On the day of the transfer, I'll have the money deposited into your account. If I might suggest, we should put it in a money market so it earns a little interest while you remain here. I'll take care of all that for you."

"Okay," I said. "Thank you."

"Franklin was quite impressed with you. He claims you're the most mature eighteen-year-old he's seen."

"I'm practically nineteen."

He laughed. "Yes, that accounts for it."

I laughed at myself. I think it was the first time I'd really laughed since I had arrived at Wyndemere. It was as if a thick black curtain had finally been lifted and we were all suddenly just people.

Mrs. Marlene began to serve our dinner.

"I take it you haven't mentioned any of this to your family," he said, filling my glass with water.

"No. They think I've taken a role in a regional theater."

He nodded. "I'd be more comfortable about it, however, if you gave me all the details concerning your family, address, phone numbers. No one else will have it but me."

What a way of subtly suggesting that something terrible could happen, I thought. He saw the look on my face.

"It's just intelligent protocol. Franklin Bliskin is probably the best maternity physician within a hundred miles. I've known him and his family for years."

"I liked him very much."

"Let's talk about you a little. I don't mean to seem so indifferent. What kind of auditions have you had? Where did you sing in England?"

Once he got me started, it seemed like I would never stop, but he was someone who really listened. Whether or not that was a necessary characteristic for a doctor like him, he homed in on everything, asked good questions, and by the time our salmon arrived, he'd told me he would like to hear me sing someday.

"Of course, things will be quite subdued here for a while."

"Yes. And your mother isn't well, either?"

He looked surprised for a moment and then nodded. "She's the type of person who would stare down Death at her door," he said. "I think her doctor, whom you met earlier, is more frightened of her than he'll admit."

He paused and smiled, but more like someone reminiscing.

"When I was younger, it was fun watching the two of them go at each other. Lovingly, of course, but like two horses tied to the same barrel and going in different directions, neither willing to turn even slightly."

"Sounds like me and my father," I said.

He snapped back to the present, but before he could ask why I had said that, Samantha appeared. There was that extraordinary light in his eyes immediately.

"Why did you let me sleep so long?" she asked. It seemed like she was asking us both.

"You're sleeping because you need it, Samantha," he said. He rose and pulled out the chair for her.

"I thought you were still sleeping, too," she told me as she sat. She sounded a bit irritated because we didn't sleep the exact same length of time.

Mrs. Marlene entered before I could respond and served her salad. There was a deep, dark look to her since Dr. Davenport's father's passing, yet she did look at me sympathetically and almost smiled.

"More test results have come in," Dr. Davenport told Samantha. "Everything is looking very good."

Brightness returned to her face. He leaned over to kiss her.

"When it's all done and it happens, we have to do something to celebrate. It will be long enough from now, won't it, Harrison?"

"Yes, it will." He thought a moment. "I'll take the two of you to that wonderful Mediterranean restaurant on the other side of Lake Wyndemere." He turned to me. "It's become Samantha's and my secret rendezvous. No one knows us out there. Worth the trip."

I nodded and looked at Samantha. She was thoughtful for a moment, and for that moment, I had the distinct feeling she hadn't intended to include me in her future celebration. If Dr. Davenport noticed, he didn't say anything. Perhaps they would discuss it later. What I did feel was how contradictory Samantha's attitude about me was and certainly would continue to be. On one hand, I was the solution to their problem, her problem mainly, but on the other, I was a reminder of that problem, too.

I wondered . . . just how incarcerated would I be once I housed their baby's embryo in my rented-out womb?

That night, when I retired to my room, I pondered the idea of writing a letter to Mummy, despite my father's vehement threat to burn it at the door. He was at work when our mail was delivered, and I had faith that my mummy would keep it from him even though it was very rare to see her hold any secrets from my father. Usually, they were very minor things like something small she had bought for the house, usually to replace something old. For as long as I could remember, she worried about spending money on anything without my father's approval first. How many times I recalled her looking covertly at something beautiful for the house and concluding, "Arthur would be just so irritated if I bought it." I used to wish I had the money to buy it later.

Every time I began the letter, I crossed out the first sentence. I tried, *I'm so sorry that I lied to you. I was not able to tell you the truth. Please understand what I'm about to tell you.* None sounded good or adequately set the stage for an explanation that I knew would drive her to tears, despite the amount of money involved. I was still struggling with it myself. Despite going through the exams and preparations, every once in a while, I had the urge to burst out of my bedroom and flee.

I was especially vulnerable to this during the period of mourning for Dr. Davenport's father. Although he hadn't come to me to discuss it, he obviously had approved of Samantha's idea to keep me well out of the public eye. She visited with me whenever she could and rattled on and on about the services, things people had said, and especially Elizabeth Davenport's condition. Perhaps not so amazingly, I had not seen her since that first day. The few times all week that Samantha thought it was safe for me to wander about the house, Elizabeth was bedridden.

Toward the middle of the following week, Dr. Davenport came to see me to tell me that Parker was taking me and Samantha to see Dr. Bliskin early in the morning, well before his regular office hours.

"He'll do a final exam, and if all is how we expect it to be, we'll make the transfer hopefully over the weekend."

He didn't come out and say it directly, but I knew that meant the creation of the embryo or embryos had been achieved. More than likely, Dr. Bliskin had shown him his potential child through a microscope. Now that it was about to happen, I felt myself tremble.

"Get a good night's rest," he said, smiling. "All is going well."

He went off to tell Samantha. I couldn't shake off the vision of him doing so and her reacting like a woman who had just been told she was about to be pregnant. I anticipated her coming to see me immediately afterward.

"Harrison told me what he just told you," she said after I had said, "Come in." She looked almost on fire with excitement, unable to stand still. "The moment I met you, I knew this would go smoothly and as quickly as possible. I know you will be happy to get it all started. Of course, you want to return to your career as soon as you can. Someday, Harrison and I, and even our child when he or she is older, will come see you perform." She stopped pacing and looked at me. "You're happy about it, right? I mean, happy we're moving so quickly?"

She looked like she would faint if I said otherwise.

I nodded.

"Okay, okay," she said, pacing again. "Get a good night's rest. I'll be right by your side." She stood there smiling at me, but looking beyond me, I thought. "This house so desperately needs a child, a future."

She hugged me quickly and left. Despite both her and Dr. Davenport's wish for me to get a good night's rest, I barely slept. It was truly like angels and demons were debating inside me, only I couldn't decide who was arguing what. Was it really an angel advising me to go home, to accept a different life from what I dreamed of having?

Samantha was there minutes after I had risen. It was as if she thought she had to be at my side from the moment I opened my eyes this morning. Perhaps she sensed the turmoil going on within me. When I looked at her at breakfast and in the limousine, I saw how nervous she was, how frightened, and how much she dreaded hearing the words *I'm sorry. I can't do this*.

But I didn't turn back. Dr. Bliskin put me at such ease with his concern and with the way he looked at me, making me feel as if this was indeed going to be my child. I couldn't imagine him treating any woman with more loving care. When we looked at each other, we seemed to share a secret beyond what Samantha and Dr. Davenport knew. I guess the simplest way to think of it was he sincerely wanted to safely deliver the baby I would carry, as much for me as for them. Perhaps I was just looking for another rationalization, but when he declared days later that it was time, I didn't turn and run as I had seen myself doing almost every day I was at Wyndemere.

On the day of the transfer, like any father who wanted to be present when his wife went to the delivery room, Dr. Davenport accompanied Dr. Bliskin. At first, neither of them would permit Samantha to be present, but she literally shed tears, and they relented. The four of us and Dr. Bliskin's nurse, Mrs. Topper, witnessed the procedure.

Afterward, I was left to rest for a while. Samantha wouldn't leave my side. She sat there, holding my hand. I had no pain of any sort, but I had a strange, ethereal feeling. It was as if I had decided to leave my body until it was all completed. I knew Samantha was holding my hand, but I didn't feel hers. I didn't feel anything.

Despite all the tests, all the medications, and all the descriptions Dr. Bliskin had given me, I did not believe what was happening or would happen. It still hadn't settled in my reality.

But I knew that it would. There were months and months ahead of me when I would wake up every day and have it re-announced. Perhaps the first thought I would have the moment I awoke was *Someone else's baby is living inside you. You won't need to look in a mirror to see the evidence as you begin to show. You will be feeling it throughout your very being*.

And one thing was definite: not a waking moment would pass when I was in Samantha's company when I wouldn't be reminded—whether through what she said, how she treated me, or what I saw in her eyes—that I was carrying her child, her future. I felt confident that more than once, in different ways, perhaps, she would also remind me that nothing of myself would be in the child I would deliver.

How would that make me feel? Relieved that there would be no evidence I was there? Or even emptier, less significant, practically like an invisible person, and very much like the ghosts that Elizabeth Davenport told Samantha still haunted the darkest corners of Wyndemere?

Samantha left me to use the bathroom, and Dr. Bliskin came in.

"How are you doing?"

"I guess all right. I don't feel . . ."

"Not yet," he said, smiling. "But someday soon you'll know it. I'm confident this implanting is going to work. You're a fertile garden."

"Never thought of myself in those terms," I said, and he laughed. "How many of these have you done?"

"A number of them, lately more than ever." He looked at me differently, I thought, or was that again my wild imagination at work? "You're a very pretty young woman, Emma, and I'm not just referring to your good looks. There's something beautiful in you that some man is going to see and be so consumed by that he won't be able to breathe unless he has you beside him."

I widened my eyes. I had never heard a doctor speak poetry, and until now, he was comforting and gentle, but I thought he was that way with all his patients . . . just a doctor with a good bedside manner.

"Thank you," I said.

"I'm going to be with you through all this, and not only because Harrison is my best friend."

I didn't know what to say.

"The day will come when I'll deliver the baby forming inside you," he said. "You'll have lived with it for so long that it won't be unusual for you to feel something, some tie to him or her emotionally. When I lift the child and place it in Samantha's waiting hands, you're going to feel like you're giving it up. But don't."

"How should I feel?"

He smiled. "Like you're giving it back," he said.

And so it began.

THIRTEEN

Most of the girls I knew who were my age didn't foresee themselves as pregnant. Some swore they would never have children, but most admitted to at least having to deal with the possibility when they had sex. They all agreed that it was unromantic, even unrealistic, to carry on about protection while in the throes of passion. Even though I was a virgin, no one seemed to mind my being there when they talked about their sexual affairs. If anything, they believed they were superior because they had experience. I could see them thinking that I should be grateful they cared to share their wisdom with me.

But they were always talking about pregnancy as if it was a sickness, almost a fatal illness, caused by failure to protect themselves or their boyfriends who failed to wear condoms. It angered them that girls were always blamed for being so stupid as to not insist that they did. A few honestly admitted they would blame themselves for losing control when things got too hot and heavy. They referred to it as a game of Russian roulette with sperm instead of a bullet. They'd say this with wily smiles across their faces, as if that was somehow an achievement, too. They weren't thinking of pregnancy as a gateway to motherhood.

I saw it as nothing else. Even though what I was doing had nothing to do with any loving relationship or another expected stage in my development as a woman, I still felt years older than the girl who had first arrived in New York to make her career as a singer. My father once told me that nothing ages you faster than the struggle to survive, and to my way of thinking, that was what I was doing: struggling to survive. The smug girls I had left back home would surely think I had gone mad. There were many days when I wondered myself if I had.

I was sure both Dr. Davenport and Dr. Bliskin were studying me for signs of regret and what might result if those symptoms became intense. After the procedure had been completed, Samantha was certainly as worried and as attentive as I had anticipated she would be. Once Dr. Bliskin confirmed the transfer had been successful, that concern increased tenfold. Everything Samantha had envisioned to ensure that the baby I carried would be healthy became reality. A nutritionist was hired to design all my meals. The descriptions were given to Mrs. Marlene, whom Samantha then told to follow them "exactly." Portions were meticulously weighed out in grams. Mrs. Marlene made big eyes at me but did what Samantha asked. Dr. Bliskin approved of everything first, of course, and then, when the baby growing inside me was determined to be a boy, Samantha might as well have become my shadow. Dr. Davenport tried unsuccessfully to get her to be less intense. He was gentle about it, always avoiding upsetting her in any way.

He tried reverse psychology.

"Don't make her nervous, Samantha. We must keep her quiet, contented, right?"

"Oh, yes," she said, with tears in her eyes. "I don't mean anything. Have I upset you, Emma?" she asked immediately.

"I'm all right," I said, but I did want to complain about how restrictive she was when it came to my movements about the house. This chair was good; this chair wasn't. I'd sink too far in that soft pillow settee and strain myself getting up. Windows were opened too wide or not wide enough near me. *Don't lift anything heavy* was a warning she might have tattooed on her forehead. There were servants for that. Sometimes, I thought she was spying on me to see if I got out of bed too quickly. She was always there to help me bathe and sometimes even to help me dress.

Perhaps even worse, Samantha was on Mrs. Cohen's back almost as much as she was on mine. She knew every pill and when it should be taken. She was there practically for every test of my blood pressure. She pummeled me and Mrs. Cohen with questions I knew she had studied and memorized relating to a variety of symptoms important to a pregnant woman, like some morning sickness and fatigue, especially during my first trimester.

When I began to take my walks, she wasn't just at my side. She was always holding my arm, keenly aware of every step I took. I think my going up and down the stairway was the most frightening for her, however. I grew to believe she waited and watched for me to start down or turn to start up and then surged forward to be right behind me.

In the beginning, I was understanding, even a little appreciative, despite the fact that she wasn't concerned about me for me but for her baby. I really tried never to be frustrated or annoyed. When Dr. Davenport softly attempted to pull her off me, I was almost amused, but as time went by, especially when I was in my second trimester, I know I was a little more irritable. My patience began to grow thinner, but I kept as much of it as I could to myself, swallowing back anything that might bring her to tears.

During this whole time, I rarely saw Elizabeth Davenport. Whenever I did, she was still wearing black. She took her dinners in her room, and her breakfast was often brought to her as well. Her interest in outside activities waned. I could tell from Dr. Davenport's remarks that he was increasingly concerned about her. He was urging her to seek therapy. I was afraid to ask or say anything, and the few times Elizabeth Davenport saw me, she looked away quickly. It was as if she couldn't stand the sight of me, especially toward the end of my sixth month, when I began to show more and had started to wear the maternity clothes Samantha had bought and hung in my closet.

I told Samantha about Elizabeth Davenport's reactions to me.

"She doesn't approve of what we're doing and especially your being so much a part of our lives," she said, her eyes always big when she referred to her. "My mother-in-law is very intense about her privacy and how much access strangers have to Wyndemere. After all this time, she still hasn't fully accepted Mrs. Marlene as a trusted member of this household. You couldn't find a more loyal person. Pay no attention to her. Don't let her upset you. Okay?"

"I'm fine. Her feelings are not my business," I said.

She smiled. "Exactly."

It also was at the end of my second trimester when Dr. Bliskin had either been asked or knew to make house calls weekly. Going to his office was no longer possible. The unstated reason was obvious. At this point, Samantha didn't want anyone but the few trusted servants to know someone other than she was pregnant at Wyndemere. I had practically disappeared inside the house by then, anyway. In fact, I had a nightmare that it absorbed me into its walls. When I told Samantha, she looked it up and revealed that strange dreams were common to pregnant women. She swore she read it in a medical book, but Mrs. Cohen didn't put too much validity in that.

After the first trimester, when the potential for a miscarriage had lessened significantly, Samantha had begun telling their friends she was pregnant. She deliberately ate more fattening and richer foods to gain weight and went to a tailor to design a belt of cushioning to give her the "baby bump." Perhaps after considering Samantha's feelings, Dr.

Davenport never celebrated the successful transfer with a special dinner out as he had once suggested. The path was clear for Samantha to claim it all. I never saw Dr. Davenport tell anyone, of course, but I had the sense that he was leaving that entirely up to her. Whenever they returned from an event or a dinner with one or more of his associates, she hurried up to my room, first to see how I was and second to describe the reactions to her announcement.

"Imagine," she said. "We've been married barely two years, and everyone's comment was something like 'It's about time.' I get the feeling that some of them thought Harrison had to marry me and they were disappointed it wasn't true."

Then she declared, "Well, now it is."

I had the eerie feeling she was standing there in front of me, waiting for me to congratulate her as well. The look on my face brought her back to earth.

"As far as they know, of course," she added.

Later, when I had a moment alone sitting outside and gazing at Lake Wyndemere, its calm surface glittering in the twilight like strings of diamonds, I smiled to myself, thinking how the world of make-believe never really leaves us. When adults pretend, we have all sorts of ways to react, ranging from accusing them of rationalizing and being unable to face reality to declaring that they are mentally ill. My father was certainly the opposite in the extreme. I couldn't even imagine him as a little boy playing with toy soldiers.

Little girls, on the other hand, easily develop imaginary relationships with their dolls and imitate their mothers. In a very real sense, Samantha was doing that now. However, her excitement, the way I could see she was blossoming, enjoying herself and her marriage, was lovely. I had no problem with that and didn't want to do or say anything to darken the glow of joy that had come into both her and Dr. Davenport's eyes.

In fact, before long, I was doing whatever I could to enhance her pretending. I eagerly shared every aspect of my pregnancy with her, helped her to empathize until I found myself occasionally feeling as if she was truly the pregnant one. Nothing brought a bright smile to her face more than my suggesting that. Sometimes it felt like we were conjoined. If I was nauseous for one reason or another, she was. When I was tired and needed to rest, she did. And when I was hungry, she ate, no matter what time of the day or how soon after we had just eaten.

"I want to know the exact moment you feel our little boy kick inside you," she told me. "No matter when, even in the middle of the night. Just come to my door and knock, okay?"

"Yes, of course," I said.

And when it happened close to my fifth month, I did exactly that so she could put her hand on my stomach and feel him, too. Maybe I was imagining it, but sometimes during the day, I would catch her putting her hand on her imitation stomach and smiling as if she actually could feel her son introducing himself.

Meanwhile, practically every day since Dr. Davenport and Samantha learned that their baby was a boy, she was working on the room that would become the nursery. She had taken over the bedroom next to hers, and, with Elizabeth Davenport's frowns of disapproval practically floating around Wyndemere, Samantha had all the furniture removed and placed in the attic for storage. She was going to replace everything. I think to keep her occupied and give me as well as the servants and Dr. Bliskin some relief, Dr. Davenport gave her carte blanche to decide every aspect of the room's decor and furnishings. It did keep her busy visiting furniture showrooms and meeting with flooring and wallpaper salespeople, and the more people saw her in what looked clearly to be pregnancy, the happier she was.

However, it was a particularly difficult time for me, because when the laborers were brought in to carpet the floor and wallpaper the room, as well as change lighting fixtures, I was confined to my room so that no outsider would see me. Once they left for the day, Samantha came running to open my door. I felt like I was being released from a prison cell, solitary confinement, although my beautiful bedroom would hardly qualify as such.

Periodically, she would lead me by the hand to the nursery and review the changes and additions with me. As soon as the furniture she had chosen was delivered and the deliverymen had left, she wanted my opinion. Having had no experience with nurseries or designing and decorating a room, I offered only compliments. Almost every time I had been in there with her, she'd asked me the same question when we left.

"You'd want your baby to be in that nursery, wouldn't you?"

I could feel the underlying flow of insecurity. After all, no matter how she pretended or how literally she imitated me, she still knew she wasn't the one carrying the child who would live in this mansion. Until the day I delivered, what I saw, felt, and heard was very important to her. She thought that might affect her child, even though Dr. Bliskin had assured her that nothing from my DNA would become part of the baby in my womb. She told me that often, but not meanly. She was simply looking for confirmation.

"Of course, he knows all about that," I said. "I'm sure that's right."

She had brought Dr. Bliskin as well as Mrs. Marlene to the nursery to see what she was doing, where she had placed the cradle in relation to the windows, and the hypoallergenic materials she had chosen for the curtains, the carpet, and even the new wallpaper.

As far as I knew, Elizabeth Davenport had yet to look at any of the changes and additions. There was no doubt that she didn't approve of the in vitro method. That got me wondering how she would react to the birth of her grandson. Would she accept him or think of him as something freakish? I was curious, but I never dared ask. Samantha seemed quite disinterested in her mother-in-law's feelings about it, anyway, but I could imagine Dr. Davenport being somewhat upset about his mother's attitude. I was sure he was trying to get her to accept what they were doing. Like those of so many older people I had known, especially my father, her beliefs and feelings were cemented in who she was and who she would always be.

As my due date drew closer, it was sweet to watch how excited Dr. Davenport and Samantha were becoming. In the short time I had been at Wyndemere, I had seen how devoted he was to her, but during these months, he seemed to adore her to the point of worship. Once he was home, he was at her side constantly. I was aware that he was going more frequently to her bedroom at night. I couldn't explain the odd feeling I was having, but it was like they saw me but didn't at times. I was hovering above and around them, a promise that would fulfill their happiest dreams. And yet when they became intimate and loving at dinner or after, I felt intrusive and retreated to the library or to my room.

During the last trimester, Dr. Bliskin's visits were more frequent. I had the sense that he was as worried about my psychological well-being as he was about my physical well-being. After all, except for Mrs. Cohen and Mrs. Marlene and Samantha, I had no female company. Not that I hadn't grown fond of Samantha, but she was flighty and childlike at times, and even though she was older than I was, I saw her as I would a younger sister. I needed contact with other people and more stimulating conversation. Knowing that I would see the baby for only a day or so after he was born, I couldn't get excited about clothes and toys. She was reading books on raising an infant and was always eager to discuss something else she had learned. Reading helped me pass the time, but I knew I looked lost and even trapped sometimes, especially to Dr. Bliskin.

"Pregnant women can feel too limited, constrained. You can develop cabin fever, even in a house this big with grounds like Wyndemere's," he began. "I always tell my patients that I don't want them ever to feel like they're recuperating from something and it will take nine months. This is not an illness; this is not a condition or a handicap. Some of my patients get what I'm saying and are determined to lead as normal a life as possible, even working into the ninth month. I had a woman recently who nearly gave birth while continuing to work at a supermarket checkout." Then he added, "But . . . I know things are different for you . . ."

I didn't have to verbalize what I was feeling. He sensed and saw it. That was the first time he offered to take a walk with me. Samantha was out shopping for more baby clothing. She returned before Franklin, as he wanted me to call him now, and I were on our way back from the lake. Sometime during our walk, I stopped thinking of him as my doctor. Our talk was more about who we were, our past, especially mine. He had been to England but only to London. I remember when we approached the house, I was thinking that he was more like a prospective boyfriend.

Samantha's reaction was mixed. She was happy to learn that I wasn't off on my own, but she looked like she was actually jealous that he was filling my non-medical time. I think Franklin sensed it and went on about how important it was for me to get good exercise.

"I wouldn't have gone shopping," she said. "I'm so sorry. Is everything all right?"

"Absolutely," he told her.

After he left, she said, "Doctors aren't supposed to have so much free time. Harrison doesn't."

I thought that was odd, especially because Dr. Davenport was spending more time than ever with her these days, and besides, why wouldn't she be even happier that Dr. Bliskin was devoting more attention to me, which was the same as saying devoting more attention to her baby?

I think she realized it later and made sure to tell me she didn't mean to sound unappreciative.

"I don't think he felt that you were," I assured her, even though I could see that he was sensitive to her reaction. As a result, he didn't take another walk with me right away, and the few times he did, Samantha came along whenever she was home and pummeled him with questions about my health and the baby's.

I was sleeping more now and moving about the mansion less. Some days I didn't want to leave the room, but Dr. Bliskin was adamant about my getting exercise. He was happy about the amount of my weight gain but made the point of telling me, "We're not home free yet."

Home was on my mind more and more these days. I had put off calling again, knowing that when I did, I would have to elaborate on my original lie. I called once and got only the answering machine. I left a vague reference to my role in the regional theater and promised to call again. I was sure both Dr. Davenport and Samantha knew this was an area of thin ice for me to tread, and so they never asked me about my family in England.

One Saturday morning, the second week into my seventh month, I placed a call. My fingers were trembling, thinking my father would answer. I almost preferred he would and then immediately hang up. It would eliminate my need to elaborate on my lies, and I would feel that I had fulfilled my obligation. But to my stunned surprise, it was Julia who answered, and like someone who had just awoken, despite the time in England being five hours later.

"Julia?" I asked, needing to confirm it was she.

"Why haven't you called? You never gave us a way to contact you. I couldn't even write a letter, send a telegram, anything."

"I'm sorry," I said, beginning to construct my fabrication, "but this has taken—"

"Daddy is dead," she said.

It was as if something had just exploded very close to my ear. I think the explosion was even ringing with her words.

"What?"

"He was walking home after work. It was raining, and people who saw him said he was having trouble opening his old umbrella. You know how he resisted replacing it. He stood there struggling with it. He hadn't been feeling well for weeks. Some nights he would sit in the living room and not say a word to either me or Mummy. He wasn't eating well, either, and Mummy was nagging him to go to the doctor, but you know how stubborn he could be."

"What happened?" I asked.

At least, I think I did. I couldn't hear myself.

That ringing continued.

"Suddenly, he stopped struggling with the umbrella. A witness said he looked up at the rain as if he could send the drops into retreat, back up to the clouds, and then he sank to the walk. The ambulance was called, but he was already gone. They couldn't revive him. His heart exploded. That's the way they put it to us, *exploded*. Why haven't you called?"

I couldn't talk.

"Mummy wanted to wait until we could find you, but she couldn't stomach him lying there in the morgue like that. She said he would be furious. She's not making very much sense these days. Why didn't you call us?"

"I couldn't," I said.

"Why couldn't you? Why, Emma? Mummy thought for sure something terrible had happened to you, too. Everyone wanted to know why you weren't at the funeral. I had no answers for them."

"Oh, Julia," I said. I was crying now, crying louder than I thought.

"*What*?" she screamed. "Why couldn't you call us at least when you knew Daddy wouldn't be home to slam the phone down at the sound of your voice? *Why*?"

I was hyperventilating, fighting to catch my breath.

"Emma. Daddy's dead. He died over a fortnight ago. Come home tomorrow. Do you hear me?"

"I . . ."

"Tomorrow."

"Can't . . ." I said.

"What? Your damn career? Your confounded selfish—"

"No, Julia. I can't because I'm seven months pregnant," I said.

Her silence brought the ringing back. I held

the receiver away from my ear and then dropped it and slowly sank to my knees and then back against the bed before sitting on the floor, my legs apart. I swung my arm and knocked over the table and the phone.

Samantha opened my bedroom door and looked in at me for only a split second before she screamed for Mrs. Cohen. I closed my eyes and wished with all my heart that I would simply die, evaporate, and be gone from everyone and everywhere. Mrs. Cohen came running, and with Samantha's help, got me off the floor and back into my bed.

Samantha saw that the phone was still off the cradle.

"What is it, Emma? What's happened?" she asked as Mrs. Cohen began to check my vitals.

"Her heart is pounding," she muttered.

"Call Dr. Bliskin," Samantha demanded. "I'll call my husband."

She went to the phone. Mrs. Cohen went into the bathroom and returned with a cool washcloth to put on my forehead.

"Are you in any pain, Emma?" she asked. Samantha was already talking to Dr. Davenport.

I shook my head. "I'm a little dizzy," I said in a loud whisper.

"What is it?" Samantha asked. She came to hold my hand.

"I called home," I said. "My father died. More than two weeks ago. They didn't know how to reach me . . ."

I closed my eyes. I was sobbing, but I couldn't feel any tears on my cheeks. Mrs. Cohen called Dr. Bliskin's office, but he was in the delivery room.

Mrs. Topper said she would give him the message, and he would surely come as soon as he could. Samantha looked like she was in a serious panic attack, and Mrs. Cohen didn't know where she should put her attention first.

"Give her something to calm her!" Samantha screamed.

"We don't want to give her anything without Dr. Bliskin, and we usually don't give sedatives to pregnant women, Mrs. Davenport. Please try to get hold of yourself. You'll do more damage if you frighten and upset Emma more than she is."

Samantha swallowed hard and nodded.

"Take deep breaths," Mrs. Cohen told her. "Let's keep everyone as composed as we can."

"I can't go home," I said, more to myself than to them. "I can't let Mummy see me like this. She won't understand. She would be terribly embarrassed. Julia said she wasn't well. It might kill her."

"It's all right. You can't travel, anyway," Samantha said. "Dr. Davenport will figure everything out for you. You'll see."

I looked at her and nodded. Dr. Davenport was so like my father, imbued with self-confidence, stalwart, and dependable. People, after all, put their lives in his hands. Their very heartbeats relied on his skill. There was no hesitation in him when he had to make a decision.

Yes, I thought, *yes. Dr. Davenport will know what I should do.*

I lay back on my pillows and closed my eyes. I knew Samantha was hovering beside me and probably wouldn't move, but I didn't want to think about her or the baby now. That last image of my father that had haunted me for so long was on the insides of my eyelids. But it started to fade, and in its place was a different image of him, an image that I cherished. I wasn't much more than four. He was laughing at the pile of pennies I had stacked very neatly for him to see. Some of them I had found on the sidewalk and washed. I was telling him to take them to the bank, where they would grow as tall as the house.

"Yes, that's good thinking, Emma," he said. He brushed my hair back, and then he kissed me on the forehead and helped me count the pennies, before putting them in a bag for him to take to the bank. It was how my first savings account was begun.

Oddly, I had never touched that money. It wasn't much, but I hadn't withdrawn it before I left. It was still there, like some promise I had made to him years ago.

"Daddy," I whispered, and fell asleep for a while.

When I opened my eyes, Dr. Davenport was there. Samantha was standing right behind him.

"I'm sorry to hear about your father," he began.

I almost uttered a revised reference to the rising of Lazarus in the Bible. *If you had been there, he would not have died.*

"I know how frustrated you must feel. Now I'm glad I asked you to give me your family's contact details."

I widened my eyes in confusion. "Why?"

"I've booked a flight to England tomorrow morning. I'm going to see your sister and your mother," he said. "I'm going to explain everything to them. I know that doesn't mean they're going to understand or approve of what you've agreed to do, but I feel it's my responsibility to lay the groundwork for what you will do afterward. I'll be sure they're all right, too."

"Harrison can help them understand," Samantha said, stepping up. "If anyone can . . ."

"I don't know that anyone can," I said.

"Then it's best he be the one to try," she said.

He smiled and reached for her hand.

"I'm frightened," I said.

He took my hand, too. "As Samantha and I are for you and your family. We'll get through it together," he promised.

I was crying. The only way I knew was that I felt a salty tear reach my lips. He wiped it away with his handkerchief.

"Franklin will be here in twenty minutes," he said. He tightened his fingers around my hand gently and then stood. "I'll try to call you from Guildford, but if not, I'll come right here when I return."

"Tell them I'm sorry."

"It goes without saying, but they'll understand that, I'm sure." He rose.

"Thank you, Harrison," Samantha said, and hugged him as if he was doing all this for her perhaps even more than for me. Maybe he was.

In the end, what difference would it make? Until their baby was born, she would cry when I did and laugh when I did. My fear that she would become my shadow had been realized. She would cry tonight for my father the way she had cried for her own. And in the morning, she would look for the same restorative hope in the sunshine pushing away the darkness.

I shared no DNA with their child, but they were now a part of me, and I was now a part of them, no matter what was written in the science books doctors quoted.

FOURTEEN

Dr. Bliskin was with me for most of the early evening after Dr. Davenport had left for the airport. He sat at my bedside, mainly trying to keep me calm. He empathized and talked about the loss of his father. He was only in his teens when his father had passed.

Before he left, Mrs. Marlene brought up some dinner for me herself. She and I had grown quite fond of each other, but the only reason I ate anything was to please Samantha. Like someone entranced by a movie, she sat there watching me eat and listening to Franklin and me talk. He wanted to stay longer, but I insisted he go home to his family. I assured him, and he assured Samantha, that I was all right. Samantha remained until I finally closed my eyes and drifted into an uneasy sleep, waking often.

Before I could even think of rising, Samantha appeared and insisted on my breakfast being brought to me. I wanted to get up, but I let her have her way, and then, after I had eaten under her watchful eye, I rose, dressed, and started down. What I wanted more than anything was to be alone. She started after me when I headed for the doorway. I turned on her sharply.

"I need some private time, Samantha. You'll have to trust that I won't do anything to jeopardize the baby."

She could see the determination in my face and swallowed back her fears. I left her in the outside entryway and walked slowly toward the lake. I knew she was going to remain there, watching my every move.

The day I left home seemed ages ago now. When you do things that are so intense and demanding, the time it takes to accomplish them flows in every direction in your memory. Pinning down when you had this feeling or that, this dream and ambition or another and all the voices and visuals associated with the efforts to achieve them, is as evasive as water you're trying to hold in your closed hand. Right now, I felt lost in a fog, desperately hoping not to cry. I feared I had made a terrible mess of everything.

In my earliest New York days, I had seen my father everywhere. I'd look out at the crowds of people walking up the sidewalk toward me and swear I saw him moving among them, until the man who resembled him had drawn closer. Sometimes, I imagined my father looking out at me from a high floor in an office building and then backing away to disappear inside. Occasionally, I heard someone shout what sounded like my name and spun around expecting him, but saw only strangers. He was constantly on my mind during those early hours, early days.

Gradually, he drifted back as my pursuit and my work to support it took all my attention and energy. I grew stronger and more independent. My father, who actually hated to see anyone give up on a personal goal, loved to quote Nietzsche: *That which doesn't kill us makes us stronger.* It was his favorite way of dealing with disappointment. I clung to it until one thing had piled on another and I had felt the desperation that had brought me to Wyndemere.

I never intended to hurt my family. I really believed that I would find success and make them proud, including my stubborn father. Guilt kept my head down this morning as I walked. Until now, I didn't feel anywhere as awkward or as heavy with the pregnancy. The true weight of what I had sold myself to do was pressing on my shoulders. I took deep breaths and paused. Foamy clouds were being torn by the high winds and shredded into wisps of themselves. I thought I could hear them screaming. Eventually, I made it to the dock and stood there watching the water lap against the wood and the rocks on the shoreline. People were already out in their boats, enjoying the sense of freedom it gave them. I could hear engines and even voices in the distance. I was awash in pure envy. Their lives seemed so carefree, like pure joy.

There was nothing left to do but finish here and go home, I thought. I'd use my money to help Mummy and Julia and find some menial job to help time pass until all my ambition took its final gasp and sank somewhere so deep inside me that years and years later, I couldn't even remember ever setting out for America.

Surely, there was a graveyard somewhere for dreams that died.

When I turned to go back to the house, I saw Samantha standing at the edge of the grass watching me. I had my hands on my stomach. Her baby was kicking more today than ever. Maybe he was angry at the waves of sadness and depression washing over him in my womb. The doctors and scientists might not be right, I thought. Something of the surrogate mother finds its way into the child after all.

Samantha rushed to join me when I drew closer.

"Are you all right?"

I nodded and let her take my arm. We returned to the mansion that was waiting to embrace us both and hold us firmly in the grasp of its shadows, the resonating echoes of every movement within, and the depth of its history. Houses like Wyndemere absorb so much sadness and joy. Mine was just another small swallow. Years from now, I imagined no one would recall it with any vividness. I would have passed through, and on my way through, I would have left a child to be nurtured within these walls, within this family.

This was possibly all I would have accomplished by coming to America.

Samantha and I spent most of the remainder of the day in the library. I slept on and off. She had begun to read *Rebecca* because I had told her how much I had enjoyed it when I was assigned to read it in school. Occasionally, she would pause to recite a paragraph or some dialogue to me. My eyes were drawn to the grandfather clock, my mind quickly calculating the time in England. Finally, right before we were to go to dinner, Dr. Davenport called to speak to me. Samantha remained at my side.

"I have some international banker friends," he began. "They checked on financial matters. Your father left your mother and sister very comfortable. You have no worries there."

I didn't even entertain the thought otherwise.

"Your father's personal physician laid the groundwork for my visit. They were naturally quite surprised—shocked, to be honest—when I told them what you were doing, but they were mostly concerned about how you were. I assured them you were sailing through it and I would make arrangements for your return. I said 'visit' because I didn't want to leave them with the belief you were finished with your career. They completely understand why it would be awkward for you simply to pop up on the scene right now. I invited them to Wyndemere, but I don't think they're ready for any travel yet. I told them you would call as soon as you were up to it.

"I wouldn't go so far as to say they approved or even understood why you've done what you've done, but there is no anger here waiting for you."

"Thank you," I said.

"I'll see you sometime tomorrow. Tell Samantha," he added.

"I will."

As soon as I hung up, I related it all to her. She clapped her hands and smiled as if everything had been made right again. It was almost as if my father had been resurrected. Nevertheless, hearing how Dr. Davenport had described Mummy and Julia, I was more relaxed and ate better than I thought I would. Mrs. Marlene insisted I be permitted a small piece of her chocolate cream pie. It wasn't on the designated menu, but Samantha didn't put up any resistance.

After dinner, Dr. Bliskin surprised us with a visit when he had finished his hospital rounds. He sat with the two of us for another hour or so before going home. I wondered about his home life, his wife, mainly. Samantha assured me they were still in love and his wife was a perfect doctor's wife, understanding, giving him the freedom he needed to attend to his patients, and keeping herself quite busy with their children and her friends.

"Just like me," she said proudly. "Just like how I'll be with my son soon."

Two days later, I called Mummy and spoke to both her and Julia. Even to myself, I sounded like a little girl again. They were still quite confused and surprised by it all but obviously had decided to push it aside and talk about my return. I promised I would come, but, like Dr. Davenport, I made it sound more like a visit. I added the fact that he had kept my New York apartment for me. Maybe because my father wasn't there to comment and complain, Julia said nothing negative about it. I think she was quite taken aback by what I had done and was still trying to wrap her mind around all she had learned.

I did less exercise during the final six weeks. Everyone was after me to do it, but I slept more. I felt like I was holding my breath the entire time. Despite all the preparations, when the moment came, it seemed like a bolt of lightning. My water broke, and Mrs. Cohen was immediately at my side. Dr. Bliskin dropped everything at his office and rushed over. Dr. Davenport did the same. I was informed that even Elizabeth Davenport stood in her doorway, watching and listening. A number of times, I had been told that I wasn't the first woman who had given birth in Wyndemere.

The baby cried in Samantha's arms. He had made no sound during the birthing, even when the umbilical cord had been cut, but the moment he was placed in her waiting hands, he wailed, and so strongly that everyone laughed. I stared with disbelief. It almost didn't seem real to me that something as miraculous as a baby, even with the kicking I had felt, had emerged from my body.

They had decided to name him Ryder and immediately began to refer to him that way. He was washed and dressed quickly. My body hadn't calmed. I still felt as if I was in the throes of it. As soon as she could, Samantha took him out of my room. Mrs. Cohen and Dr. Davenport followed her, but Dr. Bliskin remained behind to assure me I was doing well. Then Dr. Davenport returned, and he and Dr. Bliskin gave each other a look that caught my attention despite how exhausted I felt.

I was just about ready to ask what was wrong.

They both stepped up beside me.

"It wasn't part of our bargain," Dr. Davenport began, "but Franklin and I have been discussing it. He's a proponent of breastfeeding. He has all the clinical and historical evidence supporting how superior it is. You'll be here a while longer, so we thought, I thought . . . I'm willing to offer you an additional fifty thousand dollars."

They both stared down at me.

"Fifty thousand dollars!"

"It's best if it's begun within the first hour," Franklin said.

"A wet nurse," I said, more to myself. "But Samantha . . ."

"I've discussed it with her; we both discussed it with her. She wants what's best for Ryder. She'll be right beside you all the time." This time, his smile was more of a warning. "I know this is more than you expected to do, and it will keep you here longer. However, I intend to do more than just give you money. I want to see what I can do to help you get a start on your singing career, too, when the time comes."

"But . . . I was to go home to see my family."

"You can pump and store breast milk for up to two weeks if we freeze it," Franklin said. "Of course, you'll be leaking a bit," he added.

"It could give you a good reason to return to America sooner," Dr. Davenport said. "If you don't, I'll give you a good part of the fifty thousand anyway."

"How long would I . . . ?"

"Six months is good," Franklin said. "Many go longer but start to introduce foods. It varies. I've had women stop after three months, too."

"Six months?"

"I'm sorry," Dr. Davenport said. "We should have discussed this with you sooner, but . . ."

"But it took a while to convince Samantha despite what you are both claiming," I finished for him.

He nodded, and Franklin smiled.

I looked up at the ceiling. The money was overwhelming. When I was really back in New York, I wouldn't need another roommate, maybe ever. I could dress better and go to each and every audition I wanted. Maybe Dr. Davenport could get me some other opportunities. He seemed to know so many important and powerful people. Now, without being pregnant, there was no reason for me not to have more freedom here, either.

I looked at the two of them. The anxiety in their faces made me want to laugh. Perhaps I was going a little crazy.

"Okay," I said. "Bring Ryder back."

Both smiled like two successful conspirators.

I was more interested in the look on Samantha's face when she returned with Ryder. She seemed a little confused but not as upset as I had feared. I had made up my mind that if they had lied to me and this was going to disturb her, I would refuse. She cradled Ryder lovingly and gently brought him to me when Mrs. Cohen set up my pillows.

"I want to know how it feels," she said. "I want to know everything so years from now, when I tell him, he'll believe me."

I nodded, and she brought him to my breast.

As I had anticipated, time at Wyndemere was different after I had given birth and begun to breastfeed. I almost thought *when Samantha and I began to breastfeed*. I had yet to do it once without her beside me, sometimes even lying beside me, both of us touching Ryder, both amused at his hunger. Every time the question of my leaving to visit Mummy and Julia arose, I put it off. I called them often, and they were continually asking when I would arrive. *Soon, soon* was my chant. I questioned it myself. Was I growing too attached to Ryder? Was it because I didn't want to disappoint Samantha and Dr. Davenport? Was I afraid to go home, afraid to enter that house, knowing my father wouldn't be there? The very idea of visiting his grave was a nightmare.

Dr. Bliskin still stopped by from time to time. Now that Samantha wasn't worrying about my every move, she didn't join us for our walks or remain in the living room when we talked. Despite what Samantha had assured me about his marriage, he rarely mentioned his wife or even his own children, for that matter.

One night, when Dr. Davenport was home early and Franklin had stopped by, he remained for cocktails. I wasn't permitted any alcoholic beverages because I was breastfeeding, but I didn't mind. I went to the piano and played and sang some of the songs I used to sing at the Three Bears. Of course, they were all very complimentary, and Dr. Davenport reinforced his offer to "find me a great way to take off into a real singing career." I thought they had all had too much to drink. Both doctors looked like they had needed to relax or, like Mummy used to even tell my father, "Oh, Arthur, let your hair down." "What hair?" he would say, and they would laugh. There was laughter once, too, I thought.

During these months, I did a lot more with Samantha. We went shopping, had delightful lunches, and read and watched television together. Dr. Davenport seemed busier than ever. We learned that patients were coming from as far as a hundred miles away to be under his care. His reputation was growing that much.

Finally, at the start of the fourth month after Ryder's birth, I asked Dr. Davenport to make my arrangements for a visit home. He had offered to do so almost weekly during the first two months. Samantha was quite nervous about it, not so much because she was afraid of any interruption in Ryder's feeding as because of her fear of what I now saw as the possibility our friendship would end, that I wouldn't return. She actually accompanied me to the airport.

Mrs. Cohen was still at the house, mainly to care for Elizabeth Davenport, who was practically a recluse by now. Mourning her husband and seeing herself as much less in the social world had taken their toll. Aging was making her mad, too. Her plastic surgeon, perhaps afraid of Dr. Davenport, refused to perform any more procedures, claiming her skin would tear like tissue. She even stopped dyeing her hair, no longer sending for her personal stylist.

"How far we've come together," Samantha said at the departure gate. She was holding on to my hand. "I owe you so much."

"I've been paid very well," I said, smiling.

"Money is the least of it," she said.

I almost said *Not for me*, but held back, thinking she would be hurt. Instead, we hugged, and I promised to call her soon after I had arrived.

Julia met me at Heathrow Airport. She looked like she had aged worse than Elizabeth Davenport. I could almost see the shadow of depression and sadness hovering around and over her. Instead of smiling and rushing to hug me, she shook her head. It was her way of reminding me that we were too unalike to be sisters. The years between us had sifted out most of our resemblances. Who illustrated better how two siblings could grow up in the same home, the same family, and yet be so different?

"Hi," I said. I was afraid to hug her.

She nodded and took my suitcase, as if she thought I was too weak and fragile.

"I can carry it," I said.

She looked at it in her hands. "This is the one you took when you left."

"Yes."

"I promised Mummy I would not ask you mean questions. She wants your visit to go well. It is just a visit, isn't it? You're going back to that . . . place?"

"Yes," I said. "That place: America."

"All right," she said when we got into her car. "I won't ask questions. You just tell me what you want me to know."

I never stopped talking during the whole trip, describing everything I could remember, anyone I could remember, from the first day I had arrived in New York. I even told her about Lila Lester, the woman on the plane who worked for a perfume company and gave me a ride to my apartment from the airport.

Sometime on our ride home, I realized she

was finding everything I said more fascinating than she wanted. Occasionally, when I described something like my audition at a club or dealing with customers at the Last Diner, she looked at me with what I thought was more envy than disgust. Perhaps because I wanted it to be true, I told myself she was impressed with her younger sister after all. I had done things she could never imagine herself doing.

"You really wanted this career in show business," she concluded after hearing why I became a surrogate mother.

"Still do. Maybe more than ever."

When our house came into view, I felt my body tighten and my heart beat faster. The sight of our front door, the memory of when I walked out to the waiting taxi, and my father's final look of rage all came rushing back.

Julia realized something wasn't right with me. "Are you all right?"

I nodded because I was afraid to speak. He would burn my letters at the door.

We got out and approached it slowly. Whatever anger Julia had dressed herself in, especially for our confronting each other, dissipated. She looked like she was going to cry for me. She unexpectedly took my hand, and we entered the house. Mummy was waiting in the living room. She looked up at me, and without either of us saying a word, we hugged and began to cry. I thought we'd never stop.

Later, she mentioned how much weight I had gained. I think she was referring mainly to my swollen breasts, but I imagined my face was still fuller. When we had something to eat, I told her some of what I had told Julia on the way home. She listened, looking amazed most of the time. We spoke about everything we could to avoid speaking about my father, but it eventually came to that, to the day he died, to the funeral and after. Julia said she would take me to the cemetery the next day. Mummy thought it best if I went without her.

"You make your own peace in this world," she said.

There was no doubt in my mind that she had aged years since I had left, probably mostly because of my father's death. She reminded me of Elizabeth Davenport in that way, but in nothing else. I thought Mummy's sorrow was more honest and certainly less about herself.

Once, when I was explaining to Leo Abbot why I didn't want to go home, I referred to Thomas Wolfe's novel *You Can't Go Home Again*. It came to mind when I ventured out of the house and walked the streets I had walked as a child. I found myself wanting to avoid anyone I knew. Besides the questions I wouldn't answer, I feared the looks of disdain and disapproval. I never thought my hometown would become so forbidding. When I rushed back to the house, I did what I had promised, did it for myself as well, and called Samantha. I could hear how happy she was that I did call. She was crying. She talked about things Ryder had done, his smiles and gestures, and swore to me that he missed me.

"He's not pleased with his bottle," she said, and then, practically whispering, added, "It's a nipple without love."

I laughed and realized I had tears in my eyes, too. Afterward, when Julia returned from work, the moment I dreaded had come. We were going to the cemetery.

"This doesn't seem real to me," I told her on the way.

"Oh, it's real," she said. "There's nothing more real in life than death."

How deep did your dissatisfaction with yourself have to go in order for you to think like that? I wondered.

"Did you know he had all this planned out?" she asked.

"All this?"

"Their plots, of course, but also his tombstone, its size and shape and what he wanted written on it. Mummy says he did all that years ago."

Why wasn't I surprised?

The only word on his stone that surprised me was *beloved*. I didn't think I ever realized that he believed he was. It didn't seem that important to him. *Respected* and *admired* were words I would have thought of before I had thought of *beloved husband and father*.

"Do you think this is my fault?" I asked Julia as I looked at the grave.

I was pleased that she didn't reply instantly. I glanced at her and then back at the tombstone.

"No," she said, which surprised me. Julia was so much more like him. She wouldn't rationalize or fabricate. "He gave his anger free rein; he let it diminish him. There was another way. Some understanding would have helped, helped us both," she confessed.

I looked at her, surprised.

"His father shaped him and, like following a straight line, brought him to this place."

She looked away and at the other graves, a sea of them, really. I thought she had never looked so beautiful. I was jealous of her for a change, jealous of some peace she had found in herself.

"I'm not going to try to understand you, Emma. You are who you are, and you do what you do because of that. He'd still be alive today if he'd accepted that truth."

"Thank you, Julia," I said.

She smiled, and we hugged and held each other. Why, we were both thinking for sure, couldn't he be alive to see and hear us at this moment? It would have changed the world for him.

I remained with Julia and my mother, keeping myself at home, for three more days. I had come with some doubt that I would go back to Wyndemere, but with every passing hour at home, I realized more and more that I would. They realized it, too.

There were tears when I left, but there wasn't that dread. Unsaid, but heard, was the thought, the wish, *Go find yourself and your life, Emma.*

Julia promised to visit me in America. She said she would try to bring Mummy, too. And of course, I promised to visit again soon.

Promises were really the glue that held us together. They brought relief and helped us avoid disappointment and ugly truth.

As weird as it seemed, I was happy to be back at Wyndemere. Everyone there, especially baby Ryder, I thought, was happy to see me return. My guise as Samantha's college friend was restored, and people were again invited to dinners and parties at the mansion. During many of them, I was asked to sing. The only dark moment came when Elizabeth Davenport suffered a stroke. Whatever semblance of mind she clung to kept her insisting she not be moved to any facility, and Dr. Davenport hired round-the-clock nursing for her. I was told she could live for years like that.

My six months of breastfeeding were coming to an end. No one was pressuring me to remain any longer, but comments about how healthy Ryder was were always tied in one way or another to the breastfeeding. Samantha was doing all she could to keep me amused, too. During the six months, she was still buying doubles of everything she bought for herself. Every once in a while, we'd dress alike, even doing our hair alike, and go to dinner just to see the looks on Mrs. Marlene's and Dr. Davenport's faces.

In a blatant attempt to keep me from leaving, Samantha had Dr. Davenport arrange for me to have an audition at a supper club in Hillsborough. I wasn't going to do it, but it was Franklin who convinced me. Sometimes, I thought he wanted me to stay more than anyone else did.

"You know that shows are often tested outside of New York before they get there. So are performers, I imagine. Get some experience while you have free room and board," he said, smiling. "What's the harm? It's all taking you toward the same goal. In entertainment especially, experience impresses.

"I promise," he added, "we'll wean you off breast-feeding."

He took his time doing that after I auditioned and the owner hired me to sing Friday and Saturday nights. There was a wonderful piano player to accompany me. He had been playing for some famous singers when they had first begun and had a wonderful ear for picking up a melody and remembering the song. I was convinced he was making me a better singer, too.

Of course, I suspected Dr. Davenport had some influence, but the honest compliments I received from the owner and his patrons helped me build my self-confidence. Of course, both Samantha and he were often there. Parker was assigned to drive me to and from.

One night, Franklin brought his wife so I could finally meet her. I didn't know what she knew, but I sensed he had told her almost everything. She was a very pretty woman but looked at me with suspicious eyes. It made me a little uncomfortable.

Otherwise, I was never happier. I called Mummy and Julia weekly to give them updates.

"I'm happy for you," Julia told me. I had no doubt she meant it.

I was, after all, living in a mansion, part of a successful family, doing what I dreamed of doing, and having a wonderful, surprising friendship. Samantha had truly become more like a sister, both of us now caring for Ryder. The dark shadows that clung to the corners of Wyndemere were in retreat. Samantha even said that to me one day.

Perhaps they had heard her say it.

And perhaps upon hearing her say it, they had called on their brothers and sisters floating in the darkness outside, gathering in a storm of their own making.

To change everything.

FIFTEEN

Samantha had gone on a shopping spree, insisting she'd go by herself because she wanted to have a bag full of surprises, especially for me.

I had been told that the winter weather around Lake Wyndemere and Hillsborough was quite unpredictable this year. In January, there were unusually warm days. In fact, people were warned that the lake wasn't as thickly frozen over. They were discouraged from ice skating. But then, as if Nature suddenly reminded itself it was winter, the temperatures dropped dramatically. Melting snows froze. The raindrops had started and were pellets of ice before they reached the ground. Trees were straining under the weight, branches cracking.

The sun was a deceiver. When it rose over the lake on that particular Tuesday morning, it made the world outside dazzling. It was quite inviting. Dr. Davenport had an intense day of surgery and had already left for the hospital by the time

Samantha and I went down to breakfast. I had already gone in and changed Ryder so he could be brought down with us. Samantha had been up earlier but was preparing herself for the day of shopping. She liked to do her hair and dress smartly.

"I have to keep up my image," she would tell me, "of a very important and successful heart surgeon's wife."

I wouldn't call her vain or self-absorbed, as I was sure many envious women would. I saw how proud she was and understood that she felt she had to maintain that persona, almost the way one of our royals had to pay heed to tradition. She represented someone very important.

She did look beautiful, radiant, that morning. No matter what mood you were in, being around Samantha always brightened it. I had little doubt that it was the sunshine in her smile that Dr. Davenport looked forward to as soon as he returned home. Even if what he had accomplished that day was spectacular, it was still a grueling and tense journey to get there.

I wondered if my father had enjoyed the same respite when he returned home from his day. Unlike Dr. Davenport, he seemed to carry something back, some disapproval or disgust with the way most of his clients thought these days. Maybe we were the audience he sought after all. Mummy was certainly a great listener, helping him find the proper way to express his thoughts.

Ryder was making an effort to say real words and reaching for everything in sight. I was constantly aware of how bright he seemed and how handsome he would be. Whenever I looked at Dr. Davenport, Samantha, and Ryder together, I didn't feel envy as much as I felt more ambitious for my own personal future. I had come to America with only one goal in mind: to build a singing career. Thinking about love and family was put off. When I looked at them now, I told myself, *Emma, get going. Get back to New York. You're going to lose your perspective. You'll be in danger of falling in love with someone in Hillsborough and shelving anything else.*

When Samantha was ready to go, I picked up Ryder and followed her to the door. Parker had taken Dr. Davenport to the hospital, and she had wanted to be on her own, anyway. She was still being quite mysterious about her shopping plans. I was suspicious, because she was always marking one sort of anniversary or another when it pertained to my being at Wyndemere. Almost every week, she would tell me that this was when we first did this or that and then give me something that was hers, something she claimed she rarely used, like a scarf with the tag still on it.

Tracking our little anniversaries came easily to her. She remembered far more detail than I did. Perhaps I was still feeling like someone caught in a whirlwind. Everything happened so quickly that events ran into each other, but not for her. She could sit down and relive every moment in a recitation that resembled a fairy tale: *Once upon a time, the perfect surrogate came to Wyndemere . . .*

It looked like a day for fairy tales. The sky was so blue that no one would think we'd see another cloud for a week. Ryder and I said good-bye to her at the door. He had learned how to wave his little right hand. We watched her drive off, and then I took him with me to play in his playpen while I practiced some songs on the piano. He was fascinated with that, and sometimes he would just sit and listen for hours.

About an hour after lunch, I noticed that the sky had surrendered most of its blue to a rising tide of darker clouds. Wave after wave of them came out of the northeast. Mr. Stark told Mrs. Marlene that he thought the weather was undergoing a rapid change. I looked at my watch. Samantha said she was going to have lunch out and would probably head back about three. Head back from where? I wondered. She wouldn't reveal anything, but it sounded like she was going farther than usual, perhaps to Centerville, which was a bigger city with more upscale stores.

Three o'clock came and went. At four, I went to the front windows to look at the weather. The sky was completely overcast, the clouds swirling with high winds. Fifteen minutes later, a slight rain began and gradually thickened into something that resembled sleet. I could hear it scratching at the windowpanes.

Ryder was having his nap. I was pacing about the mansion. Mrs. Marlene and I looked at each other, each reflecting the other's worry.

The phone rang at a quarter to five. I was trying to keep myself from thinking anything bad by reading, but my eyes drifted off the page constantly. I held my breath and listened. Then I heard footsteps rushing down the hallway toward the library.

I sat frozen.

Mrs. Marlene appeared, her hands clasped against the base of her throat.

I stood up slowly. "What?"

"She's been in an accident. They were looking for Dr. Davenport. They wouldn't tell me anything."

I went to her and took her hand, or she took mine.

"I'll go get Mr. Stark," she said. "He'll know what to do."

I nodded and walked out behind her. Mrs. Cohen was coming down the stairs.

"What is it?" she asked immediately.

"Samantha has been in an accident. They're looking for Dr. Davenport."

She glanced at her watch. "He's out of the operating room by now," she said. She continued down and to the kitchen to get something for Mrs. Davenport.

I went to check on Ryder. He was still asleep.

Another hour passed. And then, close to six thirty, we heard the doorbell. I hurried ahead of anyone else to open it. Franklin was standing there.

He didn't have to say a word. His face spoke volumes, all of sadness and dread.

"She went off the road, at a turn, and hit the edge of a guardrail. Her car . . . it didn't stop her . . ."

"Will she be all right?"

He shook his head.

I felt as if I had submerged myself in the icy waters of Lake Wyndemere, but I wasn't cold so much as numb. Every muscle in my body seemed to lose its grip on my bones. Franklin saw what was happening to me and rushed forward to catch me before I folded up completely on the floor. My eyes closed in self-defense, trying to avoid reality. I felt him lift me under my legs and around my back to carry me inside and place me on the settee in the living room.

Mrs. Marlene had come out of the kitchen with Mr. Stark. I could hear her crying. He had already given her the dreaded news. Mrs. Cohen heard her, too, and came rushing down the stairs. She didn't need anyone to say it.

"I need a cool wet cloth," Dr. Bliskin told her.

Both she and Mrs. Marlene hurried to get one. Keeping busy was the only way to avoid hysteria.

Mr. Stark stepped up to Franklin. "I spoke to Charley Siegel at the police station. That damn Olympic Hill's been the scene of a dozen or so fatal accidents over the years. People just forget that turn. She must have been in shock. She didn't even attempt to brake."

I felt the cloth on my forehead and opened my eyes. "It can't be true," I said.

"Harrison called me," Franklin said. "He wanted me to be here to tell you and everyone. He's in a bad way. I'm worried about him. We've got to hold it together for him. He's not a man who permits his emotions a breath of air. He's choking on his sorrow."

I nodded. "He's so strong for everyone else."

"He is. That's always the case," Franklin said.

"The baby," I said, and sat up. "I'll go to him."

"Good. Stay busy," he advised.

I went up to Ryder's nursery. He was sitting up in his bed quietly. It was eerie. It was as if he knew. He didn't cry, but he didn't smile at me the way he always did, either. He seemed to be studying my face for clues. All I could do was reach in, lift him into my arms, and hold him closely, rocking from side to side as my tears began to flood my cheeks.

It was a good two hours more before Dr. Davenport came home. Parker was at his side when he entered, which was something unusual on its own. He knew Dr. Davenport was a little unsteady. Franklin immediately hugged him and spoke softly to him while the rest of us watched from the living-room doorway. Harrison nodded, and the two of them went to Dr. Davenport's office. Mrs. Marlene prepared some dinner for them and brought it there. I looked after Ryder, and after putting him to sleep hours later, I returned to the living room to wait.

"They've been in there with the doors closed all this time," Mrs. Marlene said. "I heard the phone ringing often."

I just nodded. She dabbed her eyes with her handkerchief and returned to the kitchen. Most of the staff had gathered there.

Another good half hour later, I heard, "He wants to see you."

Franklin had come so silently to the doorway that I thought he had simply appeared out of the air.

I rose. I think I was just as frightened as anything. He could see it clearly written on my face.

"He's all right. I mean, he's in some shock, but he has hold of himself. As always, he's thinking about everyone else."

"Okay."

"I'm going to go. This is my home number," he said, handing me a card. "If you need me, call me anytime. He says he has to look in on his patient tomorrow, but I'm going to arrange for Dr. Stanley to cover for him. I'll call early to tell him. See if you can get him to stay here. He'll never admit it, but he needs tender loving care."

"I understand," I said.

"I'm sorry, Emma. You probably would have been better off just going home when you ran out of money in New York. I wasn't looking out for you as much as I should have. I didn't do much to dissuade you. I was thinking selfishly of my friends, and you were just a perfect candidate, someone willing and someone who I thought could benefit from it. Don't feel obligated to do anything else."

"Whatever I do won't be because of any obligation."

"Yes, I imagine not." He stepped forward and hugged me and then turned and left.

I sucked in my breath, my sorrow, and my fear and walked slowly down the hallway to Dr. Davenport's office. He was sitting behind his desk, turned toward the portrait of Samantha in her wedding dress. He surely heard me enter but didn't look at me. I waited, holding back my tears, which made my throat ache.

Finally, he looked at me.

"You're wearing one of her dresses," he said, "one of those she had in your closet for you before you had arrived."

I hadn't realized it when I put it on. I never would think he was aware of what I wore.

"Yes. I put it on this morning before she and I went to breakfast."

He nodded, as if that made some sort of sense.

"Come in," he said, nodding at the settee.

I went to it and sat.

"I'm glad you're a cardiac surgeon. I think you'll have to sew my heart together," I said.

He smiled wanly. "Sometimes, like this morning in the OR, I feel like I could raise the dead. When I was studying, interning, I remember surgeons who walked through the hospital hallways as if they were walking on water. I think that's why historically the church and science have been at each other's throat. There's a palpable fear that science will eventually eliminate every reason to pray. Maybe I'm being punished for being part of that."

I shook my head. "Don't think like that."

"Supposedly, Marcus Aurelius, Roman emperor, had a servant assigned to follow him around, and every time Marcus received a compliment, the servant was commanded to say, 'You're only a man.'"

"You can't blame yourself for this," I said. "This isn't some act of justice or revenge."

He nodded, looked at Samantha's picture and then back at me. "Did you know your grandmother on either side?"

"My maternal one."

"Yes, I knew mine, too. She was full of superstitions. She would pounce on me whenever I got some toy I wanted and warn me not to reveal how happy I was so openly, or else the Evil Eye would see and punish me. She had me looking everywhere for some dark figure smiling with sinister delight. Maybe she was right. I had an angel, and I let everyone know I did."

"You did nothing wrong," I insisted. "She *was* an angel."

He took a deep breath and turned completely to me.

"This is getting to sound like a broken record. I know you were planning on leaving soon. I wanted to see if . . ."

"I'll stay as long as you need me," I said quickly, "and I don't want you to offer me any additional money."

He nodded. "Samantha would like that."

Now my tears came. He looked like he would crumple and turned away quickly.

"Franklin said you should stay home. He'll make sure your patient is seen."

"We'll see," he said. "Thank you."

He looked down, and I rose.

"Is there anything I can get you?"

"No. Just see to Ryder. Thank you," he said.

I left him sitting there looking completely devastated. For a moment, I imagined my father having some quiet time and perhaps regretting how badly things had gone between us. Like Dr. Davenport, he was good at keeping his sadness bound up tightly beneath his heart.

In the morning, Mrs. Marlene found him curled up, embracing himself, and asleep on the settee below Samantha's picture. She told me he looked like a little boy. After she woke him, he went up to shower and change and sit with his mother. Friends began calling almost every twenty minutes. Franklin stopped by around noon. He and Dr. Davenport then left together to make Samantha's funeral arrangements. Except for Ryder's cries and baby talk, the mansion was quiet. The shadows were deepened and hovering over us all.

Most of the time during the next few days, Dr. Davenport was home. He kept himself in his office with the doors closed. I brought Ryder in to see him whenever I could, and I suspected it was practically the only time he smiled. Mrs. Marlene brought him his meals. I had mine with Mr. Stark and Mrs. Marlene. I was beginning to feel more like another servant, but I didn't mind it. These people were, after all, my American family.

Samantha's funeral was difficult, not only because we were burying her, someone who had everything to live for, but because it was one of the most bitterly cold days on record. A surprising number of people came to the cemetery after the service. Many, I was told, were either Dr. Davenport's patients or family of one of his patients. When I looked around at the mourners, I saw their breaths puffing like smoke. No one dared utter a complaint. All were alive, after all, imagining that Samantha would have gladly endured a dozen days like this in a row if it meant she could live on to see her son grow up.

When it was over, we returned to Wyndemere, where Mrs. Marlene and some rented help prepared food for those who wanted to continue to offer Dr. Davenport comfort. A few who had met me before and remembered the cover story remarked how terrible I must feel having come to Wyndemere on what were now two very sad occasions. Most everyone saw how I was caring for

Ryder during the time he was up and about, and the story line was embellished with the revelation that I would be staying to help care for him for a while at least.

I fed him and put him to bed. By the time I returned to the grand room, most of the mourners had left. Dr. Davenport, a man who had attended the funerals of some of his patients, looked like he was there to comfort others. His lips never trembled; his eyes remained clear and his voice steady. Other people cried around him, but Dr. Bliskin moved them off as quickly as he could, as if he were there to protect his friend.

After everyone left, Dr. Davenport went up to his mother for a while and then to bed. Before he did, however, he asked me to do something that at first actually made me shiver.

"I'd feel more at ease if you would move to Samantha's bedroom, because it's right beside the nursery. Would you do that? Mrs. Cohen and the other nurse both have their hands full with my mother. Despite how she could be, she liked Samantha. She once told me that she imagined my little sister would be something like her. My little sister . . ." he said, his voice drifting off.

He had drunk far more than I had ever seen him drink, and he looked exhausted from that and from containing his sorrow. Inside, his body was surely overflowing with the hidden tears. His face was red from the alcohol he had consumed, but his eyes were darkened with the pain. He waited for my response.

"Of course, if that's what you think best, Dr. Davenport."

He nodded, his eyes fixed on me. He turned to walk away, paused, and turned back. "I think I'd be more comfortable now with you calling me Harrison. Samantha was practically the only one left in Wyndemere who did. Even my mother calls me Dr. Davenport sometimes. Lately, more than ever," he added. He closed and opened his eyes.

"If that's what you wish, of course," I said.

He took my hand for a second or two and then went to the stairway. Mrs. Marlene stepped up beside me, and both of us watched him going up, looking like a man twice his age climbing a mountain. Surely, in his mind, he was, I thought.

Mrs. Marlene and I hugged each other. I told her what Dr. Davenport had asked me to do.

She didn't look surprised. "He's not a man who's used to asking anyone for a favor. It's almost always the other way around. It's kind of you to do what you can to give him some comfort."

"Honestly," I said, "I think I'm doing it to comfort myself, keep myself from believing she's not here."

She smiled. "I'm having the same trouble. You wear her perfume, and the aroma lingers in the air, causing me to imagine she has just passed through this room or that."

"Oh."

"It's all right. I'm not afraid to remember."

We said good night, and I made my way up the stairs. I gathered what I needed from my room and stepped into Samantha's. It had been prepared the way it always was, everything neatly organized, the bedding crisp and clean, and the curtains drawn closed. She once told me that she didn't want to be woken by sunlight abruptly. She would smoothly step out of sleep, and then, "as if I controlled day and night, I open my curtains and give the sun permission to be there. You may enter now, Mr. Sun."

She giggled after saying things like that, but I loved hearing them. For a while, we were truly more like little girls growing up together in Wyndemere. And then, after I became pregnant, we were both forced to be mature and responsible. Maybe that was the real reason she wanted a surrogate to carry her child: she never wanted to give up her own childhood. Harrison Davenport certainly did whatever he could to keep her safely ensconced in that world of baubles, bangles, and beads. Living and working beside death for most of his day, it was surely an escape to come through the magnificent, castle-like entrance of Wyndemere and find his princess waiting to wash away any remnants of the darkness he had traveled in outside.

Now it had come in, and he had only the darkness now, and I think I went to bed crying over that as much as the loss of Samantha herself.

A baby monitor was beside Samantha's bed. It was what woke me early in the morning the first night I slept in her room. I went to Ryder immediately, and then, like she often did, I brought him back to her bedroom. When I was nursing him regularly, she'd call me to her room and lie beside me while I nursed him. Now he was on his bottle, and again, as she always did, I watched him feed, his eyes on me as if he was looking for approval, as if he knew he had gone elsewhere for his nourishment and wanted to be sure I wasn't upset.

Afterward, we both fell back to sleep. I wasn't

sure if I had dreamed it or not, but I thought Dr. Davenport had opened the bedroom door and stood at the foot of the bed for a while. When I did wake up, he wasn't there, of course. Ryder was still sleeping. I washed up, dressed for breakfast, and carried him down with me.

"He was up before I arrived this morning," Mrs. Marlene said. "Parker was taking him off when I pulled in. George told me he had insisted on going to his office."

"Maybe that is best," I said.

"How long do you think you will stay?" she asked.

"I don't know. I haven't given that much thought. Every time I start to, I feel terribly selfish."

She gave me a sympathetic look. "You've got to think of your future, too, not that I don't dread the day you walk out of here."

Ryder looked at both of us, suspicion in his eyes.

Mrs. Marlene laughed first, and then I did.

It sounded like the crack in a sheet of ice.

Just a little bit of light came pouring through.

As long as I had Ryder to occupy me, I would be able to hold together, I thought. It was those quiet moments alone that would be devastating.

How could I live through those?

EPILOGUE

The first time it happened, at the start, I thought I was having a dream. I would never deny to myself that I had fantasized it more than once. Franklin had told me that Harrison was at the hospital, but confining himself to administrative work, and he had not agreed to take on any new patients or surgeries. He came home at dinner to spend time with Ryder and then retreated almost immediately afterward to his office.

One night, when he came into the dining room, I decided to take the seat Samantha always took. Samantha and I used to sit on both sides of Ryder in his high chair, she always on his right, which was on Dr. Davenport's left. It felt right to me, right for Ryder, and right for Dr. Davenport. He smiled, but neither of us said anything about it.

Mrs. Marlene paused at the kitchen door. I glanced at her. She looked a little frightened but nodded. I liked that she approved.

I thought about the questions Samantha would ask Dr. Davenport at dinner and toyed with them in my mind. He hadn't been very talkative during the week, but I didn't expect he would be.

"Are you very busy?" I asked.

The way he looked at me suggested he wasn't going to answer, but he did. "I've put most everything on hold for a while. I'm catching up on reports, new research, and the like."

I nodded and continued to feed Ryder. Later that night, he looked in on me in the library. I could see that he had been drinking again or, actually, still. It was the way he was putting himself to sleep these nights.

"I should talk to you about your future," he said. "Please forgive me."

"I'm fine. Let's give it a while," I said, which obviously pleased him.

"Are you rereading that or reading it for the first time?" he asked, nodding at the copy of *Rebecca* in my hands. Samantha hadn't quite finished it. I had the feeling I was finishing it for her.

"Rereading. I've forgotten so much."

"When something is good, it shouldn't be forgotten." He stood there. I didn't know whether I should invite him to sit with me. "One of these days, we'll have you sing for us again . . . I have to look in on my mother. Good night."

"Good night."

I put the novel down after he left and sat there thinking.

Was it good that I had remained, or did I keep Samantha's death fresh in his mind simply by being here? We had been inseparable, after all. In the beginning, it was because of her concerns about my surrogacy, and then, as time passed and we talked more, a real affection was built between us. It was more of a friendship while I was nursing. I imagined that every time he saw me enter a room or come down the stairs, he was still anticipating Samantha would follow or be beside me.

But every time I gave serious consideration to leaving and returning to my life, my ambitions, I felt waves of guilt. How could I be so selfish? At least stay long enough for him to get through it. It would also be quite traumatic for Ryder to suddenly lose both of us. Or . . . was I thinking more of myself?

Julia would pounce if she knew all this. She would blame me for getting myself entangled in the Davenports' lives. I would have trouble defending myself. Ironically, she would be telling me that I had placed too much importance on money, something we both thought was true about our father.

Being a father was still very important to Dr. Davenport, but it was difficult for him. He truly enjoyed seeing Ryder and took delight in every little advancement he made, whether it was simply moving about more gracefully or learning what things were and pronouncing new words. Every smile on Dr. Davenport's face was instantly accompanied by a sign of sorrow. It manifested itself in his eyes. She wasn't there to share the joy. Almost always, he would glance at her portrait. If only I could fill that void, I thought.

Everyone noticed Dr. Davenport's drinking, but no one would dare say a word. Franklin was aware of it and visited as often as he could. His efforts were yet to have a significant effect. Night after night, I heard Dr. Davenport lumbering his way up the stairs to his room. A few times, I thought he had turned in Ryder's and my direction. I listened harder but heard nothing and fell asleep.

Then it happened.

I never heard my bedroom door open. I never heard him step up to my bed. He was naked.

"Samantha," he said. "Samantha."

God forgive me, but I said, "Yes, my darling."